Among the Shadows

LUCY MAUD MONTGOMERY (1874-1942), undoubtedly Canada's most famous author, is generally known as the creator of *Anne of Green Gables*. But *Anne* is just a small part of an oeuvre that contains nineteen other novels, as well as more than 500 short stories and 500 poems that Montgomery wrote and published between 1895 and 1940. Very few of these short stories have previously been collected in book form. In 1978 editor Rea Wilmshurst found a cache of Montgomery's scrapbooks at her birthplace in P.E.I. and compiled a bibliography of the 300 or so stories in them, in the process finding even more. *Among the Shadows* is a companion to the other three volumes of these rediscovered tales, *Akin to Anne*, *Along the Shore*, and *After Many Days*.

REA WILMSHURST has been reading and re-reading L. M. Montgomery's works all her life, and has published three articles on Montgomery's work in *Canadian Children's Literature*. She edited *Akin to Anne*, *Along the Shore*, and *After Many Days*, the other three volumes in this series of rediscovered stories, is co-author with Ruth and Delbert Russell of *Lucy Maud Montgomery: A Preliminary Bibliography* (Waterloo: University of Waterloo Press, 1986), and is associated with both the *Collected Works of John Stuart Mill* and the *Collected Works of Samuel Taylor Coleridge* as an editorial assistant.

L. M. MONTGOMERY

Among the Shadows

edited by Rea Wilmshurst

M&S

An M&S Paperback from
McClelland & Stewart Inc.
The Canadian Publishers

An M&S Paperback from McClelland & Stewart Inc.

First printing June 1992
Cloth edition printed 1990

Canadian Cataloguing in Publication Data

Montgomery, L.M. (Lucy Maud), 1874-1942
Among the shadows

"An M&S paperback."
ISBN 0-7710-6152-8

I. Wilmshurst, Rea, 1941-   . II. Title.

PS8526.O55A73   1992   C813'.52   C90-095166-4
PR9199.2.M6A73   1992

Cover illustration by Greg Ruhl
Cover design by Stephen Kenny

Printed and bound in Canada

McClelland & Stewart Inc.
The Canadian Publishers
481 University Avenue
Toronto, Ontario
M5G 2E9

Contents

Introduction

IT MAY BE a truth almost universally acknowledged that L. M. Montgomery wrote tales of sweetness and light for girls. But a full and careful reading of her novels and stories reveals strong passions, tragedy, and some spooky occurrences. There are threads from a darker web woven through her twenty novels (Alice Munro has said that in *Emily of New Moon* there is "a real sense of brooding and menace and even horror"), and through some of the tales in other collections of her short stories. In *Akin to Anne*, the first volume in this series, Montgomery dealt with unhappy topics: the separation of siblings upon the death of parents and the loneliness of people without family connections; the endings, however, were all happy. The second volume, *Along the Shore*, contains a few tales sounding even more sombre notes, and some have very unhappy endings.

So it is possible to find many elements in Montgomery "from the darker side," and the stories collected here have been chosen to illustrate this less acknowledged aspect of Canada's favourite author. Two of these tales deal with drunkenness, three with embezzlement and petty thievery, one with adultery, and one with a shot-gun marriage. Two degenerate men spoil the lives of the women who love them; another does not. We meet two murderers, one male and one female. In the stories with a supernatural basis Montgomery poignantly demonstrates her belief that the power of love could last beyond death. In all, here is an abundance of material to show her familiarity with, and sensitivity to, the shadows of life.

The Women's Temperance Movement was a great force during the last half of the nineteenth century and the first part of the twentieth. The use of alcohol was seen almost totally as abuse: many people believed there were few men who could live with drink at a happy medium, and it was women and children who suffered. Surprisingly, the drunkard in Montgomery's "The Martyrdom of Estella" is not a man but a woman, an actress who is staying for the summer in a small village. She obstructs the course of true love during her visit, but her unmasking comes in time to save Estella's and Spencer Morgan's engagement. Montgomery, of course, could nearly always see a lighter side to most things, even drunkenness, and a companion story, "The Deacon's Painkiller," presents a humorous look at the question of temperance. What *can* the deacon do to save his reputation when he has been so obviously and joyously drunk, and in church too?

Embezzlement is often called a "white-collar crime" and is therefore almost respectable. Even in Montgomery's day it could be introduced into light fiction without an author being accused of soiling the minds of her readers. In "The Redemption of John Churchill," Mr. Churchill, an embezzler, sets out on his release from prison intending to see his boy Joey, who was left in the care of an aunt when his father went to jail. He doesn't intend even to speak to the boy, just to see him. Then he expects to "go to the devil," since there is no one in his life to care whether he reforms or not. He arrives in time to hear a friend of Joey's taunting him with his criminal father.

Petty thievery in small communities does not usually go

long undiscovered and unattributed. But will exposure bring about contrition and reform, or will the thief proceed on the easier, downward path to eventual ruin? Two of Montgomery's stories in this vein have opposite resolutions. "Detected by the Camera" was written in 1897, and concludes with the harsher judgement of petty crime that one might expect from its youthful, idealistic author. (By the way, it is also one of a dozen stories that Montgomery wrote out of her interest in the developing medium of photography.) "Miss Calista's Peppermint Bottle" came thirteen years later, when Montgomery's outlook had softened. Miss Calista is one of the great company of Montgomery's spunky old maids, and has an extraordinarily independent set of ideas for her times. The young man she accuses of burgling her house has much to be thankful for.

But it did not take Montgomery thirteen years to become more tolerant. Even in 1904, when she wrote "The Man on the Train," she was able to see and portray the good side of a fugitive from justice. The man who helps poor bewildered Grandma Sheldon on her first train trip, when she not only loses her ticket but has no money to replace it and is not met at her destination, shows his better nature in his treatment of one old lady at least. As she says: "I'll never believe he was all bad – a man who would do what he did for a poor old woman like me – when he was flying for his life too. No, no, there was good in him even if he did kill that man."

The anti-hero in "A Redeeming Sacrifice" seems all bad: "A bad egg was Paul King, with a bad past and a bad future. He was shiftless and drunken; ugly tales were told of him." A handsome charmer, Paul drinks and plays cards, stays out late carousing, and flirts with every pretty girl in sight. He has made Joan Shelley, one of the loveliest girls in the village, fall in love with him and plans to marry her, but has no intention of reforming. Even in Paul, however, Montgomery is able to find a core of goodness. She doesn't give us a reformation – that would be too hard to believe in – but she does have him make the one high-minded gesture of his life.

The tales mentioned thus far take place in the usual Montgomery settings of small towns and villages, and deal with ordinary people. But "The Red Room" (1898) strikes a different note, being an early attempt at a "Gothic" thriller. Readers familiar with the tales of Miss Tomgallon in *Anne of Windy Poplars* will know that Montgomery later lightened her approach to this genre and, while not mocking it, certainly took it less seriously. Here, however, seriousness is all. Through the eyes of Beatrice, a child visiting Montressor Place, "an old-fashioned, mysterious house" (the name may well have been chosen to evoke Poe's "The Cask of Amontillado"), we are shown scenes of jealousy, adultery, and murder. The style is intentionally overwrought, adding to the weight and gloom: "He fell heavily, yet held her even in death, so that she had to wrench herself free, with a shriek that rings yet in my ears on a night when the wind wails over the rainy moors. She rushed past me unheeding, and fled down the hall like a hunted creature, and I heard the heavy door clang hollowly behind her." Can this really be our Montgomery? Most of her work used other fictional modes, but she did try the melodramatic convention from time to time.

The tale of "Min" is melodramatic too, but its presentation is more conventionally realistic. Montgomery has given us very few portraits of "fallen women," but most of those few have been strong, independent, self-willed and, to modern minds, very interesting. Min is just such a woman. Endowed with intelligence that she had no chance to develop, born with a passionate nature but given no training in self-control, Min was forced by preg-

nancy into an unwanted marriage and ostracized therefore by her community. Although she cares deeply for her
crippled child, she has lived her life burning with resentment at God and fate. She meets too late the man who
might have changed her life, but Allan Telford's love gives
her the strength on her deathbed to go hopefully into the
beyond. Montgomery seems to have little doubt of her
salvation: "Who shall say that her remorseful cry was not
heard, even at that late hour, by a Judge more merciful
than her fellow creatures?"

Before she dies, Min asks Allan if they will meet again.
He believes they will, when he dies too. But is it always
necessary to wait for death to meet again? In Montgomery's supernatural tales, people may come back from
beyond the grave to help the living by providing information or comfort. The belief that one could contact or be
contacted by the dead was taken seriously by many people at the turn of the century. Ghost stories have always
been popular, of course, but the emergence of mediums –
people adept at creating an atmosphere conducive to
apparent manifestations and messages from the beyond –
brought "spiritualism" into many lives. Montgomery
stated her views on séances in her journal on 19 July 1918:
"I have never for one moment believed in what is called
'spiritualism.' Nothing I have ever seen or read has convinced me for a moment that any communication from
the dead is possible by such means." Still, she had experi-
mented with table rapping as early as 1890, and mentions
one or two strange occurrences to do with it in her journals. It was a game for her, however, merely an evening's
amusement, not to be taken seriously.

But Montgomery obviously wanted very much to believe that love could reach from beyond the grave, and
indeed had made a pact with her dearest friend, Frederi-
ca Campbell (Frede), that when the first of them died, she

"was to come back and appear to the survivor *if* it were possible to cross the gulf." Frede died on 25 January 1919. Montgomery was with her and was devastated by her loss. On 7 February she mourned in her diary that obviously the dead could not return, since Frede had not appeared to her. But on 21 May, nervous about her elder son's health, she poignantly describes longing for Frede and wondering if she could possibly be with her in the room. Her cat Daffy was involved: "I recalled reading that animals are aware of presences which human beings cannot sense. Perhaps it was also true that those presences could influence animals.... 'Frede,' I whispered, 'if you are here *make Daff come over to me and kiss me.*'" Daffy, a most undemonstrative cat, did. Montgomery "felt sure that Frede *was* there with me and had made our old furry comrade the medium of her message. The conviction brought comfort and strength and calmness."

So if anything can bring the dead back, it is the power of love. A lover who comes to help a crossing into death is evoked in "The Girl at the Gate." Jeanette has been sitting with old Mr. Lawrence in his last hours. He tells her of his fiancée, Margaret, who, dying at the age of eighteen, had said: "Herbert, I promise that I will be true to you forever, through as many years of lonely heaven as I must know before you come. And when your time is at hand I will come to make your deathbed easy as you have made mine." A young and attractive girl who is not from the village does visit the house later that night. Is it Margaret, come to aid his passage to death, whom Jeanette sees?

The woman who returns from the grave to "The House Party at Smoky Island" comes to confess to murder, and, in so doing, saves Brenda and Anthony's marriage, a marriage that is foundering on the rocks of suspicion and doubt. The group has been telling ghost stories when Christine speaks: "'Do you remember how firmly Aunt

Elizabeth believed in ghosts?' said Christine. 'And how angry it used to make her when I laughed at the idea. I am . . . wiser now.'" She goes on to tell them that she, not Anthony, gave their cousin an overdose of chloral. When she stops speaking, and is suddenly no longer there, they realize that "none of us had ever known or heard of the girl I had called Christine."

The power of love brought both Margaret and Christine back to help their loved ones, and revenants appear purposefully and affectionately in "Miriam's Lover" and "Davenport's Story" as well. The situation in "The Closed Door" is much less loving and serene. A group of children solve the mystery of a missing family jewel when they come upon a house that none of them has ever seen before. But in that house they are "in the presence of something very evil." They pay a price for the knowledge they have gained: "They had learned that afternoon, looking into Ralph Kilbourne's eyes, more about hell than they had ever known before. They were too young to have learned so much . . ."

Montgomery's other "supernatural" tales have the atmosphere of ghost stories, but no real ghosts (if one can speak of real ghosts). A message comes to Anne in "From out the Silence," but not via a spirit. Aunt Beenie, a very earthly, unromantic, slightly batty old woman, is the agent. In one of her rare flashes of rational thought, Aunt Beenie tells Anne of a package that has been waiting for her, unopened, since her friend Edith's death. It changes everything for Anne: "All the ceaseless, gnawing, longing gone, all the bitterness. Edith was her own again, all her memories unspoiled and beautiful." She can now accept Edith's death and go on living.

"The Tryst of the White Lady" has an unearthly unreality that is eventually dispelled, and love comes to two people who may be unusual, but who are very much of this world. However, for a while both Roger Temple and his Aunt Catherine firmly believe that he has seen and been bewitched by his ancestress, Isabel Temple, who was killed by "a jilted lover, crazed by despair," on her wedding day. She does not rest quietly in her grave: "It was only to men the lovely, restless ghost appeared, and her appearance boded no good to him who saw. Roger knew this, but he had a curious longing to see her." And when he thinks he sees her: "He would not have missed it for a score of other men's lives. He had drunk of some immortal wine and was as a god. Even if she never came again, he had seen her once, and she had taught him life's great secret in that one unforgettable exchange of eyes." When Roger discovers that his beloved ghost is a mere woman, he is "dazed, wretched, lost," and believes – at least for a while – that he would rather die than have to give up his unearthly passion.

Combining both the apparent supernatural and the darker side of human nature is one of Montgomery's longest tales, "Some Fools and a Saint." What seem like supernatural happenings occur; even the old minister of the village believes that a ghost walks the house: "I heard a devilish sort of laugh . . . I can't say whether it was in my room or out of it. There was a quality in it that filled me with a sickening sort of horror . . . I admit it, Mr. Burns, that laughter was not human." The weird, mean, and petty occurrences are actually the secret, malicious deeds of a warped woman who simply wishes to make the people she lives with miserable. The tricks played cause constant disruptions in their lives and are a result of suppressed jealousy and the mistreatment she endured as a child. When she is unmasked, her pathological behaviour is explained easily: "Her father and grandfather were dipsomaniacs. You can't reform your ancestors." The demon of alcohol has appeared again.

Introduction

The publication in 1986 and 1987 of the first two volumes of L. M. Montgomery's journals revealed aspects of her life that were known to very few, and it has indeed been a revelation. An emotionally unsatisfactory childhood, a repressed adolescence, a young womanhood sacrificed to the care of an elderly grandmother, a late marriage to a man incapable of sharing her love of literature and nature: no longer can Montgomery be thought of as having no "darker side" to her life. The tales collected here show that there were occasions when Montgomery allowed what her journal editors call the "darknesses and depths" a place in her fiction.

REA WILMSHURST

The Closed Door

BEFORE RACHEL had been at Briarwold a month there was a saying that whenever she went around a corner, she went into something. Hazel was a sweet thing with dove's eyes, whom everybody loved, but Rachel was a green-eyed bantling who had been touched with faery from birth. She had an elfin face and slim brown hands that talked as eloquently as her lips, especially when she was telling Cecil and Chris tales of man-eating tigers and Hindoo superstitions she had no business to know. Her devoted missionary parents would have died of horror if they had suspected she did know them. They thought they had protected her so carefully, but Rachel was one of those predestined creatures to whom strange knowledge comes and strange things happen. Very soon after she came to Briarwold she was telling the other children fading old stories of their ancestors . . . ivory-white women and gallant men . . . which they had never heard before . . . mystic wraiths of tales which came alive when Rachel touched them. Everything seemed to come alive when Rachel touched it. When she told the simplest incident it took on a colouring of romance and mystery. She was somehow like a window through which they peeped into an unknown world.

The things she knew! For instance, she knew that if she could only open a door . . . any door . . . quickly enough, she would see strange things . . . perhaps the people who had once lived in it. But she could never open it quite quickly enough. After she told them this every room with a closed door was full of magic for Cecil and Chris. What was going on inside? Even Jane Alicut tiptoed past it, and Jane was impervious to most subtleties. She was the daughter of the new housekeeper at Briarwold . . . a pudgy, blunt-spoken lass of twelve . . . the same age as

Rachel. Cecil Latham was twelve too, and lived with his mother next door at faded, shabby Pinecroft. Chris, who matched Hazel with ten years of life, lived at Briarwold with Mr. Digby, whom she called Uncle Egerton, although he was only a second cousin of her dead mother. But though it was said they lived at these places this meant that they slept and ate there. They really did their living in the gardens and the pinewoods and the fields. Especially when Rachel and Hazel came. After India's burning suns Rachel could not get enough of the crystal homeland air and the long, green, rolling fields and the shadowy woods and the moonlight among the beeches. And of course the minute Rachel looked at the landscape she saw things none of the rest of them could.

Cecil and Chris had been good friends and had played together before Rachel came, but Chris was shy and timid and Cecil was shy and timid and they did not just hit it off. Rachel seemed to fuse everybody in an atmosphere of pixy laughter and companionship, and Hazel was like a soft strain of music in the background. So Cecil was having the happiest summer he had ever known, and even the creeping shadow ceased to haunt him.

Rachel had not been at Briarwold two weeks before she found out what the shadow at Pinecroft was. She had been curled up in the wing chair in one corner of the porch when Egerton Digby was talking with his sister-in-law in the other. The chair's back was towards them and it did not occur to Rachel that they did not know she was there. It is by no means certain that she would have gone away if it had occurred to her.

She heard only snatches. Yet enough to know that Mrs. Latham was very poor and had recently become still poorer by reason of the failure of some company ... that it was becoming doubtful if she could keep Cecil ... certainly she could not educate him.

"It will come to this," said Enid Latham in a terrible voice, "I shall have to give him up to his father's people at last. They've always been determined to have him."

Rachel knew quite well, with that uncanny prescience of hers, that Cecil's mother did not like his father's people. To give Cecil to them meant giving him up forever.

"I wish I could help you," Egerton Digby said. "If I were not so wretchedly hard up myself . . . and Chris must be provided for . . ."

"You have done far more than you should already," said Mrs. Latham. "We have no claim on you."

"If you had the Peacock Pearl, as you should have had, there would have been no such problems for you," said Mr. Digby.

He spoke so bitterly that even a less acute child than Rachel might have known that he was touching on something unspeakably painful.

"I am sure that Nora never gave Arthur Nesbitt the pearl," said Mrs. Latham with a gentle firmness. "She was gay and heedless . . . my poor, beautiful Nora . . . but she wasn't wicked. I don't believe he was her lover, Egerton. I have never believed it and I never can."

"I have never believed it either," said Egerton harshly. "But I can't be sure . . . and my doubt has eaten into my soul all these years like a corroding rust. I suppose I loved her too much. And that quarrel we had the last night of her life . . . the last time I ever saw her. If I could undo it, Enid! But nothing can be undone. Life has beaten me."

I should like to see life beat me, thought Rachel.

"If she did not give Arthur Nesbitt the pearl, what became of it?" Egerton Digby went on.

"I think if Ralph had lived he could have told us something about that," said Mrs. Latham. "He was furious because Uncle Michael left the pearl to me."

Why does she hate to mention the name of Ralph,

wondered Rachel. It sounds as if it blistered her lips.

"The pearl was an exquisite thing," said Egerton dreamily. "There is some especial charm and mystery about the jewels of the sea. And its colour . . . a moonlight blend of blue and green . . . I never saw anything so lovely. Your Uncle Michael paid fifty thousand for it . . . and loved it more than he should. Perhaps that was why it brought misfortune."

"It will kill me if I have to give Cecil up," said Mrs. Latham.

"I would welcome death," said Egerton Digby. "Perhaps on the other side of the grave I might find Nora . . . and know . . . and kiss our quarrel away."

They talked longer but they dropped their voices, and Rachel heard nothing further. She thought a great deal over what she had heard. There was a mystery. She felt that she was standing before a closed door and that if she could open it quickly enough she would see things . . . Nora and the Peacock Pearl among them. The name and idea of the pearl captivated Rachel. She had heard stories of such things in India . . . rare mysterious old gems of beauty and desire.

I must find out all about it, decided Rachel.

SHE DID NOT SAY a word to anybody of what she had heard. Rachel loved secrets. Besides, she was not going to worry Cecil any more than he was worried. But when Jane Alicut began to tell her things one night, when they were alone together in the twilight, Rachel let her talk. Rachel had already discovered how much could be found out just by letting people talk. Everybody was away from Briarwold, and Cecil was staying home because his mother had a headache, so it was an excellent chance for Jane to talk and she took it. Jane, on a lower plane, was as good as Rachel at finding out things. The crudity of her telling hurt Rachel, who loved to soften and beautify as she went along. Jane never suggested mystery. To her a spade was a spade, never a golden trowel which might turn up who knew what of treasure trove.

"I heard Ma talking to Mrs. Agar down in the village about it. Mrs. Agar told Ma everything. Mr. Digby's wife was Mrs. Latham's sister and they were dreadful fond of each other . . . Mrs. Latham and Mrs. Digby, I mean. I dunno if Mrs. Digby was as fond of her husband. Mrs. Agar said there were queer tales. She was a great beauty with a rope of black hair that fell to her feet. But she was a gay piece and Mr. Digby was jealous as jealous.

"She had a brother called Ralph who was as bad as they make 'em, but Mrs. Digby always stuck up for him and took his part. She seemed to love him more'n she loved anybody else. Then old Michael Foster . . . he was their uncle . . . up and died. He hadn't much money but he had a big pearl that was worth a king's ransom, Mrs. Agar said. He'd ruined himself to buy it. And he willed it to Mrs. Latham. Ralph was furious because he thought he should have got it. He said his uncle had promised it to him. He seemed to be sorter a favourite with the old man in spite of his goings-on. They had an awful quarrel over it, Mrs. Agar says. And then one night Mrs. Digby went home . . . her old home where Ralph and her father lived . . . to stay all night, and it was burned down and they were all burned to death in it . . . all three of 'em . . . yes, wasn't it awful! And Mr. Digby nearly went mad. He's never been the same man since, Mrs. Agar says. His hair turned white in a month. And there was a big to-do because the pearl had disappeared. It never was found either.

"Mrs. Agar says everybody thought Mrs. Digby was going to run away with Arthur Nesbitt and had given him the pearl. He was up to his eyes in debt. He went away after that and word came back that he had lots of money. A nice kettle of fish, wasn't it? Mrs. Agar says the rich society folks are all like that."

"But Mr. Digby isn't rich," said Rachel.

"No . . . he's got poor since his wife was burned to death. He just let everything slide. And of course Mrs. Latham is as poor as a church mouse . . . everyone knows that. Mrs. Agar says his father's people want Cecil. They've always hated her . . . they didn't want Cecil's father to marry her."

"You are not to tell Cecil that," said Rachel.

"Of course I won't. I like the kid and I'm sorry for him. So's Ma. I don't want to hurt his feelings," protested Jane.

"And I think you'd better not talk about that story to anyone," continued Rachel austerely. "You've talked too much about it now."

Jane stared. She had certainly felt that Rachel wanted to hear her talk. It wasn't fair that she should be snubbed like that.

"I can hold my tongue as well as the next one," she said sulkily. "You are good at listening, Miss Rachel."

Rachel smiled . . . remotely . . . mysteriously.

"You would be surprised, Jane, if you knew what I can hear sometimes," she said dreamily.

Rachel felt now that she knew all about the mystery . . . except the one thing worth knowing. The door was still closed. And she did not know how it was to be opened. She did not have the key. In this impasse Rachel betook herself to prayer. For the daughter of a missionary, Rachel did not pray overmuch. Hazel prayed sweetly and innocently every night and morning, but Rachel made a special, mystic, alluring rite of prayer. She would not make it common. Neither did she kneel down. She stood in the garden by the sundial and lifted her face to the sky with upraised hands, facing God fearlessly.

"Please open the door," she said, less as a request than

as a statement of right. "Because," she added, "you know that things can't be right until the door is opened."

PERHAPS WHAT FOLLOWED on a certain afternoon, which none of the children ever forgot, was an answer to this prayer. You will not get any of those children to discuss it with you. Nobody will talk of it, not even Jane Alicut, who is now a stout matron with a bevy of her own children round her. She tells them many tales of her old playmates at Briarwold, but she never tells the story of that haunted afternoon. She would like to think she dreamed it. When she cannot believe that, she blames it on Rachel. Very likely with justice. I think if Rachel had not been with the other children that day, they would never have stepped through the closed door.

They were to go to tea with old Great-aunt Lucy down at Mount Joy. And they were to go by a short cut through fields and woods which none of them had ever traversed before, but which Uncle Egerton described so clearly that they were quite sure they could follow it. At first they went along the wood path back of Briarwold. They had never gone quite so far into those woods before. But they felt quite at home and very happy. The woods had a friendly mood on that day. They did not always have it. Sometimes they frowned. Sometimes they were wrapped up in their own concerns. But this day they welcomed the children. There were beautiful shadows everywhere. The mosses along the path were emerald and gold. They passed through a little glen full of creamy toadstools. They found a lovely green pool with ferns around it that nobody ever seemed to have found before. Rachel was quite sure that if they waited quietly a faun would come through the trees to peep at himself in it. But they had no time to waste for Great-aunt Lucy was fussy about punctuality.

Jane was with them. Great-aunt Lucy made a point of inviting Jane because she liked her. And Jane's dog, who had no name because Jane could not find one which would suit everybody, was along too . . . a gay, light-hearted little mongrel who tore about in the woods and outran them, then sat on his haunches waiting for them to come up with him, laughing at them with his red tongue lolling from his jaws.

After the woods there was a meadow path that enticed them with daisies and was jewelled with the red of wild strawberry leaves. Then came another stretch of wood-land . . . a more shadowy place. The path ran along by a mysterious, fir-darkened brook. The children were never quite sure just when the feeling of something strange came over them. All at once they found themselves draw-ing closer together. Their light chatter failed them. Even Jane became very quiet. Rachel had been quiet all along that day, now that they came to think of it. She had walked a little apart . . . listening. She would never talk of it afterwards, so nobody knows what she was listening for or what she expected. Jane's dog was the only one of the party who kept his spirits up.

"Are you sure this is the right road?" whispered Jane nervously at last. She didn't know why she must whisper.

"It's the only road there is," said Rachel.

A little further on Cecil suddenly said, "If this is the right road, there's something wrong with it."

They stared at each other, beginning to be pale. Cecil had put their secret feeling into words.

"There is something wrong with it," said Rachel. "I've known that for some time. And I'm going to find out what it is."

They went on. It was just as well to go on as to go back, for the chill and fear were all around them now. They dared not stand still. They could not even whisper. Jane's dog had given up chasing imaginary rabbits but he trotted along sturdily, his tail curled saucily over his back.

All at once they were through the woods and out in the open. A lovely landscape of hill and meadow and homesteads spread below the hill on which they stood. They scrambled over the rotten fence and found themselves in an old, deep-rutted, grass-grown lane which ran down to join a road that went on until it reached the lake. But just beside them was a garden oddly shaped like a triangle, basking in the sunshine, full of flowers and bees and sleepy shadows. And at the tip of this garden triangle was a house.

None of them could recall having seen it before. It was a large, old-fashioned house, overgrown with vines, and the door was open. On the sun-warm sandstone step a cat was basking . . . a huge, black cat with pale-green eyes.

An odd hush lay over the windless place. Cecil remembered an old poem he had heard Uncle Egerton reading . . . a poem that spoke of a land "where the wind never blew." Had they come to it? What was this lost garden, so full of inescapable mystery? What was wrong with it?

He looked appealingly at Rachel.

"Where are we? I don't see Aunt Lucy's anywhere."

"I'm going to that house to ask," said Rachel resolutely.

Cecil did not know why he felt such a horror of doing this. He was ashamed to betray his cowardice before a girl, so he went along. They walked up the central path of the garden, past tulips and daffodils and bleeding-heart. Cecil knew what was wrong with the garden now. Tulips and daffodils and bleeding-heart had no right to be there . . . it was long past the time for them. He felt Chris's cold little hand steal into his. At the very step Jane's dog suddenly gave a low whine, turned and fled.

"I suppose he doesn't like that cat," said Jane, as if she felt called upon to explain his behaviour.

"Hush," said Cecil . . . he didn't know why.

Rachel knocked . . . but nobody came. The cat stared at them unblinkingly. The scent of lilacs came on the air, although this was late summer and lilacs are in spring. Never again, as long as he lived, could Cecil endure the scent of lilacs. Beyond they saw a large, square hall and on one side of it was a closed door.

Rachel went in and across the hall to the door. The others followed because following was a little less terrible than staying behind. They were all very cold now. Rachel's thin shoulders were shivering. But she did a strange thing. She did not knock at the door . . . she simply set her teeth, turned the knob and went in.

FOR ONCE she had done it quickly and silently enough.

They were in a beautiful, old-fashioned room. Two other people were also in it. A lady sat by a tea-table whereon were ivory candles in tall silver candlesticks and a bowl of violets. She was very beautiful. Her masses of black hair were held to her head by a golden band. She had a very fine, pale, creamy skin, and she wore a dress of black velvet with long, flowing sleeves of black lace. A great rose of dark-golden velvet was fastened to her shoulder, and the melting, pansy-hued eyes that looked at them were full of allurement and soft fire under the heavy fringing lashes.

A young man was standing by the window, playing with the tassel of the shade. He was handsome too, in a dark and splendid way, but the white hands that pulled at the tassel had terribly long, thin fingers. Cecil knew that he was in the presence of something very evil.

The young man left the window, took a cup from the table and came to the children. Cecil felt as if a dark chill night were coming towards him. But it was Rachel to whom the young man held out the cup. All the children saw the ring on his hand . . . or, rather, the three rings, fastened to each other by tiny gold chains, so that all three must be taken off or put on together. A diamond in one ring, a ruby in another, an emerald in the third, each stone held in a dragon's mouth.

Rachel shook her head and turned away. Then the lady smiled.

"You are quite right not to take it," she said. "It would not have hurt you, but you would never have been quite the same again. And you are too different already for your own good. Besides, you would have forgotten us as soon as you went out."

She rose and came towards them also. Cecil was afraid that she was going to touch him, and he knew that if she did he could not endure it. But it was by Rachel she paused. A little quivering ruby of light fell for a moment on her white neck from the stained-glass window at the far end of the room. The young man stood apart with the window for a background. There was a sneer on his face. He looked like some beautiful fallen angel . . . dark, impotent and rebellious.

The lady bent her head and said something to Rachel in a very low tone. But they all heard it.

"Tell Egerton I loved him only . . . Arthur Nesbitt was nothing to me. As for that foolish quarrel of ours . . . one forgets such things here . . . only love is remembered. But I did take the pearl . . . for Ralph. He persuaded me that Uncle Michael meant him to have it . . . that he was childish and doted when he made the will giving it to Enid. But I had not given it to him. Tell Egerton he will find the pearl among the folds of my wedding gown in the locked box in the attic. I am glad you came and opened the door. So few people would have had the courage to open it. There will be rest now. But go . . . go quickly."

They went quickly. Once outside that terrible house,

they ran blindly through the garden and down the lane. At the entrance to the wood-path they stopped and looked back.

There was no house. There was only a tangled enclosure with a growth of young trees in the centre among which were the ruins of burned walls.

"Let us go home," said Jane. "I don't care what Aunt Lucy thinks. I'm . . . I'm sick."

They got home somehow, running, stumbling, clinging together. When they got home nobody would say anything . . . could say anything . . . but Rachel. She had something to tell her Uncle Egerton and she told it, closeted with him in the library. Then she went out and flung herself down on the grass by the sundial, shaken with dreadful sobs.

"What did he say?" whispered Cecil.

"He wouldn't believe me at first, until I happened to mention the three rings the . . . the man wore. Then he said, 'The Rajah's rings . . . Ralph always wore them.' And he went to the attic."

"Was . . . was it there?"

"Yes. And he looked like . . . like a man who had got out of hell," said Rachel.

Nobody was shocked. They had learned that afternoon, looking into Ralph Kilbourne's eyes, more about hell than they had ever known before. They were too young to have learned so much . . . which was perhaps why they could never be got to say anything of it. Such things are not good for anybody to know.

"I will never open a closed door again," shuddered Rachel.

Davenport's Story

T WAS A RAINY AFTERNOON, and we had been passing the time by telling ghost stories. That is a very good sort of thing for a rainy afternoon, and it is a much better time than after night. If you tell ghost stories after dark they are apt to make you nervous, whether you own up to it or not, and you sneak home and dodge upstairs in mortal terror, and undress with your back to the wall, so that you can't fancy there is anything behind you.

We had each told a story, and had had the usual assortment of mysterious noises and death warnings and sheeted spectres and so on, down through the whole catalogue of horrors – enough to satisfy any reasonable ghost-taster. But Jack, as usual, was dissatisfied. He said our stories were all second-hand stuff. There wasn't a man in the crowd who had ever seen or heard a ghost; all our so-called authentic stories had been told us by persons who had the story from other persons who saw the ghosts.

"One doesn't get any information from that," said Jack. "I never expect to get so far along as to see a real ghost myself, but I would like to see and talk to one who had."

Some persons appear to have the knack of getting their wishes granted. Jack is one of that ilk. Just as he made the remark, Davenport sauntered in and, finding out what was going on, volunteered to tell a ghost story himself – something that had happened to his grandmother, or maybe it was his great-aunt; I forget which. It was a very good ghost story as ghost stories go, and Davenport told it well. Even Jack admitted that, but he said:

"It's only second-hand too. Did you ever have a ghostly experience yourself, old man?"

Davenport put his finger tips critically together.

"Would you believe me if I said I had?" he asked.

"No," said Jack unblushingly.

"Then there would be no use in my saying it."

"But you don't mean that you ever really had, of course?"

"I don't know. Something queer happened once. I've never been able to explain it – from a practical point of view, that is. Want to hear about it?"

Of course we did. This was exciting. Nobody would ever have suspected Davenport of seeing ghosts.

"It's conventional enough," he began. "Ghosts don't seem to have much originality. But it's first-hand, Jack, if that's what you want. I don't suppose any of you have ever heard me speak of my brother, Charles. He was my senior by two years, and was a quiet, reserved sort of fellow – not at all demonstrative, but with very strong and deep affections.

"When he left college he became engaged to Dorothy Chester. She was very beautiful, and my brother idolized her. She died a short time before the date set for their marriage, and Charles never recovered from the blow.

"I married Dorothy's sister, Virginia. Virginia did not in the least resemble her sister, but our eldest daughter was strikingly like her dead aunt. We called her Dorothy, and Charles was devoted to her. Dolly, as we called her, was always 'Uncle Charley's girl.'

"When Dolly was twelve years old Charles went to New Orleans on business, and while there took yellow fever and died. He was buried there, and Dolly half broke her childish heart over his death.

"One day, five years later, when Dolly was seventeen, I was writing letters in my library. That very morning my wife and Dolly had gone to New York en route for Europe. Dolly was going to school in Paris for a year. Business prevented my accompanying them even as far as New York, but Gilbert Chester, my wife's brother, was going with them. They were to sail on the *Aragon* the next morning.

"I had written steadily for about an hour. At last, growing tired, I threw down my pen and, leaning back in my chair, was on the point of lighting a cigar when an unaccountable impulse made me turn round. I dropped my cigar and sprang to my feet in amazement. There was only one door in the room and I had all along been facing it. I could have sworn nobody had entered, yet there, standing between me and the bookcase, was a man – and that man was my brother Charles!

"There was no mistaking him; I saw him as plainly as I see you. He was a tall, rather stout man, with curly hair and a fair, close-clipped beard. He wore the same light-grey suit which he had worn when bidding us good-bye on the morning of his departure for New Orleans. He had no hat on, but wore spectacles, and was standing in his old favourite attitude, with his hands behind him.

"I want you to understand that at this precise moment, although I was surprised beyond measure, I was not in the least frightened, because I did not for a moment suppose that what I saw was – well, a ghost or apparition of any sort. The thought that flashed across my bewildered brain was simply that there had been some absurd mistake somewhere, and that my brother had never died at all, but was here, alive and well. I took a hasty step towards him.

" 'Good heavens, old fellow!' I exclaimed. 'Where on earth have you come from? Why, we all thought you were dead!'

"I was quite close to him when I stopped abruptly. Somehow I couldn't move another step. He made no motion, but his eyes looked straight into mine.

" 'Do not let Dolly sail on the *Aragon* tomorrow,' he said in slow, clear tones that I heard distinctly.

"And then he was gone – yes, Jack, I know it is a very

conventional way of ending up a ghost story, but I have to tell you just what occurred, or at least what I thought occurred. One moment he was there and the next moment he wasn't. He did not pass me or go out of the door.

"For a few moments I felt dazed. I was wide awake and in my right and proper senses so far as I could judge, and yet the whole thing seemed incredible. Scared? No, I wasn't conscious of being scared. I was simply bewildered.

"In my mental confusion one thought stood out sharply – Dolly was in danger of some kind, and if the warning was really from a supernatural source, it must not be disregarded. I rushed to the station and, having first wired to my wife not to sail on the *Aragon*, I found that I could connect with the five-fifteen train for New York. I took it with the comfortable consciousness that my friends would certainly think I had gone out of my mind.

"I arrived in New York at eight o'clock the next morning and at once drove to the hotel where my wife, daughter and brother-in-law were staying. I found them greatly mystified by my telegram. I suppose my explanation was a very lame one. I know I felt decidedly like a fool. Gilbert laughed at me and said I had dreamed the whole thing. Virginia was perplexed, but Dolly accepted the warning unhesitatingly.

" 'Of course it was Uncle Charley,' she said confidently. 'We will not sail on the *Aragon* now.'

"Gilbert had to give in to this decision with a very bad grace, and the *Aragon* sailed that day minus three of her intended passengers.

"Well, you've all heard of the historic collision between the *Aragon* and the *Astarte* in a fog, and the fearful loss of life it involved. Gilbert didn't laugh when the news came, I assure you. Virginia and Dolly sailed a month later on the *Marseilles*, and reached the other side in safety. That's all the story, boys – the only experience of the kind I ever had," concluded Davenport.

We had many questions to ask and several theories to advance. Jack said Davenport had dreamed it and that the collision of the *Aragon* and the *Astarte* was simply a striking coincidence. But Davenport merely smiled at all our suggestions and, as it cleared up just about three, we told no more ghost stories.

*The Deacon's
Painkiller*

NDREW WAS a terrible set man. When he put his foot down, something always squashed – and stayed squashed. In this particular instance, it was poor Amy's love affair.

"No, my daughter," he said solemnly (the deacon always spoke solemnly and called Amy "my daughter" when he was going to be contrary), "I – ah, shall never consent to your marrying Dr. Boyd. He is not worthy of you."

"I'm sure a Boyd is as good as a Poultney any day," sobbed Amy. "And nobody can say a word against Frank."

"He used to drink, my daughter," said the deacon more solemnly than ever.

"He never touches a drop now," said Amy, firing up. Amy has a spice of the Barry temper. But the deacon did not get angry. There would have been more hope if he had. You can generally do something with a man who loses his temper, especially when it comes to repenting time. But Andrew never lost his temper; he just remained placid and aggravating.

"Don't you know, my poor child," he said sorrowfully, "that a man who has once been addicted to drink is liable to break out again any time? I – ah, have no faith in Dr. Boyd's reformation. Look at his father."

Amy couldn't very well look at Dr. Boyd's father, seeing that he had drunk himself to death and been safely buried in Brunswick churchyard for over fifteen years. But she knew the reference clinched the matter in the deacon's estimation. Amy had not lived with her pa for twenty years without discovering that when he began dragging people's ancestors from their tombs and hurling them at your head, you might as well stop arguing.

Amy stopped and came upstairs to me and cried instead. I couldn't do a great deal to comfort her, knowing Andrew as I did. I'd kept house for him ever since his wife, who was my sister, died; he was as fine a man as ever lived in most respects – very generous, never given to nagging; but when he'd once made up his mind on any point, you might as well try to soften the nether millstone.

For one thing, there was nothing you could use as a lever, because the deacon was such a moral man. If he'd had any little vices or foibles, he might have been vulnerable on some point. But he was so godly as to be almost painful. It's a blessing that he had no sons or they would certainly have gone to the bad by way of keeping the family to a natural average.

Before going any further with this story, I might as well clear up matters in regard to Dr. Boyd. From Andrew's statement, you might suppose that he had once been a confirmed toper. The fact was that young Frank, in spite of his father, was as sober and steady a lad as you could wish to see; but one summer, just before he went to college, he fell in with a wild set of fellows from town who were out at the beach hotel; they went somewhere to a political meeting one night and all got drunk, young Frank included, and made fearful fools of themselves; the deacon was there, representing the temperance interest, and saw them. After that he never had any use for Frank Boyd. It didn't make a mite of difference that Frank was terribly ashamed and sorry and never went with those fellows afterwards nor ever was known to taste liquor again. He got through college splendidly and came home and settled in Brunswick and worked up a fine practice. It was of no use, as far as the deacon was concerned. He persisted in regarding Dr. Frank as a reformed rake who might relapse into his evil ways at any moment. And Andrew would have excused a man for murder before he would have excused him for getting drunk.

The deacon was what his enemies – for he had plenty of enemies in spite of, or maybe because of, his goodness –

called a temperance fanatic. Now, I'm not going to decry temperance. It's the right thing, and I'm a white ribboner myself and never touch even homemade currant wine; and a little fanaticism always greases the wheels of any movement. But I'm bound to say that Andrew carried things too far. He was fairly rabid for the temperance cause; and the only man in the world he wouldn't speak to was Deacon Millar, because Deacon Millar opposed the introduction of unfermented wine for the communion and used whiskey to break up a cold.

So, all these things considered, I thought poor Amy's prospects for marrying her man were very faint indeed, and I felt nearly as bad over it as she did. I knew that Frank Boyd was her choice, once and forever. Amy is a Barry by nature, even if she is a Poultney by birth, and the Barrys never change – as *I* could testify; but this isn't my story. If they can't marry the one they set their hearts on, they never marry. And Frank Boyd was such a fine young fellow, and everybody liked and respected him. Any man in the world but Andrew would have been delighted at the thought of having him for a son-in-law.

However, I comforted Amy as well as I could and I even agreed to go and argue with her pa, although I knew I should have nothing to show for my waste of breath. And I hadn't, although I did all that mortal woman could do. I cooked a magnificent dinner with all the deacon's favourite dishes; and after he had eaten all he possibly could and twice as much as was good for him, I tackled him – and failed. And when a woman fails under *those* circumstances, she may as well fold her hands and hold her tongue.

Andrew heard all I had to say politely, as he always did, for he prided himself on his good manners; but I saw right along that it wasn't sinking in any deeper than the skin.

"No, Juliana," he said patiently, "I – ah, can never give my daughter to a reformed drunkard. I – ah, should tremble for her happiness. Besides, think how it would look if I – ah, were to allow my daughter to marry a man addicted to drink, I – ah, who am noted for my sound temperance principles. Why, it would be a handle for the liquor people to use against me. I – ah, beg of you, dear Juliana, not to refer to this painful subject again and *not* to encourage my daughter in her foolish and unfilial conduct. It will only make an unpleasantness in our peaceful home – an unpleasantness that can in no way further any wishes she or you may have unwisely formed on this subject. I – ah, feel sure that a woman of your prudence and good sense must see this clearly."

I was seeing red just then, for Andrew's "I – ah's" had put me in a regular Barry temper. But I had sense enough to hold my tongue, although I could have cried out for very rage. I took my revenge by feeding the deacon on salt codfish and scraps for a week. He never knew why, but he suffered. However, I'm bound to say he suffered meekly, with the air of a man who knew womenfolk take queer spells and have to be humoured.

FOR THE FOLLOWING MONTH the deacon's "peaceful home" had a rather uncomfortable atmosphere. Amy cried and moped and fretted, and Dr. Boyd didn't dare come near the place. Just what would have finally happened, if it hadn't been for the interposition of Providence, nobody knows. I suppose Amy would either have fretted herself to death and gone into consumption like her ma, or she would have run away with Frank and never been forgiven by her pa to the day of her death. And that would have almost killed her too, for Amy loved her pa – and with good reason, for he had always been an excellent pa to her and never before refused her anything in reason.

Meanwhile, the deacon was having troubles of his own. His party wanted to bring him out as a candidate at the next local election, and the deacon wanted to be brought out. But of course the liquor interest was dead against him, and he had some personal foes even on the temperance side; and altogether it was doubtful if he would get the nomination. But he was working hard for it, and his chances were at least as good as any other man's until the first Sunday in August came round.

The deacon felt a bit offish that morning when he got up; I could tell so much by his prayer even if I hadn't known he had a bad cold. The deacon's prayers are an infallible index to his state of health. When he is feeling well they are cheerful, and you can tell he has his own doubts about the doctrine of reprobation; but when he is a little under the weather his prayers are just like the old lady who said, "The Universalists think all the world is going to be saved, but we Presbyterians hope for better things."

There was a strong tinge of this in the deacon's prayer that Sunday morning, but that didn't prevent him from eating a big breakfast of ham and eggs and hot muffins, topping off with marmalade and cheese. The deacon *will* eat cheese, although he knows it never agrees with him; and shortly before church time it began to make trouble for the poor man.

When I came downstairs – Amy did not go to church that day, which, in the light of what came afterwards, was a fortunate thing – I found the deacon in his best black suit, sitting on the kitchen sofa with his hands clasped over his stomach and a most mournful expression of countenance.

"I – ah, have a bad attack of cramps, Juliana," he said with a groan. "They come on just as sudden. I – ah, wish you would fix me up a dose of ginger tea."

"There isn't a drop of hot water in the house," I said, "but I'll see what I can get you."

The deacon, with sundry dismal groans, followed me into the pantry. While I was measuring out the ginger, he spied a big black bottle away upon the top shelf.

"Why, there is the very thing!" he exclaimed joyfully. "Mr. Johnson's painkiller! Why didn't I think of it before?"

I felt dubious about the painkiller, for I don't believe in messing with medicines you don't know anything about, though goodness knows Mr. Johnson used enough of it, and it seemed to agree with him fine. He was a young artist who had boarded with us the summer before, and a real nice, jolly, offhanded young fellow he was. We all liked him, and he got on extra well with the deacon, agreeing with him in everything, especially as regards temperance. He wasn't strong though, poor young man, and soon after he came he told us he was subject to stomach trouble and had to take a dose of painkiller after every meal and sometimes between meals. He kept his bottle of it in the pantry, and I thought him a real good hand to take medicine, for he never made any faces swallowing that painkiller. He said it was a special mixture, tonic and painkiller combined, that his doctor had ordered for him, and it wasn't hard to take. He went away in a hurry one day in consequence of a telegram saying his mother was ill, and he forgot his bottle of tonic – a new one he had just begun on. It had been standing there on the pantry shelf ever since.

The deacon climbed up on a chair, got it down, opened it, and sniffed at it.

"I kind of like the smell," he said, as he poured out a glassful, same as he'd seen Mr. Johnson do.

"I wouldn't take too much of it," I said warningly. "You don't know how it might agree with you."

But the deacon thought he knew, and he drank it all down and smacked his lips.

"That is the nicest kind of painkiller I – ah, ever tasted, Juliana," he said. "It has a real appetizing flavour. I – ah, believe I'll take another glass; I – ah, have seen Mr. Johnson take two. Maybe it has lost its strength, standing there so long, and I – ah, do not want to risk another attack of cramp in church. It is best to make sure. I – ah, feel better already."

So went the second glass and, when I came back with my bonnet on, that misguided man was just drinking a third.

"The cramp is all gone, Juliana," he said joyfully. "That painkiller is the right kind of medicine and no mistake. I – ah, feel fine. Come on, let's go to church."

He said it in a light, hilarious sort of tone as if he'd been saying, "Let's go to a picnic." We walked to the church – it wasn't more than half a mile – and Andrew stepped along jauntily and talked about various worldly subjects. He was especially eloquent about the election and discoursed as if he were sure of the nomination. He seemed so excited that I felt real uneasy, thinking he must be feverish.

We were late as usual, for our clock is always slow; Andrew will never have it meddled with because it was his grandfather's. The minister was just giving out his text when we got there. Our pew is right at the top of the church. The Boyd pew is just behind and Dr. Frank was sitting in it all alone. I saw his face fall as I went into our pew, and I knew he was feeling disappointed because Amy hadn't come. Almost everybody else in Brunswick was there, though, and the church was full. Andrew sat down in his place with a loud, cheerful "hem," and looked beamingly around on the congregation, smiling all across his face. I'd never seen Andrew smile in church before – he was usually as grave and solemn as if he were at a funeral – and there seemed something uncanny about it. I felt real relieved when he stopped looking around and concentrated his attention on the minister, who was just warming up to his subject.

Mr. Stanley is a real fine preacher. We've had him for three years and everybody likes him. In two minutes I was lost to all worldly things, listening to his eloquence. But suddenly – all too suddenly – my thoughts were recalled to earth.

I heard the deacon make a queer sort of noise, something between a growl and a sniff, and I looked around just in time to see him jump to his feet. He was scowling and his face was purple. I'd never seen Andrew in a temper before, but now he was just mad clean through.

"I tell you, preacher, that isn't true," he shouted. "It's heresy – rank heresy – that is what it is – and as a deacon of this church I shall not let it pass unchallenged. Preacher, you've got to take that back. It ain't true and what's more, it ain't sound doctrine."

And here the deacon gave the pew back in front of him such a resounding thwack that deaf old Mrs. Prott, who sat before him and hadn't heard a word of his outburst, felt the jar and jumped up as if she had been shot. But Mrs. Prott was the only person in church who hadn't heard him, and the sensation was something I can't describe. Mr. Stanley had stopped short, with his hand outstretched, as if he were turned to stone, and his eyes were fairly sticking out of his head. They are goggle eyes at the best of times, for Mr. Stanley is no beauty with all his brains. I shall never forget the look of him at that moment.

I suppose I should have tried to calm the deacon or do something, but I was simply too thunderstruck to move or speak. The plain truth is, I thought Andrew had suddenly gone out of his mind and the horror of it froze me.

Meanwhile, the deacon, having got his second wind,

went on, punctuating his remarks with thumps on the pew back.

"Never since I was a deacon have I heard such doctrine preached from this pulpit. The idea of saying that maybe all the heathen won't be lost! You know they will be, for if they wouldn't, all the money we've been giving foreign missions would be clean wasted. You're unsound, that's what you are! We ask for bread and you give us a stone." A tremendous thwack!

Just then Dr. Boyd got up behind us. He leaned forward and tapped the deacon on the shoulder.

"Let us go out and talk it over outside, Mr. Poultney," he said quietly, as if it was all a regular part of the performance.

I expected to see the deacon fly at him, but instead, Andrew just flung his arms around Frank's neck and burst into tears.

"Yesh, lesh go out, m' dear boy," he sobbed. "Lesh leave this ungodly plache. Blesh you, m' boy! Always loved you like a son – yesh. So doesh Amy."

Dr. Boyd piloted him down the aisle. The deacon insisted on walking with his arms around Frank's neck and he sobbed all the way out. Just by the door he came to a dead stop and looked at Selena Cotton, who was sitting past the door in the first raised pew. Like myself, Selena isn't as young as she used to be; but, unlike myself, she hasn't quite given up thinking about marriage, and everybody in Brunswick knew that she had been setting her cap for the deacon ever since his wife died. The deacon knew it himself.

Dr. Boyd tried to get him to move on, but Andrew wouldn't budge until he had had his say. "Jesh in a moment, m' dear boy. Don' be in such a hurry – never be in a hurry going out of church – go shlow and dignified –

always. Look at that lady. Blesh me, she's a fine woman – fines' woman in Brunswick. But I never encouraged her, Frank, 'pon my word. I'd shcorn to trifle with a lady's affections. Yesh, yesh, I'm coming, m' dear boy."

With that, the deacon threw a kiss at the outraged Selena and walked out.

Of course I had followed them, and now Frank said to me in a low voice, "I'll drive him home – but my buggy is very narrow. Would you mind walking, Miss Barry?"

"I'll walk, of course, but tell me," I whispered anxiously, "do you think this attack is serious?"

"Not at all. I think he will soon recover and be all right," said the doctor. His face was as grave as a judge's, but I was sure I saw his eyes twinkle and I resented it. Here was Andrew either gone crazy or sickening from some dreadful disease and Dr. Boyd was laughing internally over it. I walked home in a state of mingled alarm and indignation. When I got there the doctor's buggy was tied at the gate, the doctor and Amy were sitting together on the kitchen sofa, and the deacon was nowhere to be seen.

"Where's Andrew?" I exclaimed.

"In there, sound asleep," said Frank, nodding at the door of the deacon's bedroom.

"What is the matter with him?" I persisted. I was sure that Amy had been laughing, and I wondered if I was dreaming or if everybody had gone stark mad.

"Well," said the doctor, "in plain English, he is – drunk!"

I sat down; fortunately there was a chair behind me. I don't know whether I felt more relieved or indignant.

"It's impossible!" I said. "Im – possible! The deacon never – there isn't a drop – he didn't taste a thing – why – why -"

In a flash I remembered the painkiller. I flew to the pantry, snatched the bottle, and rushed to Frank.

"It's the painkiller – Mr. Johnson's painkiller – he took an overdose of it – and maybe he's poisoned. Oh, do something for him quick! He may be dying this minute."

Dr. Frank didn't get excited. He uncorked the bottle, smelled it, and then took a swig of its contents.

"Don't be alarmed, Miss Barry," he said, smiling. "This happens to be wine; I don't know what particular kind, but it is pretty strong."

"Drunk!" I said – and then *I* began to laugh, though I've been ashamed of it ever since.

"The deacon will sleep it off," said the doctor, "and be no worse when he wakens, except that he will probably have a bad headache. The thing for us to do is to hold a consultation and decide how this incident may be turned to the best advantage."

THE DEACON SLEPT until after supper. Then we heard a feeble groan proceeding from the bedroom. I went in and Frank followed me, his face solemn in the extreme. The deacon was sitting on the side of the bed, looking woebegone and dissipated.

"How are you feeling now, Andrew?" I asked.

"I don't feel well," said the deacon. "My head is splitting. Have I been sick? I thought I was in church. I don't remember coming home. What is the matter with me, doctor?"

"The plain truth, Mr. Poultney," said young Frank deliberately, "is that you were drunk. No, sit still!" – for the deacon had bounced up alarmingly – "I am not trying to insult you. You took three doses of what you supposed to be painkiller, but which was really a very strong wine. Then you went to church and made a scene; that is all."

"All! Gracious Providence!" groaned the poor deacon, sitting dazedly down again. "You can't mean it – yes, you do. Juliana, for pity's sake, tell me what I said and did. I have dim recollections – I thought they were just bad dreams."

I told him the truth. When I got to where he had thrown a kiss at Selena Cotton, he flung up his hands in despair.

"I'm a ruined man – utterly ruined! My standing in the community is gone forever and I've lost every chance of the nomination and Selena Cotton will marry me in spite of myself with this for a handle. Oh, if I only had that Johnson here!"

"Don't worry, Deacon," said Frank soothingly. "I think you can hush the matter up with my assistance. For instance, I might gravely state to all and sundry that you had a feverish cold and took a bad attack of cramp with it; that to relieve it you imprudently took a dose of very strong painkiller left here by a boarder, which painkiller, not being suited to your ailment, went straight to your head and rendered you delirious for the time being and entirely unaccountable for your words and actions. That is all quite true, and I think people will believe me."

"That will be the very thing," said the deacon eagerly. "You'll do it, won't you, Frank?"

"I don't know," said Frank gravely. "I might do it – for my future father-in-law."

The deacon never blinked.

"Of course, of course," he declared. "You can have Amy. I've been an old idiot. But if you can get me out of this scrape, I'll agree to anything you ask."

Dr. Frank got him out of it. There was a fearful lot of gossip and clatter at first, but Frank had the same story for everyone and they finally believed him, especially as the deacon stayed meekly in bed and had any amount of medicines sent over under Frank's prescription from the drugstore. Nobody was allowed to see him. When people called to inquire for him, we told them that the doctor's orders were that he was to be kept perfectly quiet, lest any excitement might set up the brain disturbance again.

"It's *very* strange," said Selena Cotton. "If it had been anyone but Deacon Poultney, people would really have supposed that he was intoxicated."

"Yes," I assented calmly, "the doctor says there was a drug in the painkiller that is apt to have the same effect as liquor. However, I guess it has taught Andrew a lesson. He won't go drinking strange medicines again without knowing what is in them. He is thankful he has escaped as well as he has. It might have been poison."

In the long run the deacon got his nomination and won his election, and Frank got Amy. But nowadays, when the deacon has the cramp, I brew him up a good hot jorum of ginger tea. I never mention the word "painkiller" to him.

Detected
by the Camera

NE SUMMER I was attacked by the craze for amateur photography. It became chronic afterwards, and I and my camera have never since been parted. We have had some odd adventures together, and one of the most novel of our experiences was that in which we played the part of chief witness against Ned Brooke.

I may say that my name is Amy Clarke, and that I believe I am considered the best amateur photographer in our part of the country. That is all I need tell you about myself.

Mr. Carroll had asked me to photograph his place for him when the apple orchards were in bloom. He has a picturesque old-fashioned country house behind a lawn of the most delightful old trees and flanked on each side by the orchards. So I went one June afternoon, with all my accoutrements, prepared to "take" the Carroll establishment in my best style.

Mr. Carroll was away but was expected home soon, so we waited for him, as all the family wished to be photographed under the big maple at the front door. I prowled around among the shrubbery at the lower end of the lawn and, after a great deal of squinting from various angles, I at last fixed upon the spot from which I thought the best view of the house might be obtained. Then Gertie and Lilian Carroll and I got into the hammocks and swung at our leisure, enjoying the cool breeze sweeping through the maples.

Ned Brooke was hanging around as usual, watching us furtively. Ned was one of the hopeful members of a family that lived in a tumble-down shanty just across the road from the Carrolls. They were wretchedly poor, and old Brooke, as he was called, and Ned were employed a good deal by Mr. Carroll – more out of charity than anything else, I fancy.

The Brookes had a rather shady reputation. They were notoriously lazy, and it was suspected that their line of distinction between their own and their neighbours' goods was not very clearly drawn. Many people censured Mr. Carroll for encouraging them at all, but he was too kind-hearted to let them suffer actual want and, as a consequence, one or the other of them was always dodging about his place.

Ned was a lank, tow-headed youth of about fourteen, with shifty, twinkling eyes that could never look you straight in the face. His appearance was anything but prepossessing, and I always felt, when I looked at him, that if anyone wanted to do a piece of shady work by proxy, Ned Brooke would be the very lad for the business.

Mr. Carroll came at last, and we all went down to meet him at the gate. Ned Brooke also came shuffling along to take the horse, and Mr. Carroll tossed the reins to him and at the same time handed a pocketbook to his wife.

"Just as well to be careful where you put that," he said laughingly. "There's a sum in it not to be picked up on every gooseberry bush. Gilman Harris paid me this morning for that bit of woodland I sold him last fall – five hundred dollars. I promised that you and the girls should have it to get a new piano, so there it is for you."

"Thank you," said Mrs. Carroll delightedly. "However, you'd better put it back in your pocket till we go in. Amy is in a hurry."

Mr. Carroll took back the pocketbook and dropped it carelessly into the inside pocket of the light overcoat that he wore.

I happened to glance at Ned Brooke just then, and I could not help noticing the sudden crafty, eager expression that flashed over his face. He eyed the pocketbook in Mr. Carroll's hands furtively, after which he went off with the horse in a great hurry.

The girls were exclaiming and thanking their father, and nobody noticed Ned Brooke's behaviour but myself, and it soon passed out of my mind.

"Come to take the place, are you, Amy?" said Mr. Carroll. "Well, everything is ready, I think. I suppose we'd better proceed. Where shall we stand? You had better group us as you think best."

Whereupon I proceeded to arrange them in due order under the maple. Mrs. Carroll sat in a chair, while her husband stood behind her. Gertie stood on the steps with a basket of flowers in her hand, and Lilian was at one side. The two little boys, Teddy and Jack, climbed up into the maple, and little Dora, the dimpled six-year-old, stood gravely in the foreground with an enormous grey cat hugged in her chubby arms.

It was a pretty group in a pretty setting, and I thrilled with professional pride as I stepped back for a final, knowing squint at it all. Then I went to my camera, slipped in the plate, gave them due warning and took off the cap.

I took two plates to make sure and then the thing was over, but as I had another plate left I thought I might as well take a view of the house by itself, so I carried my camera to a new place and had just got everything ready to lift the cap when Mr. Carroll came down and said:

"If you girls want to see something pretty, come to the back field with me. That will wait till you come back, won't it, Amy?"

So we all betook ourselves to the back field, a short distance away, where Mr. Carroll proudly displayed two of the prettiest little Jersey cows I had ever seen.

We returned to the house by way of the back lane and, as we came in sight of the main road, my brother Cecil drove up and said that if I were ready, I had better go home with him and save myself a hot, dusty walk.

The Carrolls all went down to the fence to speak to

Cecil, but I dashed hurriedly down through the orchard, leaped over the fence into the lawn and ran to the somewhat remote corner where I had left my camera. I was in a desperate hurry, for I knew Cecil's horse did not like to be kept waiting, so I never even glanced at the house, but snatched off the cap, counted two and replaced it.

Then I took out my plate, put it in the holder and gathered up my traps. I suppose I was about five minutes at it all and I had my back to the house the whole time, and when I laid all my things ready and emerged from my retreat, there was nobody to be seen about the place.

As I hurried up through the lawn, I noticed Ned Brooke walking at a smart pace down the lane, but the fact did not make any particular impression on me at the time, and was not recalled until afterwards.

Cecil was waiting for me, so I got in the buggy and we drove off. On arriving home I shut myself up in my dark room and proceeded to develop the first two negatives of the Carroll housestead. They were both excellent, the first one being a trifle the better, so that I decided to finish from it. I intended also to develop the third, but just as I finished the others, a half-dozen city cousins swooped down upon us and I had to put away my paraphernalia, emerge from my dark retreat and fly around to entertain them.

The next day Cecil came in and said:

"Did you hear, Amy, that Mr. Carroll has lost a pocket-book with five hundred dollars in it?"

"No!" I exclaimed. "How? When? Where?"

"Don't overwhelm a fellow. I can answer only one question – last night. As to the 'how,' they don't know, and as to the 'where' – well, if they knew that, there might be some hope of finding it. The girls are in a bad way. The money was to get them their longed-for piano, it seems, and now it's gone."

"But how did it happen, Cecil?"

"Well, Mr. Carroll says that Mrs. Carroll handed the pocketbook back to him at the gate yesterday, and he dropped it in the inside pocket of his overcoat –"

"I saw him do it," I cried.

"Yes, and then, before he went to be photographed, he hung his coat up in the hall. It hung there until the evening, and nobody seems to have thought about the money, each supposing that someone else had put it carefully away. After tea Mr. Carroll put on the coat and went to see somebody over at Netherby. He says the thought of the pocketbook never crossed his mind; he had forgotten all about putting it in that coat pocket. He came home across the fields about eleven o'clock and found that the cows had broken into the clover hay, and he had a great chase before he got them out. When he went in, just as he entered the door, the remembrance of the money flashed over him. He felt in his pocket, but there was no pocketbook there; he asked his wife if she had taken it out. She had not, and nobody else had. There was a hole in the pocket, but Mr. Carroll says it was too small for the pocket-book to have worked through. However, it must have done so – unless someone took it out of his pocket at Netherby, and that is not possible, because he never had his coat off, and it was in an inside pocket. It's not likely that they will ever see it again. Someone may pick it up, of course, but the chances are slim. Mr. Carroll doesn't know his exact path across the fields, and if he lost it while he was after the cows, it's a bluer show still. They've been searching all day, of course. The girls are awfully disappointed."

A sudden recollection came to me of Ned Brooke's face as I had seen it the day before at the gate, coupled with the remembrance of seeing him walking down the lane at a quick pace, so unlike his usual shambling gait, while I ran through the lawn.

"How do they know it was lost?" I said. "Perhaps it was stolen before Mr. Carroll went to Netherby."

"They think not," said Cecil. "Who would have stolen it?"

"Ned Brooke. I saw him hanging around. And you never saw such a look as came over his face when he heard Mr. Carroll say there was five hundred dollars in that pocket-book."

"Well, I did suggest to them that Ned might know something about it, for I remembered having seen him go down the lane while I was waiting for you, but they won't hear of such a thing. The Brookes are kind of protégés of theirs, you know, and they won't believe anything bad of them. If Ned did take it, however, there's not a shadow of evidence against him."

"No, I suppose not," I answered thoughtfully, "but the more I think it over, the more I'm convinced that he took it. You know, we all went to the back field to look at the Jerseys, and all that time the coat was hanging there in the hall, and not a soul in the house. And it was just after we came back that I saw Ned scuttling down the lane so fast."

I mentioned my suspicions to the Carrolls a few days afterwards, when I went down with the photographs, and found that they had discovered no trace of the lost pocketbook. But they seemed positively angry when I hinted that Ned Brooke might know more about its whereabouts than anyone else. They declared that they would as soon think of suspecting one of themselves as Ned, and altogether they seemed so offended at my suggestion that I held my peace and didn't irritate them by any more suppositions.

Afterwards, in the excitement of our cousins' visit, the matter passed out of my mind completely. They stayed two weeks, and I was so busy the whole time that I never got a chance to develop that third plate and, in fact, I had forgotten all about it.

One morning soon after they went away, I remembered the plate and decided to go and develop it. Cecil went with me, and we shut ourselves up in our den, lit our ruby lantern and began operations.

I did not expect much of the plate, because it had been exposed and handled carelessly, and I thought that it might prove to be underexposed or light-struck. So I left Cecil to develop it while I prepared the fixing bath. Cecil was whistling away when suddenly he gave a tremendous "whew" of astonishment and sprang to his feet.

"Amy, Amy, look here!" he cried.

I rushed to his side and looked at the plate as he held it up in the rosy light. It was a splendid one, and the Carroll house came out clear, with the front door and the steps in full view.

And there, just in the act of stepping from the threshold, was the figure of a boy with an old straw hat on his head and – in his hand – the pocketbook!

He was standing with his head turned towards the corner of the house as if listening, with one hand holding his ragged coat open and the other poised in mid-air with the pocketbook, as if he were just going to put it in his inside pocket. The whole scene was as clear as noonday, and nobody with eyes in his head could have failed to recognize Ned Brooke.

"Goodness!" I gasped. "In with it – quick!"

And we doused the thing into the fixing bath and then sat down breathlessly and looked at each other.

"I say, Amy," said Cecil, "what a sell this will be on the Carrolls! Ned Brooke couldn't do such a thing – oh, no! The poor injured boy at whom everyone has such an unlawful pick! I wonder if this will convince them."

"Do you think they can get it all back?" I asked. "It's not likely he would have dared to use any of it yet."

"I don't know. We'll have a try, anyhow. How long before this plate will be dry enough to carry down to the Carrolls as circumstantial evidence?"

"Three hours or thereabouts," I answered, "but perhaps sooner. I'll take two prints off when it is ready. I wonder what the Carrolls will say."

"It's a piece of pure luck that the plate should have turned out so well after the slap-dash way in which it was taken and used. I say, Amy, isn't this quite an adventure?"

At last the plate was dry, and I printed two proofs. We wrapped them up carefully and marched down to Mr. Carroll's.

You never saw people so overcome with astonishment as the Carrolls were when Cecil, with the air of a statesman unfolding the evidence of some dreadful conspiracy against the peace and welfare of the nation, produced the plate and the proofs, and held them out before them.

Mr. Carroll and Cecil took the proofs and went over to the Brooke shanty. They found only Ned and his mother at home. At first Ned, when taxed with his guilt, denied it, but when Mr. Carroll confronted him with the proofs, he broke down in a spasm of terror and confessed all. His mother produced the pocketbook and the money – they had not dared to spend a single cent of it – and Mr. Carroll went home in triumph.

Perhaps Ned Brooke ought not to have been let off so easily as he was, but his mother cried and pleaded, and Mr. Carroll was too kind-hearted to resist. So he did not punish them at all, save by utterly discarding the whole family and their concerns. The place got too hot for them after the story came out, and in less than a month all moved away – much to the benefit of Mapleton.

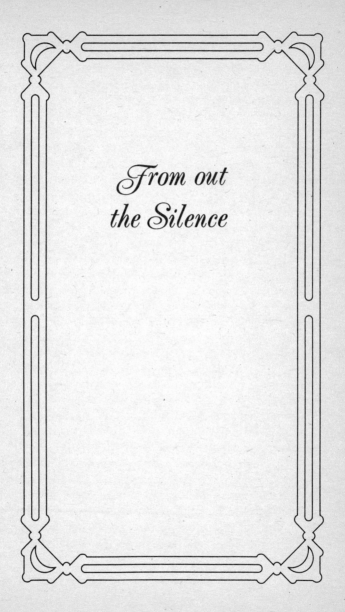

*From out
the Silence*

NNE HAMILTON had wakened from a dream of Edith. It is a strange thing to dream of the dead. There in your dream they are living, but still you know somehow that they are dead. It was the first time she had dreamed of Edith since her death, but although they had been walking together, Edith's face was averted – always averted. So the dream was no comfort to her, and her memory of Edith's face in life was becoming so blurred and indistinct.

Anne had a strange defect – or rather lack of a faculty. She could not remember faces which she had not seen for some time. She could not call up before her mind's eye a picture of them as other people seemed able to do. Edith had been dead for six months, and she was forgetting what her old friend had looked like.

There was no picture to help her. Edith had never had a photograph taken. It was an odd kink of hers. She was determined that no picture of her should exist after her death. Anne had never been able to budge her an inch on this point.

It was six months since Edith had died, but it was a year since they had quarrelled. That foolish, senseless quarrel over scapegrace Jim Harvey! It had come up like a flash out of the blue. They had often enough talked of Jim Harvey before and they had never quarrelled, although they always disagreed. Anne had no use – never had had any use – for Jim Harvey. Edith had always loved and defended him. That they should quarrel over him was unthinkable, yet they had done it. Edith had been worried over something that day. Perhaps Anne had been a little tactless. Something had been touched on the raw. And they had quarrelled bitterly after thirty years of flawless friendship. They would have made up if Edith had lived, Anne was desperately sure of that. But she left soon after for her trip abroad, and in Italy the telegram, sent by a cousin who knew nothing of their quarrel, had reached her, telling her that Edith was suddenly dead. Anne buried her face in the pillow and moaned as she always did when she recalled the anguish of that moment.

When she came home the autumn rains were beating down on Edith's grave, and there was nothing for her to do on stormy winter evenings that followed but sit alone and think of her lost friend. She could not even find alleviation of her pain in books. Everything she read reminded her of Edith. They had read and talked over so many books. There were poems and passages all through them that Edith had marked. If it had not been for the quarrel, these things would have comforted her. Now they were like a knife thrust through her heart.

Owlwood was shut up and tenantless. Never again could she look up to the hill and see Edith's light on it. And Edith had died in bitterness with her – without a word of love or remembrance. There lay the intolerable sting. Anne would have given anything she possessed to have known that Edith had thought kindly of her before death – had wished for reconciliation. She could not have done so when she had left no message. The Hamiltons had all been so bitter and unrelenting when they had quarrelled. Edith had gone away into the silence from which forevermore no word of reconciliation could come.

Anne's loneliness through the winter that followed her return to Glenellyn was terrible. She had always been a rather distant, reserved woman, reputed proud, and had no other intimate friend. Edith and she had been all in all to each other. They were almost of an age and had been friends from girlhood. Edith's young husband had died so soon after their marriage that it never seemed to Anne that Edith had really been married at all. Alastair Graham had left his wife a fortune, and Owlwood was a thing of beauty; but she had spent as much time in Anne's modest little home on the outskirts of Croyden as she did in her own.

Anne had known enough of grief in her life to know that, in time, even the bitterest memory fades out into a not unpleasing sweetness and dearness of recollection when there is no poison in it. She knew that, if it had not been for the quarrel and the fact that Edith had made no gesture of reconciliation even when she had known she was dying, her memories of Edith would have been her companions and comforters. She would have been free to imagine that Edith was still there, free to think of her in the moonlit twilights they had loved, in the garden where they had talked among the flowers they had planted. The jokes they had savoured together would still have an echo of merriment; even their old silences – silence with Edith had been more eloquent than talk with another woman – would be beautiful to recall.

But now . . .

"My days are nothing but ghosts," said Anne bitterly.

They would never be anything but ghosts. And she was not old – only forty-eight. Long years might be before her – bitter, empty years. All her memories poisoned and rankling.

"If there had been one word – just one word. If she had only mentioned my name!"

The misery of her dream of Edith's averted face went with her all day. Everything was embittered for her by it – the loveliness of her garden, the beloved willow-ware pattern plates Edith had given her two Christmases ago, the golden silence of her sun porch, the beautiful moods of the shadowy hill to the westward of Glenellyn, the soft, new-mooned skies, the tree they had planted together in memory of a soldier cousin who had died in the war. Jim Harvey had escaped the draft by some chicanery. It was something Anne had said concerning this that had brought about their quarrel. She had often said worse things than that to Edith about Jim Harvey – that frank, friendly, charming scoundrel. Edith had never flared up over them. She had always agreed sadly that he was by way of being a bad egg.

"But I can't help liking him," she used to protest whimsically. "He will be liked. I know everything you say of him is true. I know I ought to be ashamed of a relation who is a slacker and an embezzler. I am ashamed of him – and I keep on liking him. I think it was because he was such an adorable baby. Even you can't deny that. I loved him as soon as I saw him and I can't seem to get over loving people once I begin. You can abuse him as much as you like, Anne. My brain agrees with every word you say. But my heart simply won't. If I knew where he was I'd try to help him in some way."

She had always been so good-natured over Anne's viewpoint. And then to flare up as she did and tear asunder the bonds of a lifetime! Anne could never understand it.

Cousin Lida dropped in that evening, full of family gossip as usual. Anne couldn't bear Cousin Lida now. She and Edith used to have so much fun over Cousin Lida. She really was a comical old dear. Anne remembered how Edith used to "take her off."

"That Maureen thing is out of the hospital," she said.

Anne winced. "That Maureen thing" was Jim's wife, the pretty, common little hairdresser he had married. None of the family except Edith had ever taken any notice of her. After Jim had escaped arrest for embezzlement by departing for shores unknown, she had opened up her shop again and managed to support herself and her children and her childish old aunt. Then she had to go to the hospital for a serious operation.

"She looks dreadful, and she hasn't a cent," went on Cousin Lida. "She couldn't keep up the rent of the shop, so she's lost it. It's a judgement on her, no doubt."

Anne found herself smiling painfully over what Edith would have made of that. Maureen was not the person any cousin of the Hamiltons should have married, but Anne didn't know just what she had done to deserve a "judgement." She had been faithful to her scapegrace husband and she had done her best to look after his children.

"What is to become of her?" asked Anne.

"Heaven knows," said Cousin Lida in a voice that sounded very dubious of heaven's knowledge. "It's a pity Edith isn't alive. She would have helped her, I don't doubt. I know she meant to leave her something in her will, but she went so sudden, poor dear, she hadn't time to make one. It should be a warning for us all. John Alec ought to do something. He got all Edith's money because he was her half-brother. But he always hated Jim and he won't lift a finger to help the poor widow."

"I'll look after her," said Anne.

She was even more amazed than Cousin Lida over her own speech. Until she found herself saying it, she had no idea of such a thing. But Edith would have done it.

"You! But I thought . . . and how can you? You haven't got more than enough for yourself," protested Cousin Lida, a little outrage in her tone. Anne was stripping them all of any excuse for not helping Maureen.

"I've house room for them," said Anne. "And they can be fed somehow."

A SCORE OF TIMES during the summer that followed, Anne asked herself why she had been such a fool. She never felt reconciled to what she had done. It hadn't been necessary really. Maureen could have put the children and her aunt in some home and found some way of supporting herself. Instead, she, Anne, had saddled herself with their support and – worse still – their companionship. Anne did not mind the pinching and scrimping made necessary to stretch her little income over six people, to say nothing of two dogs and a cat. But it was unbearable to have her home overrun and her life turned upside-down and inside-out. For that was what it felt like.

One couldn't exactly hate any of them – Anne would have felt rather better if she could have hated them. Maureen was such a good-hearted, vulgar little soul. She jested at everything Anne held sacred and laughed and talked and told stories in excruciating grammar from morning to night. She told all the details of her operation to everyone who came to the house. She slammed doors and entertained her women friends loudly after Anne had gone to bed. She had plucked eyebrows and shallow blue eyes with no thought behind them. She had no idea what reticence meant. She was constantly and cheerfully suggesting changes that would improve Glenellyn. Anne was horrified at the thought of any change. She was passionately loyal to her home – all its virtues, all its faults. And Maureen would pat her condescendingly on the shoulder and tell her she was a darling old thing and nothing should be changed if she didn't want it.

Anne tried to like the children. They were not unlovable. But the things they did! There was hardly a day they didn't smash something. Maureen never tried to control them.

"I was bossed to death when I was a kid," she said. "My children ain't going to be repressed like that. They're going to enjoy their childhood."

Perhaps they enjoyed it, but nobody else did. And Jimmy was sick more than half the time.

"He always takes everything that comes along," Maureen would say philosophically – and leave the nursing to Anne and Aunt Beenie.

Aunt Beenie was the one Anne detested most. She reproached herself for this. Poor old Aunt Beenie! Well-meaning, harmless, but terrible.

There was something so uncanny about her. She had lost her memory almost completely and constantly muttered to herself in a senile fashion Anne found peculiarly repulsive – even more so than her sudden fits of inane laughter. Then memory would return for a few moments and Aunt Beenie would astonish everybody by some quite rational remark or well-told story.

People wondered how Anne Hamilton could endure the gang at all. She wondered herself. Life was a kind of nightmare. She had no peace – no quiet – no Edith. For she had quite forgotten Edith's face now and she could find nothing but pain still in all her memories of their companionship. That unhealed quarrel must fester forever. In a way Maureen and her family were a blessing. They kept her from thinking. She had no chance to think. Some of Maureen's friends were always coming or going; the children were always getting into scrapes; the dog was always bringing in bones or tearing up the garden; Aunt Beenie was always wandering off and getting lost or locking herself in the bathroom and forgetting how to unlock it.

"I often wonder why you don't kick us all out," laughed Maureen the day Jenny had ruined the new hall wallpaper with greasy fingerprints.

Anne might have wondered if she hadn't known. Edith would have looked after Maureen. She was doing it for Edith's sake – Edith who had died hating her.

On the day Maureen and the children and Aunt Beenie went off to the city to visit friends, Anne gazed about her with a sigh of relief. A whole day to be alone! She looked lovingly at her old books, her piano, her pictures, her garden. How she would savour them again! She had locked the dog up in the toolshed and shut Jenny's kitten in the cellar. Yesterday the kitten had disorganized the household by having a fit and crawling into a hole in the kitchen wall behind the stove. Anne had to send for men to tear out half the kitchen wall to rescue it. She had been so angry that she had meant to have the kitten disposed of. But Jenny and Jimmy had screamed themselves black in the face over the mere thought of it, and Maureen had pleaded and Aunt Beenie had cried bitterly without the least idea what she was crying about . . . and Anne had yielded.

But today was her own. A ripe autumn day, with the pale gold of aspens behind the garden. She went out and sat near them. She would do nothing for one blessed hour – nothing but sit there in the beautiful silence.

And then she saw Aunt Beenie coming around the corner of the house.

Anne knew what had happened. Aunt Beenie had run away from Maureen at the station; Maureen had shrugged her shoulders and laughed and gone on the train. Aunt Beenie would turn up safe. She always did.

Any day – every day – comes to an end. Anne thought that particular one never would. She couldn't lock Aunt Beenie up in the toolshed or the cellar. Neither could she stop her from talking. Aunt Beenie's tongue was never still for one moment. She asked the same questions over and over again and cried if Anne wouldn't answer them. And she wound up the day by falling down the back porch steps.

She did not hurt herself in the least. Anne got her into the sun room and made her lie down on the couch. Aunt Beenie was strangely obedient, and had suddenly become quiet. She lay there in silence for a time with her eyes shut. Anne sat, spent, in her rocking chair. She was tired out physically and mentally. She felt that she must scream if

Aunt Beenie started talking again. Aunt Beenie did, and her first words startled Anne.

"It was kind of nice of Edith to send you her picture, wasn't it?"

HER TONE was quite rational, but there was no sense in such a remark. Anne closed her eyes. It had begun again. Could she bear to hear Aunt Beenie talk about Edith?

"It was a real good picture of her," Aunt Beenie went on in a moving, musing tone. "She said she'd always hated the idea of having her picture took, but she had the artist feller paint it for you. It was like her – my, it was like her, colour and all. She had such a pretty colour – and her red hair wasn't a mite grey. As for her eyes – well, they weren't just eyes in that picture, they were her. What have you done with it? I've never seen it around."

"I don't know what you're talking of," said Anne unsteadily. "There isn't any picture of Edith in existence."

"Oh, yes, there is." Aunt Beenie was looking very cunning. "I saw it, I'm telling you. She showed it to me, to poor old Aunt Beenie. I was up at Owlwood the very day afore she died. She showed me the picture and told me it was for you. She'd writ you a letter too. She put 'em both in a book of yours she'd borryed and said she was going to send them to you in Italy for your birthday. I seen it. You can't fool Aunt Beenie. I'm old but I'm awfully cute."

Aunt Beenie laughed and kept on laughing. Her brief interval of sense was over.

Anne got up shakily and went into the library. She walked like a woman in a dream. The book – it had been sent to her when Edith's sister-in-law had stripped Owlwood. Anne had never even unwrapped it; she had hidden it away from sight at the back of a drawer – that book she and Edith had read and marked and cried and laughed over.

She took it out, removed the paper wrapping, opened it. There was the letter and the picture – a water-colour sketch of Edith. Unbelievably like – the pretty auburn hair, the eyes; Aunt Beenie had been right. They were Edith.

Anne sat down trembling in a chair to read the letter – the letter from Edith.

"Dearest of dear Annes," Edith had written in her beautiful, unique hand. "I've just had a picture painted for you. Sally's boy has been visiting me. He's an artist of repute and he's done the fair thing by me. Flattered me a little, as was proper. I want you to remember me as more beautiful than I really am.

"Did we fancy we had a quarrel? And did you imagine that you went off to Italy in a huff with me? Dreams all. There's no such thing as a quarrel between us – couldn't be, when I love you so much and you love me. We'll just never think of it again. I'm sending this letter and the picture for your birthday. I hope it will get there in time. And I want you to come home soon, old dear. Because . . .

"I saw my doctor today. He gives me a year if I'm careful.

"I'm content. I want to go while I'm still strong and folks will miss me. I've always had a horror of living long enough to lose my wits – like Maureen's Aunt Beenie.

"On the whole I'm well satisfied with life. I've had some splendid moments, some great vivid emotions, some wonderful hours of vision. Yes, it was well worth living. And there's always been you.

"So hurry home to me. I want to have one more good laugh yet before I die and only with you can I have it. And we'll walk over the old hill, over the frosted ferny woodside – all the old familiar places we've loved. And we'll ask all the old unanswered questions, little caring that there is no answer so long as we are ignorant together."

The letter was unfinished. Edith was not to have her

year – not even another day of it. But it said all that Anne wanted to know.

Anne was still sitting there in the twilight when Maureen blew in, with the children tumbling over each other behind her.

"All in the dark? Beats me how anyone can like sitting in the dark. It gives me the heebie-jeebies. But I've got news – and a job. Fancy! I met up with my old crony, Elinor Honway, today – her hubby has a first-class hairdressing establishment – wants an assistant – and little Maureen has landed the job with a healthy salary. Boy, but it was luck! I'm going right in tomorrow. I'll get a flat and take the kids and Aunt Beenie. Lord, won't I be glad to be in town again! Croyden's the limit, believe you me. Not but what I know you've been decent, and I'll never forget it."

Maureen switched on the light.

"Why – you've been crying. What's wrong? Aunt Beenie been plaguing the life out of you?"

"No, dear." Anne was very calm; she felt that she would always be calm henceforth. All the ceaseless, gnawing longing gone, all the bitterness. Edith was her own again, all her memories unspoiled and beautiful. "I'm really very happy. I've just had a message out of the silence – Aunt Beenie gave it to me."

Maureen stared, then shrugged.

"Sometimes I think you're nearly as nutty as Aunt Beenie," she said candidly. "But what's the odds as long as you're happy?"

"What indeed?" said Anne.

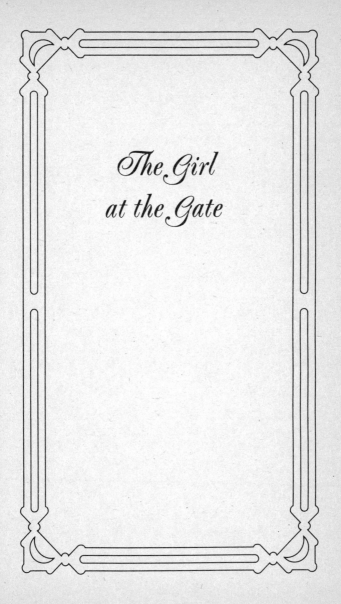

The Girl
at the Gate

OMETHING VERY STRANGE happened the night old Mr. Lawrence died. I have never been able to explain it and I have never spoken of it except to one person and she said that I dreamed it. I did not dream it . . . I saw and heard, waking.

We had not expected Mr. Lawrence to die then. He did not seem very ill . . . not nearly so ill as he had been during his previous attack. When we heard of his illness I went over to Woodlands to see him, for I had always been a great favourite with him. The big house was quiet, the servants going about their work as usual, without any appearance of excitement. I was told that I could not see Mr. Lawrence for a little while, as the doctor was with him. Mrs. Yeats, the housekeeper, said the attack was not serious and asked me to wait in the blue parlour, but I preferred to sit down on the steps of the big, arched front door. It was an evening in June. Woodlands was very lovely; to my right was the garden, and before me was a little valley abrim with the sunset. In places under the big trees it was quite dark even then.

There was something unusually still in the evening . . . a stillness as of waiting. It set me thinking of the last time Mr. Lawrence had been ill . . . nearly a year ago in August. One night during his convalescence I had watched by him to relieve the nurse. He had been sleepless and talkative, telling me many things about his life. Finally he told me of Margaret.

I knew a little about her . . . that she had been his sweetheart and had died very young. Mr. Lawrence had remained true to her memory ever since, but I had never heard him speak of her before.

"She was very beautiful," he said dreamily, "and she was only eighteen when she died, Jeanette. She had wonderful pale-golden hair and dark-brown eyes. I have a little ivory miniature of her. When I die it is to be given to you, Jeanette. I have waited a long while for her. You know she promised she would come."

I did not understand his meaning and kept silence, thinking that he might be wandering a little in his mind.

"She promised she would come and she will keep her word," he went on. "I was with her when she died. I held her in my arms. She said to me, 'Herbert, I promise that I will be true to you forever, through as many years of lonely heaven as I must know before you come. And when your time is at hand I will come to make your deathbed easy as you have made mine. I will come, Herbert.' She solemnly promised, Jeanette. We made a death-tryst of it. And I know she will come."

He had fallen asleep then and after his recovery he had not alluded to the matter again. I had forgotten it, but I recalled it now as I sat on the steps among the geraniums that June evening. I liked to think of Margaret . . . the lovely girl who had died so long ago, taking her lover's heart with her to the grave. She had been a sister of my grandfather, and people told me that I resembled her slightly. Perhaps that was why old Mr. Lawrence had always made such a pet of me.

Presently the doctor came out and nodded to me cheerily. I asked him how Mr. Lawrence was.

"Better . . . better," he said briskly. "He will be all right tomorrow. The attack was very slight. Yes, of course you may go in. Don't stay longer than half an hour."

Mrs. Stewart, Mr. Lawrence's sister, was in the sickroom when I went in. She took advantage of my presence to lie down on the sofa a little while, for she had been up all the preceding night. Mr. Lawrence turned his fine old silver head on the pillow and smiled a greeting. He was a very handsome old man; neither age nor illness had marred his finely modelled face or impaired the flash of his keen, steel-blue eyes. He seemed quite well and talked naturally and easily of many commonplace things.

At the end of the doctor's half-hour I rose to go. Mrs. Stewart had fallen asleep and he would not let me wake her, saying he needed nothing and felt like sleeping himself. I promised to come up again on the morrow and went out.

It was dark in the hall, where no lamp had been lighted, but outside on the lawn the moonlight was bright as day. It was the clearest, whitest night I ever saw. I turned aside into the garden, meaning to cross it, and take the short way over the west meadow home. There was a long walk of rose bushes leading across the garden to a little gate on the further side . . . the way Mr. Lawrence had been wont to take long ago when he went over the fields to woo Margaret. I went along it, enjoying the night. The bushes were white with roses, and the ground under my feet was all snowed over with their petals. The air was still and breezeless; again I felt that sensation of waiting . . . of expectancy. As I came up to the little gate I saw a young girl standing on the other side of it. She stood in the full moonlight and I saw her distinctly.

She was tall and slight and her head was bare. I saw that her hair was a pale gold, shining somewhat strangely about her head as if catching the moonbeams. Her face was very lovely and her eyes large and dark. She was dressed in something white and softly shimmering, and in her hand she held a white rose . . . a very large and perfect one. Even at the time I found myself wondering where she could have picked it. It was not a Woodlands rose. All the Woodlands roses were smaller and less double.

She was a stranger to me, yet I felt that I had seen her or someone very like her before. Possibly she was one of Mr. Lawrence's many nieces who might have come up to Woodlands upon hearing of his illness.

As I opened the gate I felt an odd chill of positive fear. Then she smiled as if I had spoken my thought.

"Do not be frightened," she said. "There is no reason you should be frightened. I have only come to keep a tryst."

The words reminded me of something, but I could not recall what it was. The strange fear that was on me deepened. I could not speak.

She came through the gateway and stood for a moment at my side.

"It is strange that you should have seen me," she said, "but now behold how strong and beautiful a thing is faithful love – strong enough to conquer death. We who have loved truly love always – and this makes our heaven."

She walked on after she had spoken, down the long rose path. I watched her until she reached the house and went up the steps. In truth I thought the girl was someone not quite in her right mind. When I reached home I did not speak of the matter to anyone, not even to inquire who the girl might possibly be. There seemed to be something in that strange meeting that demanded my silence.

The next morning word came that old Mr. Lawrence was dead. When I hurried down to Woodlands I found all in confusion, but Mrs. Yeats took me into the blue parlour and told me what little there was to tell.

"He must have died soon after you left him, Miss Jeanette," she sobbed, "for Mrs. Stewart wakened at ten o'clock and he was gone. He lay there, smiling, with such a strange look on his face as if he had just seen something that made him wonderfully happy. I never saw such a look on a dead face before."

"Who is here besides Mrs. Stewart?" I asked.

"Nobody," said Mrs. Yeats. "We have sent word to all his friends but they have not had time to arrive here yet."

"I met a young girl in the garden last night," I said

slowly. "She came into the house. I did not know her but I thought she must be a relative of Mr. Lawrence's."

Mrs. Yeats shook her head.

"No. It must have been somebody from the village, although I didn't know of anyone calling after you went away."

I said nothing more to her about it.

After the funeral Mrs. Stewart gave me Margaret's miniature. I had never seen it or any picture of Margaret before. The face was very lovely – also strangely like my own, although I am not beautiful. It was the face of the young girl I had met at the gate!

The House Party
at Smoky Island

HEN MADELINE STANWYCK asked me to join her house party at Smoky Island I was not at first disposed to do so. It was too early in the season, for one thing; for another, there would be mosquitoes. One mosquito can keep me more awake than a bad conscience, and there are always millions of mosquitoes in Muskoka.

"No, no, the season for them is over," Madeline assured me. Madeline would say anything to get her way.

"The mosquito season is never over in Muskoka," I said, as grumpily as anyone could speak to Madeline. "They thrive up there at zero. And even if by some miracle there are no mosquitoes, I've no hankering to be chewed to pieces by blackflies."

Even Madeline did not dare to say there would be no blackflies, so she wisely fell back on her Madelinity.

"Please come, for my sake," she said wistfully. "It wouldn't be a real party for me if you weren't there, Jim, darling."

I am Madeline's favourite cousin, twenty years her senior, and she calls everybody darling when she wants to get something out of him. Not but that Madeline . . . but this story is not about Madeline. It is about an occurrence which took place at Smoky Island. None of us pretends to understand it except the Judge, who pretends to understand everything. But he really understands it no better than the rest of us. His latest explanation is that we were all hypnotized and in the state of hypnosis saw and remembered things we couldn't otherwise have seen or remembered. But even he cannot explain who or what hypnotized us.

I decided to yield, but not all at once.

"Has your Smoky Island housekeeper still got that detestable white parrot?" I asked.

"Yes, but it is *much* better mannered than it used to be," assured Madeline. "And you know you have always liked her cat."

"Who'll be in your party? I'm rather finicky as to the company I keep."

Madeline grinned.

"You know I never invite anyone but interesting people to my parties" – I bowed to the implied compliment – "with a dull one or two to show off the sparkle of the rest of us" – I did not bow this time – "Consuelo Anderson, Aunt Alma, Professor Tennant and his wife, Dick Lane, Tod Newman, Senator Malcolm and Mrs. Senator, Old Nosey, Min Ingram, Judge Warden, Mary Harland, and a few Bright Young Things to amuse *me*."

I ran over the list in my mind, not disapprovingly. Consuelo was a very fat girl with a B.A. degree. I liked her because she could sit still for a longer time than any woman I know. Tennant was professor of something he called the New Pathology – an insignificant little man with a gigantic intellect. Dick Lane was one of those coming men who never seem to arrive, but a frank, friendly, charming fellow enough. Mary Harland was a comfortable spinster, Tod an amusing little fop, Aunt Alma a sweet, silvery-haired thing like a Whistler mother. Old Nosey – whose real name was Miss Alexander and who never let anyone forget that she had nearly sailed on the *Luisitania* – and the Malcolms had no terrors for me, although the Senator always called his wife "Kittens." And Judge Warden was an old crony of mine. I did not like Min Ingram, who had a rapier-like tongue, but she could be ignored, along with the Bright Young Things.

"Is that all?" I asked cautiously.

"Well . . . Dr. Armstrong and Brenda, of course," said Madeline, eying me as if it were not at all of course.

"Is that . . . wise?" I said slowly.

Madeline crumpled.

"Of course not," she said miserably. "It will likely spoil everything. But John insists on it . . . you know he and Anthony Armstrong have been pals all their lives. And Brenda and I have always been chummy. It would look so funny if we didn't have them. I don't know what has got into her. We all *know* Anthony never poisoned Susette."

"Brenda doesn't know it, apparently," I said.

"Well, she ought to!" snapped Madeline. "As if Anthony could have poisoned anyone! But that's one of the reasons I particularly want you to come."

"Ah, now we're getting at it. But why *me*?"

"Because you've more influence over Brenda than anyone else . . . oh, yes, you have. If you could get her to open up - talk to her - you might help her. Because . . . if something doesn't help her soon, she'll be beyond help. You know that."

I knew it well enough. The case of the Anthony Armstrongs was worrying us all. We saw a tragedy being enacted before our eyes and we could not lift a finger to help. For Brenda would not talk and Anthony had never talked.

The story, now five years old, was known to all of us, of course. Anthony's first wife had been Susette Wilder. Of the dead nothing but good, so I will say of Susette only that she was beautiful and rich. Very beautiful and very rich. Luckily her fortune had come to her unexpectedly by the death of an aunt and cousin after she had married Anthony, so that he could not be accused of fortune-hunting. He had been wildly in love with Susette at first, but after they had been married a few years I don't think he had much affection left for her. None of the rest of us had ever had any to begin with. When word came back from California - where Anthony had taken her one winter for her nerves - that she was dead, I don't suppose anyone felt any regret, nor any suspicion when we heard that she had died from an overdose of chloral; rather mysteriously, to be sure, for Susette was neither careless nor suicidally inclined. There were some ugly rumours, especially when it became known that Anthony had inherited her entire fortune under her will, but nobody ever dared say much openly. We, who knew and loved Anthony, never paid any heed to the hints. And when, two years later, he married Brenda Young, we were all glad. Anthony, we said, would have some real happiness now.

For a time he did have it. Nobody could doubt that he and Brenda were ecstatically happy. Brenda was a sincere, spiritual creature, lovely after a fashion totally different from Susette. Susette had had golden hair and eyes as cool and green as fluorspar. Brenda had slim, dark distinction, hair that blended with the dusk, and eyes so full of twilight that it was hard to say whether they were blue or grey. She loved Anthony so terribly that sometimes I thought she was tempting the gods.

Then . . . slowly, subtly, remorselessly . . . the change set in. We began to feel that there was something wrong – very wrong – between the Armstrongs. They were no longer quite so happy . . . they were not happy at all . . . they were wretched. Brenda's old delightful laugh was never heard, and Anthony went about his work with an air of abstraction that didn't please his patients. His practice had fallen off a while before Susette's death, but it had picked up and grown wonderfully. Now it began dropping again. And the worst of it was that Anthony didn't seem to care. Of course he didn't need it from a financial point of view, but he had always been so keenly interested in his work.

I don't know if it were merely surmise or whether Brenda had let a word slip, but we all knew or felt that she was possessed by a horrible suspicion. There was some whisper of an anonymous letter, full of vile innuendoes, that had started the trouble. I never knew the rights of that, but I did know that Brenda had become a haunted woman.

Had Anthony given Susette that overdose of chloral – given it purposely?

If she had been the kind of woman who talks things out, some of us might have saved her. But she wasn't. It's my belief that she never said a word to Anthony of the cold horror of distrust that was poisoning her life. But he must have felt she suspected him, and between them was the chill and shadow of a thing that must not be spoken of.

At the time of Madeline's house party the state of affairs between the Armstrongs was such that Brenda had almost reached the breaking point. Anthony's nerves were tense too, and his eyes were almost as tragic as hers. We were all ready to hear that Brenda had left him or done something more desperate still. And nobody could do a thing to help, not even I, in spite of Madeline's foolish hopes. *I* couldn't go to Brenda and say, "Look here, you know, Anthony never thought of such a thing as poisoning Susette." After all, in spite of our surmises, the trouble might be something else altogether. And if she did suspect him, what proof could I offer her that would root the obsession out of her mind?

I hardly thought the Armstrongs would go to Smoky Island, but they did. When Anthony turned on the wharf and held out his hand to assist Brenda from the motorboat, she ignored it, stepping swiftly off without any assistance and running up through the rock garden and the pointed firs. I saw Anthony go very white. I felt a little sick myself. If matters had come to such a pass that she shrank from his mere touch, disaster was near.

Smoky Island was in a little blue Muskoka lake, and the house was called the Wigwam ... probably because nothing on earth could be less like a wigwam. The Stanwyck money had made a wonderful place of it, but even the Stanwyck money could not buy fine weather. Madeline's party was a flop. It rained every day more or less for the week, and though we all tried heroically to make the best of things, I don't think I ever spent a more unpleasant time. The parrot's manners were no better in spite of Madeline's assurances. Min Ingram had brought an aloof, disdainful dog with her that everyone hated because he despised us all. Min herself kept passing out needle-like insults when she saw anyone in danger of being comfortable. I thought the Bright Young Things seemed to hold *me* responsible for the weather. All our nerves got edgy except Aunt Alma's. Nothing ever upset Aunt Alma. She prided herself a bit on that.

On Saturday the weather wound up with a regular downpour and a wind that rushed out of the black-green pines to lash the Wigwam and then rushed back like a maddened animal. The air was as full of torn, flying leaves as of rain, and the lake was a splutter of tossing waves. This charming day ended in a dank, streaming night.

And yet things had seemed a bit better than any day yet. Anthony was away. He had got some mysterious telegram just after breakfast, had taken the small motorboat and gone to the mainland. I was thankful, for I felt I could no longer endure seeing a man's soul tortured as his was. Brenda had kept her room all day on the good old plea of a headache. I won't say it wasn't a relief. We all felt the strain between her and Anthony like a tangible thing.

"Something . . . *something* . . . is going to happen," Madeline kept saying to me. She was really worse than the parrot, and I told her so.

After dinner we all gathered around the fireplace in the hall, where a cheerful fire of white birchwood was glowing, for although it was June the evening was cold. I settled back with a sigh of relief. After all, nothing lasted forever, and this infernal house party would be over on Monday. Besides, it was really quite comfortable and cheerful here, despite rattling windows and wailing winds and rain-swept panes. Madeline turned out the electric lights, and the firelight was kind to the women, who all looked quite charming. Some of the Bright Young Things sat cross-legged on the floor with arms around one another quite indiscriminately as far as sex was concerned . . . except one languid, sophisticated creature in orange velvet and long amber earrings, who sat on a low stool with a lapful of silken housekeeper's cat, giving everyone an excellent view of the bones in her spine. Min's dog posed haughtily on the rug, and the parrot in his cage was quiet – for him – only telling us once in a while that he or someone else was devilish clever. Mrs. Howey, the housekeeper, insisted on keeping him in the hall, and Madeline had to wink at it because it was hard to get a housekeeper in Muskoka even for a Wigwam.

The Judge was looking like a chuckle because he had solved a jigsaw puzzle that had baffled everyone, and the Professor and Senator, who had been arguing stormily all day, were basking in each other's regard for a foeman worthy of his steel. Consuelo was sitting still, as usual. Mrs. Tennant and Aunt Alma were knitting pullovers. Kittens, her fat hands folded across her satin stomach, was surveying her Senator adoringly, and Miss Nosey was taking everything in. We were, for the time being, a con-tented, congenial bunch of people, and I did not see why Madeline should have suddenly proposed that we all tell a ghost story, but she did. It was an ideal night for ghost stories, she averred. She hadn't heard any for ages and she understood that everybody had had at least one super-natural occurrence in his or her life.

"I haven't," growled the Judge contemptuously.

"I suppose," said Professor Tennant a little belligerently, "that you would call anyone an ass who believed in ghosts?"

The Judge carefully fitted his fingertips together before he replied.

"Oh, dear, no. I would not so insult asses."

"Of course if you don't *believe* in ghosts, they can't happen," said Consuelo.

"Some people are able to see ghosts and some are not," announced Dick Lane. "It's simply a gift."

"A gift I was not dowered with," said Kittens complacently.

Mary Harland shuddered. "What a dreadful thing it would be if the dead really came back!"

" 'From ghaisties and ghoulies and lang-legged beasties / And things that go bump in the night / Good Lord, deliver us,' " quoted Tod flippantly.

But Madeline was not to be side-tracked. Her little elfish face under its crown of russet hair was alive with determination.

"We're going to spook a bit," she said resolutely. "This is just the sort of night for ghosts to walk. Only of course they can't walk here because the Wigwam isn't haunted, I'm sorry to say. Wouldn't it be heavenly to live in a haunted house? Come now, everyone must tell a ghost story. Professor Tennant, you lead off. Something nice and creepy, please."

To my surprise, the Professor did lead off, although Mrs. Tennant's expression plainly informed us that she didn't approve of juggling with ghosts. He told a very good story too – punctuated with snorts from the Judge – about a house he knew which had been haunted by the voice of a dead child, who joined in every conversation bitterly and vindictively. The child had, of course, been ill-treated and murdered, and its body was eventually found under the hearthstone of the library. Then Dick told a tale about a dead dog who avenged his master, and Consuelo amazed me by spinning a really gruesome yarn of a ghost who came to the wedding of her lover with her rival . . . Consuelo said she knew the people. Tod knew a house in which you heard voices and footfalls where no voices or footfalls could be, and even Aunt Alma told of "a white lady with a cold hand" who asked you to dance with her. If you were reckless enough to accept the invitation, you never lost the feeling of her cold hand in yours. This chilly apparition was always garbed in the costume of the seventies.

"Fancy a ghost in a crinoline," giggled a Bright Young Thing.

Min Ingram, of all people, had seen a ghost and took it quite seriously.

"Well, show me a ghost and I'll believe in it," said the Judge, with another snort.

"Isn't he devilish clever?" croaked the parrot.

Just at this point Brenda drifted downstairs and sat down behind us all, her tragic eyes burning out of her white face. I had a feeling that there, in that calm, untroubled scene, full of good-humoured, tolerant, amused, commonplace people, a human heart was burning at a stake in agony.

Something fell over us with Brenda's coming. Min Ingram's dog suddenly whined and flattened himself out on the rug. It occurred to me that it was the first time I had ever seen him looking like a real dog. I wondered idly what had frightened him. The housekeeper's cat sat up, its back bristling, slid from the orange-velvet lap and slunk out of the hall. I had a queer sensation in the roots of what hair I have left, so I turned hastily to the slim, dark girl on the oak settle at my right.

"You haven't told us a ghost story yet, Christine. It's your turn."

Christine smiled. I saw the Judge looking admiringly at her ankles, sheathed in what I believe are called chiffon hose. The Judge always had an eye for a pretty ankle. As for me, I was wondering why I couldn't recall Christine's last name and why I felt as if I had been impelled in some odd way to make that commonplace remark to her.

"Do you remember how firmly Aunt Elizabeth believed in ghosts?" said Christine. "And how angry it used to make her when I laughed at the idea. I am . . . wiser now."

"I remember," said the Senator in a dreamy way.

"It was your Aunt Elizabeth's money that went to the first Mrs. Armstrong, wasn't it?" said one of the Bright Young Things, nicknamed Tweezers. It was an abominable thing for anyone to say, right there before Brenda. But nobody seemed horrified. I had another odd feeling that it *had* to be said and who but Tweezers would say it? I had another feeling . . . that ever since Brenda's entrance every trifle was important, every tone was of profound significance, every word had a hidden meaning. Was I developing nerves?

"Yes," said Christine evenly.

"Do you suppose Susette Armstrong really took that overdose of chloral on purpose?" went on Tweezers unbelievably.

Not being near enough to Tweezers to assassinate her, I looked at Brenda. But Brenda gave no sign of having heard. She was staring fixedly at Christine.

"No," said Christine. I wondered how she knew, but there was no question whatever in my mind that she *did* know it. She spoke as one having authority. "Susette had no intention of dying. And yet she was doomed, although she never suspected it. She had an incurable disease which would have killed her in a few months. Nobody knew that except Anthony and me. And she had come to hate Anthony so. She was going to change her will the very next day . . . leave everything away from him. She told me so. I was furious. Anthony, who had spent his life doing good to suffering creatures, was to be left poor and struggling again, after his practice had been all shot to pieces by Susette's goings-on. I had loved Anthony ever since I had known him. He didn't know it . . . but Susette did. Trust her for that. She used to twit me with it. Not that it mattered . . . I knew he would never care for me. But I saw my chance to do something for him and I took it. *I* gave Susette that overdose of chloral. I loved him enough for that . . . and for *this*."

Somebody screamed. I have never known whether it was Brenda or not. Aunt Alma – who was never upset over anything – was huddled in her chair in hysterics. Kittens, her fat figure shaking, was clinging to her Senator, whose foolish, amiable face was grey – absolutely grey. Min Ingram was on her knees, and the Judge was trying to keep his hands from shaking by clenching them together. His lips were moving and I know I caught the word "God." As for Tweezers and all the rest of her gang, they were no longer Bright Young Things but simply shivering, terrified children.

I felt sick – very, very sick. *Because there was no one on the oak settle and none of us had ever known or heard of the girl I had called Christine.*

At that moment the hall door opened and a dripping Anthony entered. Brenda flung herself hungrily against him, wet as he was.

"Anthony, Anthony, forgive me," she sobbed.

Something good to see came into Anthony's worn face.

"Have you been frightened, darling?" he said tenderly. "I'm sorry I was so late. There was really no danger. I waited to get an answer to my wire to Los Angeles. You see

99

I got word this morning that Christine Latham had been killed in a motor accident yesterday evening. She was Susette's second cousin and nurse . . . a dear, loyal little thing. I was very fond of her. I'm sorry you've had such an anxious evening, sweetheart."

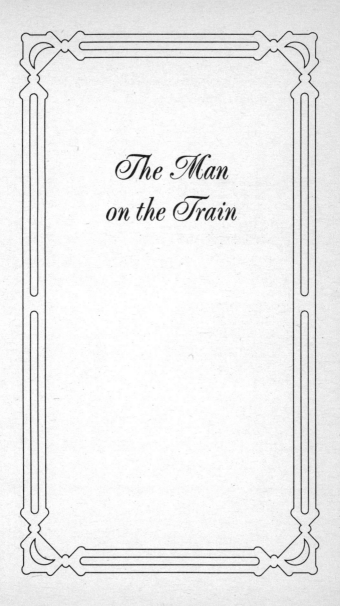

The Man
on the Train

HEN THE TELEGRAM CAME from William George, Grandma Sheldon was all alone with Cyrus and Louise. And Cyrus and Louise, aged respectively twelve and eleven, were not very much good, Grandma thought, when it came to advising what was to be done. Grandma was "all in a flutter, dear, oh dear," as she said.

The telegram said that Delia, William George's wife, was seriously ill down at Green Village, and William George wanted Samuel to bring Grandma down immediately. Delia had always thought there was nobody like Grandma when it came to nursing sick folks.

But Samuel and his wife were both away – had been away for two days and intended to be away for five more. They had driven to Sinclair, twenty miles away, to visit with Mrs. Samuel's folks for a week.

"Dear, oh dear, what shall I do?" said Grandma.

"Go right to Green Village on the evening train," said Cyrus briskly.

"Dear, oh dear, and leave you two alone!" cried Grandma.

"Louise and I will do very well until tomorrow," said Cyrus sturdily. "We will send word to Sinclair by today's mail, and Father and Mother will be home by tomorrow night."

"But I never was on the cars in my life," protested Grandma nervously. "I'm – I'm so frightened to start alone. And you never know what kind of people you may meet on the train."

"You'll be all right, Grandma. I'll drive you to the station, get you your ticket, and put you on the train. Then you'll have nothing to do until the train gets to Green Village. I'll send a telegram to Uncle William George to meet you."

"I shall fall and break my neck getting off the train," said

Grandma pessimistically. But she was wondering at the same time whether she had better take the black valise or the yellow, and whether William George would be likely to have plenty of flaxseed in the house.

It was six miles to the station, and Cyrus drove Grandma over in time to catch a train that reached Green Village at nine o'clock.

"Dear, oh dear," said Grandma, "what if William George's folks ain't there to meet me? It's all very well, Cyrus, to say that they will be there, but you don't know. And it's all very well to say not to be nervous because everything will be all right. If you were seventy-five years old and had never set foot on the cars in your life you'd be nervous too, and you can't be sure that everything will be all right. You never know what sort of people you'll meet on the train. I may get on the wrong train or lose my ticket or get carried past Green Village or get my pocket picked. Well, no, I won't do that, for not one cent will I carry with me. You shall take back home all the money you don't need to get my ticket. Then I shall be easier in my mind. Dear, oh dear, if it wasn't that Delia is so seriously ill I wouldn't go one step."

"Oh, you'll be all right, Grandma," assured Cyrus.

He got Grandma's ticket for her and Grandma tied it up in the corner of her handkerchief. Then the train came in and Grandma, clinging closely to Cyrus, was put on it. Cyrus found a comfortable seat for her and shook hands cheerily.

"Good-bye, Grandma. Don't be frightened. Here's the *Weekly Argus*. I got it at the store. You may like to look over it."

Then Cyrus was gone, and in a minute the station house and platform began to glide away.

Dear, oh dear, what has happened to it? thought Grandma in dismay. The next moment she exclaimed aloud, "Why, it's us that's moving, not it!"

Some of the passengers smiled pleasantly at Grandma. She was the variety of old lady at which people do smile pleasantly; a grandma with round, pink cheeks, soft, brown eyes, and lovely snow-white curls is a nice person to look at wherever she is found.

After a while Grandma, to her amazement, discovered that she liked riding on the cars. It was not at all the disagreeable experience she had expected it to be. Why, she was just as comfortable as if she were in her own rocking chair at home! And there was such a lot of people to look at, and many of the ladies had such beautiful dresses and hats. After all, the people you met on a train, thought Grandma, are surprisingly like the people you meet off it. If it had not been for wondering how she would get off at Green Village, Grandma would have enjoyed herself thoroughly.

Four or five stations farther on the train halted at a lonely-looking place consisting of the station house and a barn, surrounded by scrub woods and blueberry barrens. One passenger got on and, finding only one vacant seat in the crowded car, sat right down beside Grandma Sheldon.

Grandma Sheldon held her breath while she looked him over. Was he a pickpocket? He didn't appear like one, but you can never be sure of the people you meet on the train. Grandma remembered with a sigh of thankfulness that she had no money.

Besides, he seemed really very respectable and harmless. He was quietly dressed in a suit of dark-blue serge with a black overcoat. He wore his hat well down on his forehead and was clean shaven. His hair was very black, but his eyes were blue – nice eyes, Grandma thought. She always felt great confidence in a man who had bright, open, blue eyes. Grandpa Sheldon, who had died so long ago, four years after their marriage, had had bright blue eyes.

To be sure, he had fair hair, reflected Grandma. It's real odd to see such black hair with such light blue eyes. Well, he's real nice looking, and I don't believe there's a mite of harm in him.

The early autumn night had now fallen and Grandma could not amuse herself by watching the scenery. She bethought herself of the paper Cyrus had given her and took it out of her basket. It was an old weekly a fortnight back. On the first page was a long account of a murder case with scare heads, and into this Grandma plunged eagerly. Sweet old Grandma Sheldon, who would not have harmed a fly and hated to see even a mousetrap set, simply revelled in the newspaper accounts of murders. And the more shocking and cold-blooded they were, the more eagerly did Grandma read of them.

This murder story was particularly good from Grandma's point of view; it was full of "thrills." A man had been shot down, apparently in cold blood, and his supposed murderer was still at large and had eluded all the efforts of justice to capture him. His name was Mark Hartwell, and he was described as a tall, fair man, with full auburn beard and curly, light hair.

"What a shocking thing!" said Grandma aloud.

Her companion looked at her with a kindly, amused smile.

"What is it?" he asked.

"Why, this murder at Charlotteville," answered Grandma, forgetting, in her excitement, that it was not safe to talk to people you meet on the train. "It just makes my blood run cold to read about it. And to think that the man who did it is still around the country somewhere – plotting other murders, I haven't a doubt. What is the good of the police?"

"They're dull fellows," agreed the dark man.

"But I don't envy that man his conscience," said Grandma solemnly – and somewhat inconsistently, in view of her statement about the other murders that were being plotted. "What must a man feel like who has the blood of a fellow creature on his hands? Depend upon it, his punishment has begun already, caught or not."

"That is true," said the dark man quietly.

"Such a good-looking man too," said Grandma, looking wistfully at the murderer's picture. "It doesn't seem possible that he can have killed anybody. But the paper says there isn't a doubt."

"He is probably guilty," said the dark man, "but nothing is known of his provocation. The affair may not have been so cold-blooded as the accounts state. Those newspaper fellows never err on the side of undercolouring."

"I really think," said Grandma slowly, "that I would like to see a murderer – just one. Whenever I say anything like that, Adelaide – Adelaide is Samuel's wife – looks at me as if she thought there was something wrong about me. And perhaps there is, but I do, all the same. When I was a little girl, there was a man in our settlement who was suspected of poisoning his wife. She died very suddenly. I used to look at him with such interest. But it wasn't satisfactory, because you could never be sure whether he was really guilty or not. I never could believe that he was, because he was such a nice man in some ways and so good and kind to children. I don't believe a man who was bad enough to poison his wife could have any good in him."

"Perhaps not," agreed the dark man. He had absent-mindedly folded up Grandma's old copy of the *Argus* and put it in his pocket. Grandma did not like to ask him for it, although she would have liked to see if there were any more murder stories in it. Besides, just at that moment the conductor came around for tickets.

Grandma looked in the basket for her handkerchief. It was not there. She looked on the floor and on the seat and under the seat. It was not there. She stood up and shook herself – still no handkerchief.

"Dear, oh dear," exclaimed Grandma wildly, "I've lost my ticket – I always knew I would – I told Cyrus I would! Oh, where can it be?"

The conductor scowled unsympathetically. The dark man got up and helped Grandma search, but no ticket was to be found.

"You'll have to pay the money then, and something extra," said the conductor gruffly.

"I can't – I haven't a cent of money," wailed Grandma. "I gave it all to Cyrus because I was afraid my pocket would be picked. Oh, what shall I do?"

"Don't worry. I'll make it all right," said the dark man. He took out his pocketbook and handed the conductor a bill. That functionary grumblingly made the change and marched onward, while Grandma, pale with excitement and relief, sank back into her seat.

"I can't tell you how much I am obliged to you, sir," she said tremulously. "I don't know what I should have done. Would he have put me off right here in the snow?"

"I hardly think he would have gone to such lengths," said the dark man with a smile. "But he's a cranky, disobliging fellow enough – I know him of old. And you must not feel overly grateful to me. I am glad of the opportunity to help you. I had an old grandmother myself once," he added with a sigh.

"You must give me your name and address, of course," said Grandma, "and my son – Samuel Sheldon of Midverne – will see that the money is returned to you. Well, this is a lesson to me! I'll never trust myself on a train again, and all I wish is that I was safely off this one. This fuss has worked my nerves all up again."

"Don't worry, Grandma. I'll see you safely off the train when we get to Green Village."

"Will you, though? Will you, now?" said Grandma eagerly. "I'll be real easy in my mind, then," she added with a returning smile. "I feel as if I could trust you for anything – and I'm a real suspicious person too."

They had a long talk after that – or, rather, Grandma talked and the dark man listened and smiled. She told him all about William George and Delia and their baby and about Samuel and Adelaide and Cyrus and Louise and the three cats and the parrot. He seemed to enjoy her accounts of them too.

When they reached Green Village station he gathered up Grandma's parcels and helped her tenderly off the train.

"Anybody here to meet Mrs. Sheldon?" he asked of the station master.

The latter shook his head. "Don't think so. Haven't seen anybody here to meet anybody tonight."

"Dear, oh dear," said poor Grandma. "This is just what I expected. They've never got Cyrus's telegram. Well, I might have known it. What shall I do?"

"How far is it to your son's?" asked the dark man.

"Only half a mile – just over the hill there. But I'll never get there alone this dark night."

"Of course not. But I'll go with you. The road is good – we'll do finely."

"But that train won't wait for you," gasped Grandma, half in protest.

"It doesn't matter. The Starmont freight passes here in half an hour and I'll go on her. Come along, Grandma."

"Oh, but you're good," said Grandma. "Some woman is proud to have you for a son."

The man did not answer. He had not answered any of the personal remarks Grandma had made to him in her conversation.

They were not long in reaching William George Sheldon's house, for the village road was good and Grandma was smart on her feet. She was welcomed with eagerness and surprise.

"To think that there was no one to meet you!" exclaimed William George. "But I never dreamed of your coming by train, knowing how you were set against it. Telegram? No, I got no telegram. S'pose Cyrus forgot to send it. I'm most heartily obliged to you, sir, for looking after my mother so kindly."

"It was a pleasure," said the dark man courteously. He had taken off his hat, and they saw a curious scar, shaped like a large, red butterfly, high up on his forehead under his hair. "I am delighted to have been of any assistance to her."

He would not wait for supper – the next train would be in and he must not miss it.

"There are people looking for me," he said with his curious smile. "They will be much disappointed if they do not find me."

He had gone, and the whistle of the Starmont freight had blown before Grandma remembered that he had not given her his name and address.

"Dear, oh dear, how are we ever going to send that money to him?" she exclaimed. "And he so nice and goodhearted!"

Grandma worried over this for a week in the intervals of looking after Delia. One day William George came in with a large city daily in his hands. He looked curiously at Grandma and then showed her the front-page picture of a man, clean-shaven, with an oddly shaped scar high up on his forehead.

"Did you ever see that man, Mother?" he asked.

"Of course I did," said Grandma excitedly. "Why, it's the man I met on the train. Who is he? What is his name? Now, we'll know where to send –"

"That is Mark Hartwell, who shot Amos Gray at Charlotteville three weeks ago," said William George quietly.

Grandma looked at him blankly for a moment.

"It couldn't be," she gasped at last. "That man a murderer! I'll never believe it!"

"It's true enough, Mother. The whole story is here. He had shaved his beard and dyed his hair and came near getting clear out of the country. They were on his trail the day he came down in the train with you and lost it because of his getting off to bring you here. His disguise was so perfect that there was little fear of his being recognized so long as he hid that scar. But it was seen in Montreal and he was run to earth there. He has made a full confession."

"I don't care," cried Grandma valiantly. "I'll never believe he was all bad – a man who would do what he did for a poor old woman like me, when he was flying for his life too. No, no, there was good in him even if he did kill that man. And I'm sure he must feel terrible over it."

In this view Grandma persisted. She never would say or listen to a word against Mark Hartwell, and she had only pity for him whom everyone else condemned. With her own trembling hands she wrote him a letter to accompany the money Samuel sent before Hartwell was taken to the penitentiary for life. She thanked him again for his kindness to her and assured him that she knew he was sorry for what he had done and that she would pray for him every night of her life. Mark Hartwell had been hard and defiant enough, but the prison officials told that he cried like a child over Grandma Sheldon's little letter.

"There's nobody all bad," says Grandma when she

relates the story. "I used to believe a murderer must be, but I know better now. I think of that poor man often and often. He was so kind and gentle to me – he must have been a good boy once. I write him a letter every Christmas and I send him tracts and papers. He's my own little charity. But I've never been on the cars since and I never will be again. You never can tell what will happen to you or what sort of people you'll meet if you trust yourself on a train."

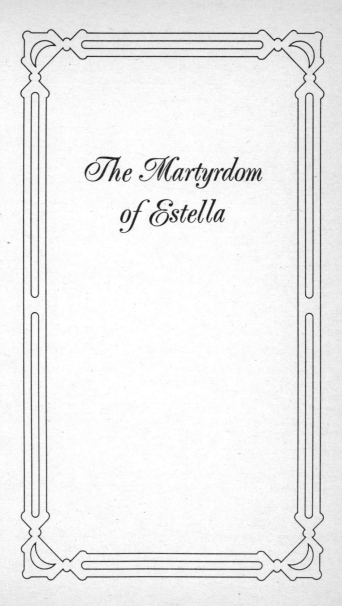

The Martyrdom
of Estella

STELLA WAS WAITING under the poplars at the gate for Spencer Morgan. She was engaged to him, and he always came to see her on Saturday and Wednesday evenings. It was after sunset, and the air was mellow and warm-hued. The willow trees along the walk and the tall birches in the background stood out darkly distinct against the lemon-tinted sky. The breath of mint floated out from the garden, and the dew was falling heavily.

Estella leaned against the gate, listening for the sound of wheels and dreamily watching the light shining out from the window of Vivienne LeMar's room. The blind was up and she could see Miss LeMar writing at her table. Her profile was clear and distinct against the lamplight.

Estella reflected without the least envy that Miss LeMar was very beautiful. She had never seen anyone who was really beautiful before – beautiful with the loveliness of the heroines in the novels she sometimes read or the pictures she had seen.

Estella Bowes was not pretty. She was a nice-looking girl, with clear eyes, rosy cheeks, and a pervading air of the content and happiness her life had always known. She was an orphan and lived with her uncle and aunt. In the summer they sometimes took a boarder for a month or two, and this summer Miss LeMar had come. She had been with them about a week. She was an actress from the city and had around her all the glamour of a strange, unknown life. Nothing was known about her. The Bowes liked her well enough as a boarder. Estella admired and held her in awe. She wondered what Spencer would think of this beautiful woman. He had not yet seen her.

It was quite dark when he came. Estella opened the gate for him, but he got out of his buggy and walked up the lane beside her with his arm about her. Miss LeMar's light had removed to the parlour where she was singing, accompanying herself on the cottage organ. Estella felt annoyed. The parlour was considered her private domain on Wednesday and Saturday night, but Miss LeMar did not know that.

"Who is singing?" asked Spencer. "What a voice she has!"

"That's our new boarder, Miss LeMar," answered Estella. "She's an actress and sings and does everything. She is awfully pretty, Spencer."

"Yes?" said the young man indifferently.

He was not in the least interested in the Bowes' new boarder. Indeed, he considered her advent a nuisance. He pressed Estella closer to him, and when they reached the garden gate he kissed her. Estella always remembered that moment afterwards. She was so supremely happy.

Spencer went off to put up his horse, and Estella waited for him on the porch steps, wondering if any other girl in the world could be quite so happy as she was, or love anyone as much as she loved Spencer. She did not see how it could be possible, because there was only one Spencer.

When Spencer came back she took him into the parlour, half shyly, half proudly. He was a handsome fellow, with a magnificent physique. Miss LeMar stopped singing and turned around on the organ stool as they entered. The little room was flooded with a mellow light from the pink-globed lamp on the table, and in the soft, shadowy radiance she was as beautiful as a dream. She wore a dress of crepe, cut low in the neck. Estella had never seen anyone dressed so before. To her it seemed immodest.

She introduced Spencer. He bowed awkwardly and sat stiffly down by the window with his eyes riveted on Miss Lemar's face. Estella, catching a glimpse of herself in the old-fashioned mirror above the mantel, suddenly felt a cold chill of dissatisfaction. Her figure had never seemed to her so stout and stiff, her brown hair so dull and prim, her complexion so muddy, her features so commonplace. She wished Miss LeMar would go out of the room.

Vivienne LeMar watched the two faces before her; a hard gleam, half mockery, half malice, flashed into her eyes and a smile crept about her lips. She looked straight in Spencer Morgan's honest blue eyes and read there the young man's dazzled admiration. There was contempt in the look she turned on Estella.

"You were singing when we came in," said Spencer. "Won't you go on, please? I am very fond of music."

Miss LeMar turned again to the organ. The gleaming curves of her neck and shoulders rose out of their filmy sheathings of lace. Spencer, sitting where he could see her face with its rose-leaf bloom and the ringlets of golden hair clustering about it, gazed at her, unheeding of aught else. Estella saw his look. She suddenly began to hate the black-eyed witch at the organ – and to fear her as well. Why did Spencer look at her like that? She wished she had not brought him in at all. She felt commonplace and angry, and wanted to cry.

Vivienne LeMar went on singing, drifting from one sweet love song into another. Once she looked up at Spencer Morgan. He rose quickly and went to her side, looking down at her with a strange fire in his eyes.

Estella got up abruptly and left the room. She was angry and jealous, but she thought Spencer would follow her. When he did not, she could not believe it. She waited on the porch for him, not knowing whether she were more angry or miserable. She would not go back into the room. Vivienne LeMar had stopped singing. She could hear a low murmur of voices. When she had waited there an hour, she went in and upstairs to her room with ostentatious footsteps. She was too angry to cry or to realize what had happened, and still kept hoping all sorts of impossible things as she sat by her window.

It was ten o'clock when Spencer went away and Vivienne LeMar passed up the hall to her room. Estella clenched her hands in an access of helpless rage. She was very angry, but under her fury was a horrible ache of pain. It could not be only three hours since she had been so happy! It must be more than that! What had happened? Had she made a fool of herself? Ought she to have behaved in any other way? Perhaps Spencer had come out to look for her after she had gone upstairs and, not finding her, had gone back to Miss LeMar to show her he was angry. This poor hope was a small comfort. She wished she had not acted as she had. It looked spiteful and jealous, and Spencer did not like people who were spiteful and jealous. She would show him she was sorry when he came back, and it would be all right.

She lay awake most of the night, thinking out plausible reasons and excuses for Spencer's behaviour, and trying to convince herself that she had exaggerated everything absurdly. Towards morning she fell asleep and awoke hardly remembering what had happened. Then it rolled back upon her crushingly.

But she rose and dressed in better spirits. It had been hardest to lie there and do nothing. Now the day was before her and something pleasant might happen. Spencer might come back in the evening. She would be doubly nice to him to make up.

Mrs. Bowes looked sharply at her niece's dull eyes and pale cheeks at the breakfast table. She had her own thoughts of things. She was a large, handsome woman with a rather harsh face.

"Did you go upstairs last night and leave Spencer Morgan with Miss LeMar?" she asked bluntly.

"Yes," muttered Estella.

"Did you have a quarrel with him?"

"No."

"What made you act so queer?"

"I couldn't help it," faltered the girl.

The food she was eating seemed to choke her. She wished she were a hundred miles away from everyone she ever knew.

Mrs. Bowes gave a grunt of dissatisfaction.

"Well, I think it is a pretty queer piece of business. But if you are satisfied, it isn't anyone else's concern, I suppose. He stayed with her till ten o'clock and when he left she did everything but kiss him – and she asked him to come back too. I heard."

"Aunt!" protested the girl.

She felt as if her aunt were striking her blow after blow on a sensitive, quivering spot. It was bad enough to know it all, but to hear it put into such cold, brutal words was more than she could endure. It seemed to make every-thing so horribly sure.

"I guess I had a right to listen, hadn't I, with such goings on in my own house? You're a little fool, Estella Bowes! I don't believe that LeMar girl is a bit better than she ought to be. I wish I'd never taken her to board, and if you say so, I'll send her packing right off and not give her a chance to make mischief atween folks."

Estella's suffering found vent in a burst of anger.

"You needn't do anything of the sort!" she cried. "It's all nonsense about Spencer – it was my fault – and anyhow, if he is so easily led away as that, I am sure I don't want him! I wish to goodness, Aunt, you'd leave me alone!"

"Oh, very well!" returned Mrs. Bowes in an offended tone. "It was for your own good I spoke. You know best, I suppose. If you don't care, I don't know that anyone else need."

Estella went about her work like one in a dream. A great

hatred had sprung up in her heart against Vivienne LeMar. The simple-hearted country girl felt almost murderous. The whole day seemed like a nightmare to her. When night came she dressed herself with feverish care, for she could not quell the hope that Spencer would surely come again. But he did not; and when she went up to bed, it did not seem as if she could live through the night. She lay staring wide-eyed through the darkness until dawn. She wished that she might cry, but no tears came to her relief.

Next day she went to work with furious energy. When her usual tasks were done, she ransacked the house for other employment. She was afraid if she stopped work for a moment she would go mad. Mrs. Bowes watched her with a grim pity.

At night she walked to prayer meeting in the school-house a mile away. She always went, and Spencer was generally on hand to see her home. He was not there tonight. She wished she had not come. It was dreadful to have to sit still and think. She did not hear a word the minister said.

She had to walk home with a crowd of girls and nerve herself to answer their merry sallies that no one might suspect. She was tortured by the fear that everyone knew her shame and humiliation and was pitying her. She got hysterically gay, but underneath all she was constantly trying to assign a satisfactory reason for Spencer's non-appearance. He was often kept away, and of course he was a little cross at her yet, as was natural. If he had come before her then, she could have gone down in the very dust at his feet and implored his forgiveness.

When she reached home she went into the garden and sat down. The calm of the night soothed her. She felt happier and more hopeful. She thought over all that had passed between her and Spencer and all his loving assurances, and the recollection comforted her. She was almost happy when she went in.

Tomorrow is Sunday, she thought when she wakened in the morning. Her step was lighter and her face brighter. Mrs. Bowes seemed to be in a bad humour. Presently she said bluntly:

"Do you know that Spencer Morgan was here last night?"

Estella felt the cold tighten round her heart. Yet underneath it sprang up a wild, sweet hope.

"Spencer here! I suppose he forgot it was prayer meeting night. What did he say? Why didn't you tell him where I was?"

"I don't know that he forgot it was prayer meeting night," returned Mrs. Bowes with measured emphasis. " 'Tisn't likely his memory has failed so all at once. He didn't ask where you was. He took good care to go before you got home too. Miss LeMar entertained him. I guess she was quite capable of it."

Estella bent over her dishes in silence. Her face was deadly white.

"I'll send her away," said Mrs. Bowes pityingly. "When she's gone, Spencer will soon come back to you."

"No, you won't!" said Estella fiercely. "If you do, she'll only go over to Barstows', and it would be worse than ever. I don't care – I'll show them both I don't care! As for Spencer coming back to me, do you think I want her leavings? He's welcome to go."

"He's only just fooled by her pretty face," persisted Mrs. Bowes in a clumsy effort at consolation. "She's just turning his head, the hussy, and he isn't really in his proper senses. You'll see, he'll be ashamed of himself when he comes to them again. He knows very well in his heart that you're worth ten girls like her."

Estella faced around.

"Aunt," she said desperately, "you mean well, I know, but you're killing me! I can't stand it. For pity's sake, don't say another word to me about this, no matter what happens. And don't keep looking at me as if I were a martyr! She watches us and it would please her to think I cared. I don't – and I mean she shall see I don't. I guess I'm well rid of a fellow as fickle as he is, and I've sense enough to know it."

She went upstairs then, tearing off her turquoise engagement ring as she climbed the steps. All sorts of wild ideas flashed through her head. She would go down and confront Vivienne LeMar – she would rush off and find Spencer and throw his ring at him, no matter where he was – she would go away where no one would ever see her again. Why couldn't she die? Was it possible people could suffer like this and yet go on living?

"I don't care – I don't care!" she moaned, telling the lie aloud to herself, as if she hoped that by this means she would come to believe it.

When twilight came she went out to the front steps and leaned her aching head against the honeysuckle trellis. The sun had just set and the whole world swam in dusky golden light. The wonderful beauty frightened her. She felt like a blot on it.

While she stood there, a buggy came driving up the lane and wheeled about at the steps. In it was Spencer Morgan.

Estella saw him and, in spite of the maddening throb of hope that seemed suddenly to transfigure the world for her, her pride rose in arms. Had Spencer come the night before, he would have found her loving and humble. Even now, had she but been sure that he had come to see her, she would have unbent. But was it the other? The torturing doubt stung her to the quick.

She waited, stubbornly resolved that she would not speak first. It was not in her place. Spencer Morgan flicked his horse sharply with his whip. He dared not look at Estella, but he felt her uncompromising attitude. He was miserably ashamed of himself, and he felt angry at Estella for his shame.

"Do you care to come for a drive?" he asked awkwardly, with a covert glance at the parlour windows.

Estella caught the glance and her jealous perception instantly divined its true significance. Her heart died within her. She did not care what she said.

"Oh," she cried with a toss of her head, "it's not me you want - it's Miss LeMar, isn't it? She's away at the shore. You'll find her there, I dare say."

Still, in spite of all, she perversely hoped. If he would only make any sign, the least in the world, that he was sorry - that he still loved her - she could forgive him everything. When he drove away without another word, she could not believe it again. Surely he would not go - surely he knew she did not mean it - he would turn back before he got to the gate.

But he did not. She saw him disappear around the turn of the road. She could not see if he took the shore lane further on, but she was sure he would. She was furious at herself for acting as she had done. It was all her fault again! Oh, if he would only give her another chance!

She was in her room when she heard the buggy drive up again. She knew it was Spencer and that he had brought Vivienne LeMar home. Acting on a sudden wild impulse, the girl stepped out on the landing and confronted her rival as she came up the stairs.

The latter paused at sight of the white face and anguished eyes. There was a little mocking smile on her lovely face.

"Miss LeMar," said Estella in a quivering voice, "what do you mean by all this? You know I'm engaged to Spencer Morgan!"

Miss LeMar laughed softly.

"Really? If you are engaged to the young man, my dear Miss Bowes, I would advise you to look after him more sharply. He seems very willing to flirt, I should say."

She passed on to her room with a malicious smile. Estella shrank back against the wall, humiliated and baffled. When she found herself alone, she crawled back to her room and threw herself face downward on the bed, praying that she might die.

But she had to live through the horrible month that followed – a month so full of agony that she seemed to draw every breath in pain. Spencer never sought her again; he went everywhere with Miss LeMar. His infatuation was the talk of the settlement. Estella knew that her story was in everyone's mouth, and her pride smarted; but she carried a brave front outwardly. No one should say she cared.

She believed that the actress was merely deluding Spencer for her own amusement and would never dream of marrying him. But one day the idea occurred to her that she might. Estella had always told herself that even if Spencer wanted to come back to her she would never take him back, but now, by the half-sick horror that came over her, she knew how strong the hope had really been and despised herself more than ever.

One evening she was alone in the parlour. She had lit the lamp and was listlessly arranging the little room. She looked old and worn. Her colour was gone and her eyes were dull. As she worked, the door opened and Vivienne LeMar walked or, rather, reeled into the room.

Estella dropped the book she held and gazed at her as one in a dream. The actress's face was flushed and her hair was wildly disordered. Her eyes glittered with an unearthly light. She was talking incoherently. The air was heavy with the fumes of brandy.

Estella laughed hysterically. Vivienne LeMar was grossly intoxicated. This woman whom Spencer Morgan worshipped, for whom he had forsaken her, was reeling about the room, laughing idiotically, talking wildly in a thick voice. If he could but see her now!

Estella turned white with the passion of the wild idea that had come to her. Spencer Morgan should see this woman in her true colours.

She lost no time. Swiftly she left the room and locked the door behind her on the maudlin, babbling creature inside. Then she flung a shawl over her head and ran from the house. It was not far to the Spencer homestead. She ran all the way, hardly knowing what she was doing. Mrs. Morgan answered her knock. She gazed in bewilderment at Estella's wild face.

"I want Spencer," said the girl through her white lips.

The elder woman stepped back in dumb amazement. She knew and rued her son's folly. What could Estella want with him?

The young man appeared in the doorway. Estella caught him by the arm and pulled him outside.

"Miss LeMar wants you at once," she said hoarsely. "At once – you are to come at once!"

"Has anything happened to her?" cried Spencer savagely. "Is she ill – is she – what is the matter?"

"No, she is not ill. But she wants you. Come at once."

He started off bareheaded. Estella followed him up the road breathlessly. Surely it was the strangest walk ever a girl had, she told herself with mirthless laughter. She pushed the key into his hand at the porch.

"She's in the parlour," she said wildly. "Go in and look at her, Spencer."

Spencer snatched the key and fitted it into the door. He was full of fear. Had Estella gone out of her mind? Had she done anything to Vivienne? Had she –

As he entered, the actress reeled to her feet and came to meet him. He stood and gazed at her stupidly. This could not be Vivienne, this creature reeking with brandy, uttering such foolish words! What fiend was this in her likeness?

He grew sick at heart and brain; she had her arms about him. He tried to push her away, but she clung closer, and her senseless laughter echoed through the room. He flung her from him with an effort and rushed out through the hall and down the road like a madman. Estella, watching him, felt that she was avenged. She was glad with a joy more pitiful than grief.

Vivienne LeMar left the cottage the next day. Mrs. Bowes, suspecting some mystery, questioned Estella sharply, but could find out nothing. The girl kept her own counsel stubbornly. The interest and curiosity of the village centred around Spencer Morgan, and his case was well discussed. Gossip said that the actress had jilted him and that he was breaking his heart about it. Then came the rumour that he was going West.

Estella heard it apathetically. Life seemed ended for her. There was nothing to look forward to. She could not even look back. All the past was embittered. She had never met Spencer since the night she went after him. She sometimes wondered what he must think of her for what she had done. Did he think her unwomanly and revengeful? She did not care. It was rather a relief to hear that he was going away. She would not be tortured by the fear of meeting him then. She was sure he would never come back to her. If he did, she would never forgive him.

One evening in early harvest Estella was lingering by the lane gate at twilight. She had worked slavishly all day and was very tired, but she was loath to go into the house, where her trouble always seemed to weigh on her more heavily. The dusk, sweet night seemed to soothe her as it always did.

She leaned her head against the poplar by the gate. How long Spencer Morgan had been standing by her she did not know, but when she looked up he was there. In the dim light she could see how haggard and hollow-eyed he had grown. He had changed almost as much as herself.

The girl's first proud impulse was to turn coldly away and leave him. But some strange tumult in her heart kept her still. What had he come to say?

There was a moment's fateful silence. Then Spencer spoke in a muffled voice.

"I couldn't go away without seeing you once more, Estella, to say good-bye. Perhaps you won't speak to me. You must hate me. I deserve it."

He paused, but she said no word. She could not. After a space, he went wistfully on.

"I know you can never forgive me – no girl could. I've behaved like a fool. There isn't any excuse to be made for me. I don't think I could have been in my right senses, Estella. It all seems like some bad dream now. When I saw her that night, I came to my right mind, and I've been the most miserable man alive ever since. Not for her – but because I'd lost you. I can't bear to live here any longer, so I am going away. Will you say good-bye, Estella?"

Still she did not speak. There were a hundred things she wanted to say but she could not say them. Did he mean that he loved her still? If she were sure of that, she could forgive him anything, but her doubt rendered her mute.

The young man turned away despairingly from her rigid attitude. So be it – he had brought his fate on himself.

He had gone but a few steps when Estella suddenly found her voice with a gasp.

"Spencer!" He came swiftly back. "Oh, Spencer – do – you – do you love me still?"

He caught her hands in his.

"Love you – oh, Estella, yes, yes! I always have. That

other wasn't love – it was just madness. When it passed I hated life because I'd lost you. I know you can't forgive me, but, oh –''

He broke down. Estella flung her arms around his neck and put her face up to his. She felt as if her heart must break with its great happiness. He understood her mute pardon. In their kiss the past was put aside. Estella's martyrdom was ended.

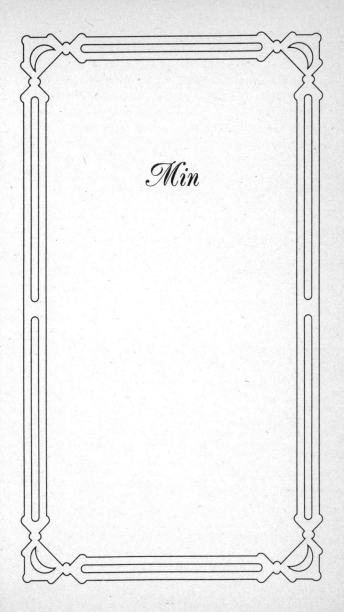

Min

HE MORNING SUN HUNG, a red, lustreless ball, in the dull grey sky. A light snow had fallen in the night and the landscape, crossed by spider-like trails of fences, was as white and lifeless as if wrapped in a shroud.

A young man was driving down the road to Rykman's Corner; the youthful face visible above the greatcoat was thoughtful and refined, the eyes deep blue and peculiarly beautiful, the mouth firm yet sensitive. It was not a handsome face, but there was a strangely subtle charm about it.

The chill breathlessness of the air seemed prophetic of more snow. The Reverend Allan Telford looked across the bare wastes and cold white hills and shivered, as if the icy lifelessness about him were slowly and relentlessly creeping into his own heart and life.

He felt utterly discouraged. In his soul he was asking bitterly what good had come of all his prayerful labours among the people of this pinched, narrow world, as rugged and unbeautiful in form and life as the barren hills that shut them in.

He had been two years among them and he counted it two years of failure. He had been too outspoken for them; they resented sullenly his direct and incisive tirades against their pet sins. They viewed his small innovations on their traditional ways of worship with disfavour and distrust and shut him out of their lives with an ever-increasing coldness. He had meant well and worked hard and he felt his failure keenly.

His thoughts reverted to a letter received the preceding day from a former classmate, stating that the pastorate of a certain desirable town church had become vacant and hinting that a call was to be moderated for him unless he signified his unwillingness to accept.

Two years before, Allan Telford, fresh from college and full of vigorous enthusiasm and high ideas, would have said:

"No, that is not for me. My work must lie among the poor and lowly of earth as did my Master's. Shall I shrink from it because, to worldly eyes, the way looks dreary and uninviting?"

Now, looking back on his two years' ministry, he said wearily:

"I can remain here no longer. If I do, I fear I shall sink down into something almost as pitiful as one of these canting, gossiping people myself. I can do them no good – they do not like or trust me. I will accept this call and go back to my own world."

Perhaps the keynote of his failure was sounded in his last words, "my own world." He had never felt, or tried to feel, that this narrow sphere was his own world. It was some lower level to which he had come with good tidings and honest intentions but, unconsciously, he had held himself above it, and his people felt and resented this. They expressed it by saying he was "stuck-up."

Rykman's Corner came into view as he drove over the brow of a long hill. He hated the place, knowing it well for what it was – a festering hot-bed of gossip and malice, the habitat of all the slanderous rumours and innuendoes that permeated the social tissue of the community. The newest scandal, the worst-flavoured joke, the latest details of the most recent quarrel, were always to be had at Rykman's store.

As the minister drove down the hill, a man came out of a small house at the foot and waited on the road. Had it been possible Telford would have pretended not to see him, but it was not possible, for Isaac Galletly meant to be seen and hailed the minister cheerfully.

"Good mornin', Mr. Telford. Ye won't mind giving me a lift down to the Corner, I dessay?"

Telford checked his horse reluctantly and Galletly crawled into the cutter. He was that most despicable of created beings, a male gossip, and he spent most of his time travelling from house to house in the village, smoking his pipe in neighbourly kitchens and fanning into an active blaze all the smouldering feuds of the place. He had been nicknamed "The Morning Chronicle" by a sarcastic schoolteacher who had sojourned a winter at the Corner. The name was an apt one and clung. Telford had heard it.

I suppose he is starting out on his rounds now, he thought.

Galletly plunged undauntedly into the conversational gap.

"Quite a fall of snow last night. Reckon we'll have more 'fore long. That was a grand sermon ye gave us last Sunday, Mr. Telford. Reckon it went home to some folks, judgin' from all I've heard. It was needed and that's a fact. 'Live peaceably with all men' – that's what I lay out to do. There ain't a house in the district but what I can drop into and welcome. 'Tain't everybody in Rykman's Corner can say the same."

Galletly squinted out of the corner of his eye to see if the minister would open on the trail of this hint. Telford's passive face was discouraging but Galletly was not to be baffled.

"I s'pose ye haven't heard about the row down at Palmers' last night?"

"No."

The monosyllable was curt. Telford was vainly seeking to nip Galletly's gossip in the bud. The name of Palmer conveyed no especial meaning to his ear. He knew where the Palmer homestead was, and that the plaintive-faced, fair-haired woman, whose name was Mrs. Fuller and who came to church occasionally, lived there. His knowledge went no further. He had called three times and found nobody at home – at least, to all appearances. Now he was fated to have the whole budget of some vulgar quarrel forced on him by Galletly.

"No? Everyone's talkin' of it. The long and short of it is that Min Palmer has had a regular up-and-down row with Rose Fuller and turned her and her little gal out of doors. I believe the two women had an awful time. Min's a Tartar when her temper's up – and that's pretty often. Nobody knows how Rose managed to put up with her so long. But she has had to go at last. Goodness knows what the poor critter'll do. She hasn't a cent nor a relation – she was just an orphan girl that Palmer brought up. She is at Raw-lingses now. Maybe when Min cools off, she'll let her go back but it's doubtful. Min hates her like p'isen."

To Telford this was all very unintelligible. But he understood that Mrs. Fuller was in trouble of some kind and that it was his duty to help her if possible, although he had an odd and unaccountable aversion to the woman, for which he had often reproached himself.

"Who is this woman you call Min Palmer?" he said coldly. "What are the family circumstances? I ought to know, perhaps, if I am to be of any service – but I have no wish to hear idle gossip."

His concluding sentence was quite unheeded by Galletly.

"Min Palmer's the worst woman in Rykman's Corner – or out of it. She always was an odd one. I mind her when she was a girl – a saucy, black-eyed baggage she was! Handsome, some folks called her. I never c'd see it. Her people were a queer crowd and Min was never brung up right – jest let run wild all her life. Well, Rod Palmer took to dancin' attendance on her. Rod was a worthless scamp. Old Palmer was well off and Rod was his only child, but

this Rose lived there and kept house for them after Mis'
Palmer died. She was a quiet, well-behaved little creetur.
Folks said the old man wanted Rod to marry her – dunno if
'twas so or not. In the end, howsomever, he had to marry
Min. Her brother got after him with a horse-whip, ye
understand. Old Palmer was furious but he had to give in
and Rod brought her home. She was a bit sobered down
by her trouble and lived quiet and sullen-like at first. Her
and Rod fought like cat and dog. Rose married Osh Fuller,
a worthless, drunken fellow. He died in a year or so and
left Rose and her baby without a roof over their heads.
Then old Palmer went and brought her home. He set great
store by Rose and he c'dn't bear Min. Min had to be civil to
Rose as long as old Palmer lived. Fin'lly Rod up and died
and 'twasn't long before his father went too. Then the
queer part came in. Everyone expected that he'd purvide
well for Rose and Min'd come in second best. But no will
was to be found. I don't say but what it was all right, mind
you. I may have my own secret opinion, of course. Old
Palmer had a regular mania, as ye might say, for makin'
wills. He'd have a lawyer out from town every year and
have a new will made and the old one burnt. Lawyer Bell
was there and made one 'bout eight months 'fore he died.
It was s'posed he'd destroyed it and then died 'fore he'd
time to make another. He went off awful sudden. Anyway,
everything went to Min's child – to Min as ye might say.
She's been boss. Rose still stayed on there and Min let her,
which was more than folks expected of her. But she's
turned her out at last. Min's in one of her tantrums now
and 'tain't safe to cross her path.''

''What is Mrs. Fuller to do?'' asked Telford anxiously.

''That's the question. She's sickly – can't work much –
and then she has her leetle gal. Min was always jealous of
that child. It's a real purty, smart leetle creetur and old
Palmer made a lot of it. Min's own is an awful-looking

thing – a cripple from the time 'twas born. There's no doubt 'twas a jedgement on her. As for Rose, no doubt the god of the widow and fatherless will purvide for her."

In spite of his disgust, Telford could not repress a smile at the tone, half-whine, half-snuffle, with which Galletly ended up.

"I think I had better call and see this Mrs. Palmer," he said slowly.

" 'Twould be no airthly use, Mr. Telford. Min'd slam the door in your face if she did nothing worse. She hates ministers and everything that's good. She hasn't darkened a church door for years. She never had any religious tendency to begin with, and when there was such a scandal about her, old Mr. Dinwoodie, our pastor then – a godly man, Mr. Telford – he didn't hold no truck with evildoers – he went right to her to reprove and rebuke her for her sins. Min, she flew at him. She vowed then she'd never go to church again, and she never has. People hereabouts has talked to her and tried to do her good, but it ain't no use. Why, I've heard that woman say there was no God. It's a fact, Mr. Telford – I have. Some of our ministers has tried to visit her. They didn't try it more than once. The last one – he was about your heft – he got a scare, I tell you. Min just caught him by the shoulder and shook him like a rat! Didn't see it myself but Mrs. Rawlings did. Ye ought to hear her describin' of it."

Galletly chuckled over the recollection, his wicked little eyes glistening with delight. Telford was thankful when they reached the store. He felt that he could not endure this man's society any longer.

Nevertheless, he felt strangely interested. This Min Palmer must at least be different from the rest of the Cornerites, if only in the greater force of her wickedness. He almost felt as if her sins on the grand scale were less blameworthy than the petty vices of her censorious neighbours.

Galletly eagerly joined the group of loungers on the dirty wet platform, and Telford passed into the store. A couple of slatternly women were talking to Mrs. Rykman about "the Palmer row." Telford made his small purchases hastily. As he turned from the counter, he came face to face with a woman who had paused in the doorway to survey the scene with an air of sullen scorn. By some subtle intuition Telford knew that this was Min Palmer.

The young man's first feeling was one of admiration for the woman before him, who, in spite of her grotesque attire and defiant, unwomanly air, was strikingly beautiful. She was tall, and not even the man's ragged overcoat which she wore could conceal the grace of her figure. Her abundant black hair was twisted into a sagging knot at her neck, and from beneath the old fur cap looked out a pair of large and brilliant black eyes, heavily lashed, and full of a smouldering fire. Her skin was tanned and coarsened, but the warm crimson blood glowed in her cheeks with a dusky richness, and her face was a perfect oval, with features chiselled in almost classic regularity of outline.

Telford had a curious experience at that moment. He seemed to see, looking out from behind this external mask of degraded beauty, the semblance of what this woman might have been under more favouring circumstance of birth and environment, wherein her rich, passionate nature, potent for either good or evil, might have been trained and swayed aright until it had developed grandly out into the glorious womanhood the Creator must have planned for her. He knew, as if by revelation, that this woman had nothing in common with the narrow, self-righteous souls of Rykman's Corner. Warped and perverted though her nature might be, she was yet far nobler than those who sat in judgement upon her.

Min made some scanty purchases and left the store quickly, brushing unheedingly past the minister as she did so. He saw her step on a rough wood-sleigh and drive down the river road. The platform loungers had been silent during her call, but now the talk bubbled forth anew. Telford was sick at heart as he drove swiftly away. He felt for Min Palmer a pity he could not understand or analyze. The attempt to measure the gulf between what she was and what she might have been hurt him like the stab of a knife.

He made several calls at various houses along the river during the forenoon. After dinner he suddenly turned his horse towards the Palmer place. Isaac Galletly, comfortably curled up in a neighbour's chimney corner, saw him drive past.

"Ef the minister ain't goin' to Palmers' after all!" he chuckled. "He's a set one when he does take a notion. Well, I warned him what to expect. If Min claws his eyes out, he'll only have himself to blame."

Telford was not without his own misgivings as he drove into the Palmer yard. He tied his horse to the fence and looked doubtfully about him. Untrodden snowdrifts were heaped about the front door, so he turned towards the kitchen and walked slowly past the bare lilac trees along the fence. There was no sign of life about the place. It was beginning to snow again, softly and thickly, and the hills and river were hidden behind a misty white veil.

He lifted his hand to knock, but before he could do so, the door was flung open and Min herself confronted him on the threshold.

She did not now have on the man's overcoat which she had worn at the store, and her neat, close-fitting home-spun dress revealed to perfection the full, magnificent curves of her figure. Her splendid hair was braided about her head in a glossy coronet, and her dark eyes were ablaze with ill-suppressed anger. Again Telford was overcome by a sense of her wonderful loveliness. Not all the years of bondage to ill-temper and misguided will had been able to blot out the beauty of that proud, dark face.

She lifted one large but shapely brown hand and pointed to the gate.

"Go!" she said threateningly.

"Mrs. Palmer," began Telford, but she silenced him with an imperious gesture.

"I don't want any of your kind here. I hate all you ministers. Did you come here to lecture me? I suppose some of the Corner saints set you on me. You'll never cross my threshold."

Telford returned her defiant gaze unflinchingly. His dark-blue eyes, magnetic in their power and sweetness, looked gravely, questioningly, into Min's stormy orbs. Slowly the fire and anger faded out of her face and her head drooped.

"I ain't fit for you to talk to anyway," she said with a sort of sullen humility. "Maybe you mean well but you can't do me any good. I'm past that now. The Corner saints say I'm possessed of the devil. Perhaps I am – if there is one."

"I do mean well," said Telford slowly. "I did not come here to reprove you. I came to help you if I could – if you needed help, Mrs. Palmer –"

"Don't call me that," she interrupted passionately. She flung out her hands as if pushing some loathly, invisible thing from her. "I hate the name – as I hated all who ever bore it. I never had anything but wrong and dog-usage from them all. Call me Min – that's the only name that belongs to me now. Go – why don't you go? Don't stand there looking at me like that. I'm not going to change my mind. I don't want any praying and whining round me. I've been well sickened of that. Go!"

Telford threw back his head and looked once more into her eyes. A long look passed between them. Then he silently lifted his cap and, with no word of farewell, he turned and went down to the gate. A bitter sense of defeat and disappointment filled his heart as he drove away.

Min stood in the doorway and watched the sleigh out of sight down the river road. Then she gave a long, shivering sigh that was almost a moan.

"If I had met that man long ago," she said slowly, as if groping vaguely in some hitherto unsounded depth of consciousness, "I would never have become what I am. I felt that as I looked at him – it all came over me with an awful sickening feeling – just as if we were standing alone somewhere out of the world where there was no need of words to say things. He doesn't despise me – he wouldn't sneer at me, bad as I am, like those creatures up there. He could have helped me if we had met in time, but it's too late now."

She locked her hands over her eyes and groaned, swaying her body to and fro as one in mortal agony. Presently she looked out again with hard, dry eyes.

"What a fool I am!" she said bitterly. "How the Corner saints would stare if they saw me! I suppose some of them do –" with a glance at the windows of a neighbouring house. "Yes, there's Mrs. Rawlings staring out and Rose peeking over her shoulder."

Her face hardened. The old sway of evil passion reasserted itself.

"She shall never come back here – never. Oh, she was a sweet-spoken cat of a thing – but she had claws. I've been blamed for all the trouble. But if ever I had a chance, I'd tell that minister how she used to twit and taunt me in that sugary way of hers – how she schemed and plotted against me as long as she could. More fool I to care what he thinks either! I wish I were dead. If 'twasn't for the child, I'd go and drown myself at that black springhole down there – I'd be well out of the way."

* * *

IT WAS A DULL grey afternoon a week afterwards when Allan Telford again walked up the river road to the Palmer place. The wind was bitter and he walked with bent head to avoid its fury. His face was pale and worn and he looked years older.

He paused at the rough gate and leaned over it while he scanned the house and its surroundings eagerly. As he looked, the kitchen door opened and Min, clad in the old overcoat, came out and walked swiftly across the yard.

Telford's eyes followed her with pitiful absorption. He saw her lead a horse from the stable and harness it into a wood-sleigh loaded with bags of grain. Once she paused to fling her arms about the animal's neck, laying her face against it with a caressing motion.

The pale minister groaned aloud. He longed to snatch her forever from that hard, unwomanly toil and fold her safely away from jeers and scorn in the shelter of his love. He knew it was madness – he had told himself so every hour in which Min's dark, rebellious face had haunted him – yet none the less was he under its control.

Min led the horse across the yard and left it standing before the kitchen door; she had not seen the bowed figure at the gate. When she reappeared, he saw her dark eyes and the rose-red lustre of her face gleam out from under the old crimson shawl wrapped about her head.

As she caught the horse by the bridle, the kitchen door swung heavily to with a sharp, sudden bang. The horse, a great, powerful, nervous brute, started wildly and then reared in terror.

The ice underfoot was glib and treacherous. Min lost her foothold and fell directly under the horse's hoofs as they came heavily down. The animal, freed from her detaining hand, sprang forward, dragging the laden sleigh over the prostrate woman.

It had all passed in a moment. The moveless figure lay where it had fallen, one outstretched hand still grasping the whip. Telford sprang over the gate and rushed up the slope like a madman. He flung himself on his knees beside her.

"Min! Min!" he called wildly.

There was no answer. He lifted her in his arms and staggered into the house with his burden, his heart stilling with a horrible fear as he laid her gently down on the old lounge in one corner of the kitchen.

The room was a large one and everything was neat and clean. The fire burned brightly, and a few green plants were in blossom by the south window. Beside them sat a child of about seven years who turned a startled face at Telford's reckless entrance.

The boy had Min's dark eyes and perfectly chiselled features, refined by suffering into cameo-like delicacy, and the silken hair fell in soft, waving masses about the spiritual little face. By his side nestled a tiny dog, with satin ears and paws fringed as with ravelled silk.

Telford paid heed to nothing, not even the frightened child. He was as one distraught.

"Min," he wailed again, striving tremblingly to feel her pulse while cold drops came out on his forehead.

Min's face was as pallid as marble, save for one heavy bruise across the cheek and a cruel cut at the edge of the dark hair, from which the blood trickled down on the pillow.

She opened her eyes wonderingly at his call, looking up with a dazed, appealing expression of pain and dread. A low moan broke from her white lips. Telford sprang to his feet in a tumult of quivering joy.

"Min, dear," he said gently, "you have been hurt – not seriously, I hope. I must leave you for a minute while I run for help – I will not be long."

"Come back," said Min in a low but distinct tone.

He paused impatiently.

"It is of no use to get help," Min went on calmly. "I'm dying – I know it. Oh, my God!"

She pressed her hand to her side and writhed. Telford turned desperately to the door. Min raised her arm.

"Come here," she said resolutely.

He obeyed mutely. She looked up at him with bright, unquailing eyes.

"Don't you go one step – don't leave me here to die alone. I'm past help – and I've something to say to you. I must say it and I haven't much time."

Telford hardly heeded her in his misery.

"Min, let me go for help – let me do something," he implored. "You must not die – you must not!"

Min had fallen back, gasping, on the blood-stained pillow.

He knelt beside her and put his arm about the poor, crushed body.

"I must hurry," she said faintly. "I can't die with it on my mind. Rose – it's all hers – all. There was a will – he made it – old Gran'ther Palmer. He always hated me. I found it before he died – and read it. He left everything to her – not a cent to me nor his son's child – we were to starve – beg. I was like a madwoman. When he died – I hid the will. I meant – to burn it – but I never could. It's tortured me – night and day – I've had no peace. You'll find it in a box – in my room. Tell her – tell Rose – how wicked I've been. And my boy – what will become of him? Rose hates him – she'll turn him out – or ill-treat him –"

Telford lifted his white, drawn face.

"I will take your child, Min. He shall be to me as my own son."

An expression of unspeakable relief came into the dying woman's face.

"It is good – of you. I can die – in peace – now. I'm glad to die – to get clear of it all. I'm tired – of living so. Perhaps – I'll have a chance – somewhere else. I've never – had any – here."

The dark eyes drooped – closed. Telford moaned shudderingly.

Once again Min opened her eyes and looked straight into his.

"If I had met you – long ago – you would have – loved me – and I would have been – a good woman. It is well for us – for you – that I am – dying. Your path will be clear – you will be good and successful – but you will always – remember me."

Telford bent and pressed his lips to Min's pain-blanched mouth.

"Do you think – we will – ever meet again?" she said faintly. "Out there – it's so dark – God can never – forgive me – I've been so – wicked."

"Min, the all-loving Father is more merciful than man. He will forgive you, if you ask Him, and you will wait for me till I come. I will stay here and do my duty – I will try hard –"

His voice broke. Min's great black eyes beamed out on him with passionate tenderness. The strong, deep, erring nature yielded at last. An exceeding bitter cry rose to her lips.

"Oh, God – forgive me – forgive me!"

And with the cry, the soul of poor suffering, sinning, sinned-against Min Palmer fled – who shall say whither? Who shall say that her remorseful cry was not heard, even at that late hour, by a Judge more merciful than her fellow creatures?

Telford still knelt on the bare floor, holding in his arms the dead form of the woman he loved – his, all his, in death, as she could never have been in life. Death had bridged the gulf between them.

The room was very silent. To Min's face had returned something of its girlhood's innocence. The hard, unlovely lines were all smoothed out. The little cripple crept timidly up to Telford, with the silky head of the dog pressed against his cheek. Telford gathered the distorted little body to his side and looked earnestly into the small face – Min's face, purified and spiritualized. He would have it near him always. He bent and reverently kissed the cold face, the closed eyelids and the blood-stained brow of the dead woman. Then he stood up.

"Come with me, dear," he said gently to the child.

THE DAY AFTER the funeral, Allan Telford sat in the study of his little manse among the encircling wintry hills. Close to the window sat Min's child, his small, beautiful face pressed against the panes, and the bright-eyed dog beside him.

Telford was writing in his journal.

"I shall stay here – close to her grave. I shall see it every time I look from my study window – every time I stand in my pulpit – every time I go in and out among my people. I begin to see wherein I have failed. I shall begin again patiently and humbly. I wrote today to decline the C—— church call. My heart and my work are here."

He closed the book and bowed his head on it. Outside the snow fell softly; he knew that it was wrapping that new-made grave on the cold, fir-sentinelled hillside with a stainless shroud of infinite purity and peace.

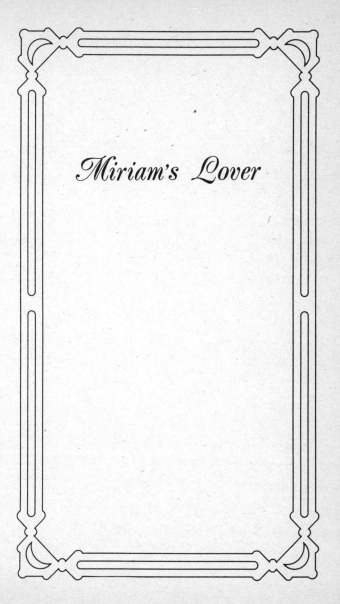

Miriam's Lover

HAD BEEN READING a ghost story to Mrs. Sefton, and I laid it down at the end with a little shrug of contempt.

"What utter nonsense!" I said.

Mrs. Sefton nodded abstractedly above her fancywork.

"That is. It is a very commonplace story indeed. I don't believe the spirits of the departed trouble themselves to revisit the glimpses of the moon for the purpose of frightening honest mortals – or even for the sake of hanging around the favourite haunts of their existence in the flesh. If they ever appear, it must be for a better reason than that."

"You don't surely think that they ever do appear?" I said incredulously.

"We have no proof that they do not, my dear."

"Surely, Mary," I exclaimed, "you don't mean to say that you believe people ever do or can see spirits – ghosts, as the word goes?"

"I didn't say I believed it. I never saw anything of the sort. I neither believe nor disbelieve. But you know queer things do happen at times – things you can't account for. At least, people who you know wouldn't lie say so. Of course, they may be mistaken. And I don't think that everybody can see spirits either, provided they are to be seen. It requires people of a certain organization – with a spiritual eye, as it were. We haven't all got that – in fact, I think very few of us have. I dare say you think I'm talking nonsense."

"Well, yes, I think you are. You really surprise me, Mary. I always thought you the least likely person in the world to take up with such ideas. Something must have come under your observation to develop such theories in your practical head. Tell me what it was."

"To what purpose? You would remain as sceptical as ever."

"Possibly not. Try me; I may be convinced."

"No," returned Mrs. Sefton calmly. "Nobody ever is convinced by hearsay. When a person has once seen a spirit – or thinks he has – he thenceforth believes it. And when somebody else is intimately associated with that person and knows all the circumstances – well, he admits the possibility, at least. That is my position. But by the time it gets to the third person – the outsider – it loses power. Besides, in this particular instance the story isn't very exciting. But then – it's true."

"You have excited my curiosity. You must tell me the story."

"Well, first tell me what you think of this. Suppose two people, both sensitively organized individuals, loved each other with a love stronger than life. If they were apart, do you think it might be possible for their souls to communicate with each other in some inexplicable way? And if anything happened to one, don't you think that that one could and would let the spirit of the other know?"

"You're getting into too deep waters for me, Mary," I said, shaking my head. "I'm not an authority on telepathy, or whatever you call it. But I've no belief in such theories. In fact, I think they are all nonsense. I'm sure you must think so too in your rational moments."

"I dare say it is all nonsense," said Mrs. Sefton slowly, "but if you had lived a whole year in the same house with Miriam Gordon, you would have been tainted too. Not that she had 'theories' – at least, she never aired them if she had. But there was simply something about the girl herself that gave a person strange impressions. When I first met her I had the most uncanny feeling that she was all spirit – soul – what you will! no flesh, anyhow. That feeling wore off after a while, but she never seemed like other people to me.

"She was Mr. Sefton's niece. Her father had died when she was a child. When Miriam was twenty her mother had married a second time and went to Europe with her husband. Miriam came to live with us while they were away. Upon their return she was herself to be married.

"I had never seen Miriam before. Her arrival was unexpected, and I was absent from home when she came. I returned in the evening, and when I saw her first she was standing under the chandelier in the drawing room. Talk about spirits! For five seconds I thought I had seen one.

"Miriam was a beauty. I had known that before, though I think I hardly expected to see such wonderful loveliness. She was tall and extremely graceful, dark – at least her hair was dark, but her skin was wonderfully fair and clear. Her hair was gathered away from her face, and she had a high, pure, white forehead, and the straightest, finest, blackest brows. Her face was oval, with very large and dark eyes.

"I soon realized that Miriam was in some mysterious fashion different from other people. I think everyone who met her felt the same way. Yet it was a feeling hard to define. For my own part I simply felt as if she belonged to another world, and that part of the time she – her soul, you know – was back there again.

"You must not suppose that Miriam was a disagreeable person to have in the house. On the contrary, it was the very reverse. Everybody liked her. She was one of the sweetest, most winsome girls I ever knew, and I soon grew to love her dearly. As for what Dick called her 'little queernesses' – well, we got used to them in time.

"Miriam was engaged, as I have told you, to a young Harvard man named Sidney Claxton. I knew she loved him very deeply. When she showed me his photograph, I liked his appearance and said so. Then I made some teasing remark about her love-letters – just for a joke, you know. Miriam looked at me with an odd little smile and said quickly:

"'Sidney and I never write to each other.'

"'Why, Miriam!' I exclaimed in astonishment. 'Do you mean to tell me you never hear from him at all?'

"'No, I did not say that. I hear from him every day – every hour. We do not need to write letters. There are better means of communication between two souls that are in perfect accord with each other.'

"'Miriam, you uncanny creature, what do you mean?' I asked.

"But Miriam only gave another queer smile and made no answer at all. Whatever her beliefs or theories were, she would never discuss them.

"She had a habit of dropping into abstracted reveries at any time or place. No matter where she was, this, whatever it was, would come over her. She would sit there, perhaps in the centre of a gay crowd, and gaze right out into space, not hearing or seeing a single thing that went on around her.

"I remember one day in particular; we were sewing in my room. I looked up and saw that Miriam's work had dropped on her knee and she was leaning forward, her lips apart, her eyes gazing upward with an unearthly expression.

"'Don't look like that, Miriam!' I said, with a little shiver. 'You seem to be looking at something a thousand miles away!'

"Miriam came out of her trance or reverie and said, with a little laugh:

"'How do you know but that I was?'

"She bent her head for a minute or two. Then she lifted it again and looked at me with a sudden contraction of her level brows that betokened vexation.

"'I wish you hadn't spoken to me just then,' she said.

'You interrupted the message I was receiving. I shall not get it at all now.'

" 'Miriam,' I implored. 'I so wish, my dear girl, that you wouldn't talk so. It makes people think there is something queer about you. Who in the world was sending you a message, as you call it?'

" 'Sidney,' said Miriam simply.

" 'Nonsense!'

" 'You think it is nonsense because you don't understand it,' was her calm response.

"I recall another event was when some caller dropped in and we had drifted into a discussion about ghosts and the like – and I've no doubt we all talked some delicious nonsense. Miriam said nothing at the time, but when we were alone I asked her what she thought of it.

" 'I thought you were all merely talking against time,' she retorted evasively.

" 'But, Miriam, do you really think it is possible for ghosts –'

" 'I detest that word!'

" 'Well, spirits then – to return after death, or to appear to anyone apart from the flesh?'

" 'I will tell you what I know. If anything were to happen to Sidney – if he were to die or be killed – he would come to me himself and tell me.'

"One day Miriam came down to lunch looking pale and worried. After Dick went out, I asked her if anything were wrong.

" 'Something has happened to Sidney,' she replied, 'some painful accident – I don't know what.'

" 'How do you know?' I cried. Then, as she looked at me strangely, I added hastily, 'You haven't been receiving any more unearthly messages, have you? Surely, Miriam, you are not so foolish as to really believe in that!'

" 'I know,' she answered quickly. 'Belief or disbelief has

153

nothing to do with it. Yes, I have had a message. I know that some accident has happened to Sidney – painful and inconvenient but not particularly dangerous. I do not know what it is. Sidney will write me that. He writes when it is absolutely necessary.'

" 'Aerial communication isn't perfected yet then?' I said mischievously. But, observing how really worried she seemed, I added, 'Don't fret, Miriam. You may be mistaken.'

"Well, two days afterwards she got a note from her lover – the first I had ever known her to receive – in which he said he had been thrown from his horse and had broken his left arm. It had happened the very morning Miriam received her message.

"Miriam had been with us about eight months when one day she came into my room hurriedly. She was very pale.

" 'Sidney is ill – dangerously ill. What shall I do?'

"I knew she must have had another of those abominable messages – or thought she had – and really, remembering the incident of the broken arm, I couldn't feel as sceptical as I pretended to. I tried to cheer her, but did not succeed. Two hours later she had a telegram from her lover's college chum, saying that Mr. Claxton was dangerously ill with typhoid fever.

"I was quite alarmed about Miriam in the days that followed. She grieved and fretted continually. One of her troubles was that she received no more messages; she said it was because Sidney was too ill to send them. Anyhow, she had to content herself with the means of communication used by ordinary mortals.

"Sidney's mother, who had gone to nurse him, wrote every day, and at last good news came. The crisis was over and the doctor in attendance thought Sidney would recover. Miriam seemed like a new creature then, and rapidly recovered her spirits.

"For a week reports continued favourable. One night we went to the opera to hear a celebrated prima donna. When we returned home Miriam and I were sitting in her room, chatting over the events of the evening.

"Suddenly she sat straight up with a sort of convulsive shudder, and at the same time – you may laugh if you like – the most horrible feeling came over me. I didn't see anything, but I just felt that there was something or someone in the room besides ourselves.

"Miriam was gazing straight before her. She rose to her feet and held out her hands.

" 'Sidney!' she said.

"Then she fell to the floor in a dead faint.

"I screamed for Dick, rang the bell and rushed to her.

"In a few minutes the whole household was aroused, and Dick was off posthaste for the doctor, for we could not revive Miriam from her death-like swoon. She seemed as one dead. We worked over her for hours. She would come out of her faint for a moment, give us an unknowing stare and go shudderingly off again.

"The doctor talked of some fearful shock, but I kept my own counsel. At dawn Miriam came back to life at last. When she and I were left alone, she turned to me.

" 'Sidney is dead,' she said quietly. 'I saw him – just before I fainted. I looked up, and he was standing between me and you. He had come to say farewell.'

"What could I say? Almost while we were talking a telegram came. He was dead – he had died at the very hour at which Miriam had seen him."

Mrs. Sefton paused, and the lunch bell rang.

"What do you think of it?" she queried as we rose.

"Honestly, I don't know what I think of it," I answered frankly.

Miss Calista's
Peppermint Bottle

ISS CALISTA was perplexed. Her nephew, Caleb Cramp, who had been her right-hand man for years and whom she had got well broken into her ways, had gone to the Klondike, leaving her to fill his place with the next best man; but the next best man was slow to appear, and meanwhile Miss Calista was looking about her warily. She could afford to wait a while, for the crop was all in and the fall ploughing done, so that the need of a successor to Caleb was not as pressing as it might otherwise have been. There was no lack of applicants, such as they were. Miss Calista was known to be a kind and generous mistress, although she had her "ways," and insisted calmly and immovably upon wholehearted compliance with them. She had a small, well-cultivated farm and a comfortable house, and her hired men lived in clover. Caleb Cramp had been perfection after his kind, and Miss Calista did not expect to find his equal. Nevertheless, she set up a certain standard of requirements; and although three weeks, during which Miss Calista had been obliged to put up with the immature services of a neighbour's boy, had elapsed since Caleb's departure, no one had as yet stepped into his vacant and coveted shoes.

Certainly Miss Calista was somewhat hard to please, but she was not thinking of herself as she sat by her front window in the chilly November twilight. Instead, she was musing on the degeneration of hired men, and reflecting that it was high time the wheat was thrashed, the house banked, and sundry other duties attended to.

Ches Maybin had been up that afternoon to negotiate for the vacant place, and had offered to give satisfaction for smaller wages than Miss Calista had ever paid. But he had met with a brusque refusal, scarcely as civil as Miss

Calista had bestowed on drunken Jake Stinson from the Morrisvale Road.

Not that Miss Calista had any particular prejudice against Ches Maybin, or knew anything positively to his discredit. She was simply unconsciously following the example of a world that exerts itself to keep a man down when he is down and prevent all chance of his rising. Nothing succeeds like success, and the converse of this is likewise true – that nothing fails like failure. There was not a person in Cooperstown who would not have heartily endorsed Miss Calista's refusal.

Ches Maybin was only eighteen, although he looked several years older, and although no flagrant misdoing had ever been proved against him, suspicion of such was not wanting. He came of a bad stock, people said sagely, adding that what was bred in the bone was bound to come out in the flesh. His father, old Sam Maybin, had been a shiftless and tricky rascal, as everybody knew, and had ended his days in the poorhouse. Ches's mother had died when he was a baby, and he had come up somehow, in a hand-to-mouth fashion, with all the cloud of heredity hanging over him. He was always looked at askance, and when any mischief came to light in the village, it was generally fastened on him as a convenient and handy scapegoat. He was considered sulky and lazy, and the local prophets united in predicting a bad end for him sooner or later; and, moreover, diligently endeavoured by their general treatment of him to put him in a fair way to fulfil their predictions. Miss Calista, when she had shut Chester Maybin out into the chill gloom of the November dusk, dismissed him from her thoughts. There were other things of more moment to her just then than old Sam Maybin's hopeful son.

There was nobody in the house but herself, and although this was neither alarming nor unusual, it was unusual – and Miss Calista considered it alarming – that the sum of five hundred dollars should at that very moment be in the upper right-hand drawer of the sideboard, which sum had been up to the previous day safe in the coffers of the Millageville bank. But certain unfavourable rumours were in course of circulation about that same institution, and Miss Calista, who was nothing if not prudent, had gone to the bank that very morning and withdrawn her deposit. She intended to go over to Kerrytown the very next day and deposit it in the Savings Bank there. Not another day would she keep it in the house, and, indeed, it worried her to think she must keep it even for the night, as she had told Mrs. Galloway that afternoon during a neighbourly back-yard chat.

"Not but what it's safe enough," she said, "for not a soul but you knows I've got it. But I'm not used to have so much by me, and there are always tramps going round. It worries me somehow. I wouldn't give it a thought if Caleb was here. I s'pose being all alone makes me nervous."

Miss Calista was still rather nervous when she went to bed that night, but she was a woman of sound sense and was determined not to give way to foolish fears. She locked doors and windows carefully, as was her habit, and saw that the fastenings were good and secure. The one on the dining-room window, looking out on the back yard, wasn't; in fact, it was broken altogether; but, as Miss Calista told herself, it had been broken just so for the last six years, and nobody had ever tried to get in at it yet, and it wasn't likely anyone would begin tonight.

Miss Calista went to bed and, despite her worry, slept soon and soundly. It was well on past midnight when she suddenly wakened and sat bolt upright in bed. She was not accustomed to waken in the night, and she had the impression of having been awakened by some noise. She listened breathlessly. Her room was directly over the dining-room, and an empty stovepipe hole opened up through the ceiling of the latter at the head of her bed.

There was no mistake about it. Something or some person was moving about stealthily in the room below. It wasn't the cat – Miss Calista had shut him in the woodshed before she went to bed, and he couldn't possibly get out. It must certainly be a beggar or tramp of some description.

Miss Calista might be given over to nervousness in regard to imaginary thieves, but in the presence of real danger she was cool and self-reliant. As noiselessly and swiftly as any burglar himself, Miss Calista slipped out of bed and into her clothes. Then she tip-toed out into the hall. The late moonlight, streaming in through the hall windows, was quite enough illumination for her purpose, and she got downstairs and was fairly in the open doorway of the dining-room before a sound betrayed her presence.

Standing at the sideboard, hastily ransacking the neat contents of an open drawer, stood a man's figure, dimly visible in the moonlight gloom. As Miss Calista's grim form appeared in the doorway, the midnight marauder turned with a start and then, with an inarticulate cry, sprang, not at the courageous lady, but at the open window behind him.

Miss Calista, realizing with a flash of comprehension that he was escaping her, had a woman-like impulse to get a blow in anyhow; she grasped and hurled at her unceremonious caller the first thing that came to hand – a bottle of peppermint essence that was standing on the.sideboard.

The missile hit the escaping thief squarely on the shoulder as he sprang out of the window, and the fragments of glass came clattering down on the sill. The next moment Miss Calista found herself alone, standing by the sideboard in a half-dazed fashion, for the whole thing had passed with such lightning-like rapidity that it almost seemed as if it were the dissolving end of a bad dream. But the open drawer and the window, where the bits of glass were glistening in the moonlight, were no dream. Miss Calista recovered herself speedily, closed the window, lit the lamp, gathered up the broken glass, and set up the chairs which the would-be thief had upset in his exit. An examination of the sideboard showed the precious five hundred safe and sound in an undisturbed drawer.

Miss Calista kept grim watch and ward there until morning, and thought the matter over exhaustively. In the end she resolved to keep her own counsel. She had no clue whatever to the thief's whereabouts or identity, and no good would come of making a fuss, which might only end in throwing suspicion on someone who might be quite innocent.

When the morning came Miss Calista lost no time in setting out for Kerrytown, where the money was soon safely deposited in the bank. She heaved a sigh of relief when she left the building.

I feel as if I could enjoy life once more, she said to herself. Goodness me, if I'd had to keep that money by me for a week itself, I'd have been a raving lunatic by the end of it.

Miss Calista had shopping to do and friends to visit in town, so that the dull autumn day was well nigh spent when she finally got back to Cooperstown and paused at the corner store to get a bundle of matches.

The store was full of men, smoking and chatting around the fire, and Miss Calista, whose pet abomination was tobacco smoke, was not at all minded to wait any longer than she could help. But Abiram Fell was attending to a previous customer, and Miss Calista sat grimly down by the counter to wait her turn.

The door opened, letting in a swirl of raw November

evening wind and Ches Maybin. He nodded sullenly to Mr. Fell and passed down the store to mutter a message to a man at the further end.

Miss Calista lifted her head as he passed and sniffed the air as a charger who scents battle. The smell of tobacco was strong, and so was that of the open boxes of dried herring on the counter, but plainly, above all the com-mingled odours of a country grocery, Miss Calista caught a whiff of peppermint, so strong as to leave no doubt of its origin. There had been no hint of it before Ches Maybin's entrance.

The latter did not wait long. He was out and striding along the shadowy road when Miss Calista left the store and drove smartly after him. It never took Miss Calista long to make up her mind about anything, and she had weighed and passed judgement on Ches Maybin's case while Mr. Fell was doing up her matches.

The lad glanced up furtively as she checked her fat grey pony beside him.

"Good evening, Chester," she said with brisk kindness. "I can give you a lift, if you are going my way. Jump in, quick – Dapple is a little restless."

A wave of crimson, duskily perceptible under his sun-burned skin, surged over Ches Maybin's face. It almost seemed as if he were going to blurt out a blunt refusal. But Miss Calista's face was so guileless and her tone so friendly, that he thought better of it and sprang in beside her, and Dapple broke into an impatient trot down the long hill lined with its bare, wind-writhen maples.

After a few minutes' silence Miss Calista turned to her moody companion.

"Chester," she said, as tranquilly as if about to ask him the most ordinary question in the world, "why did you climb into my house last night and try to steal my money?"

Ches Maybin started convulsively, as if he meant to

spring from the buggy at once, but Miss Calista's hand was on his arm in a grasp none the less firm because of its gentleness, and there was a warning gleam in her grey eyes.

"It won't mend matters trying to get clear of me, Chester. I know it was you and I want an answer – a truthful one, mind you – to my question. I am your friend, and I am not going to harm you if you tell me the truth."

Her clear and incisive gaze met and held irresistibly the boy's wavering one. The sullen obstinacy of his face relaxed.

"Well," he muttered finally, "I was just desperate, that's why. I've never done anything real bad in my life before, but people have always been down on me. I'm blamed for everything, and nobody wants anything to do with me. I'm willing to work, but I can't get a thing to do. I'm in rags and I haven't a cent, and winter's coming on. I heard you telling Mrs. Galloway yesterday about that money. I was behind the fir hedge and you didn't see me. I went away and planned it all out. I'd get in some way – and I meant to use the money to get away out west as far from here as I could, and begin life there, where nobody knew me, and where I'd have some sort of a chance. I've never had any here. You can put me in jail now, if you like – they'll feed and clothe me there, anyhow, and I'll be on a level with the rest."

The boy had blurted it all out sullenly and half-chokingly. A world of rebellion and protest against the fate that had always dragged him down was couched in his voice.

Miss Calista drew Dapple to a standstill before her gate.

"I'm not going to send you to jail, Chester. I believe you've told me the truth. Yesterday you wanted me to give you Caleb's place and I refused. Well, I offer it to you now. If you'll come, I'll hire you, and give you as good wages as I gave him."

Ches Maybin looked incredulous.

"Miss Calista, you can't mean it."

"I do mean it, every word. You say you have never had a chance. Well, I am going to give you one – a chance to get on the right road and make a man of yourself. Nobody shall ever know about last night's doings from me, and I'll make it my business to forget them if you deserve it. What do you say?"

Ches lifted his head and looked her squarely in the face.

"I'll come," he said huskily. "It ain't no use to try and thank you, Miss Calista. But I'll live my thanks."

And he did. The good people of Cooperstown held up their hands in horror when they heard that Miss Calista had hired Ches Maybin, and prophesied that the deluded woman would live to repent her rash step. But not all prophecies come true. Miss Calista smiled serenely and kept on her own misguided way. And Ches Maybin proved so efficient and steady that the arrangement was continued, and in due time people outlived their old suspicions and came to regard him as a thoroughly smart and trustworthy young man.

"Miss Calista has made a man of Ches Maybin," said the oracles. "He ought to be very grateful to her."

And he was. But only he and Miss Calista and the peppermint bottle ever knew the precise extent of his gratitude, and they never told.

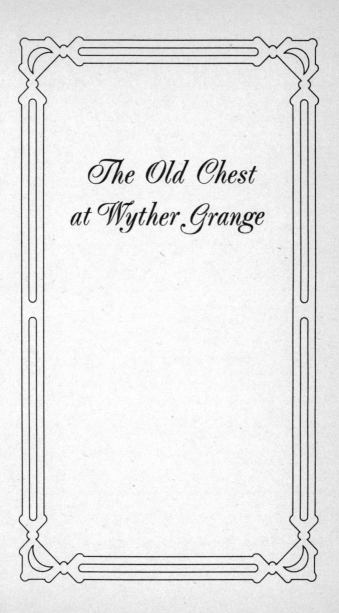

*The Old Chest
at Wyther Grange*

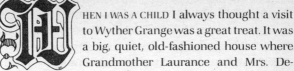HEN I WAS A CHILD I always thought a visit to Wyther Grange was a great treat. It was a big, quiet, old-fashioned house where Grandmother Laurance and Mrs. De-Lisle, my Aunt Winnifred, lived. I was a favourite with them, yet I could never overcome a certain awe of them both. Grandmother was a tall, dignified old lady with keen black eyes that seemed veritably to bore through one. She always wore stiffly-rustling gowns of rich silk made in the fashion of her youth. I suppose she must have changed her dress occasionally, but the impression on my mind was always the same, as she went trailing about the house with a big bunch of keys at her belt – keys that opened a score of wonderful old chests and boxes and drawers. It was one of my dearest delights to attend Grandmother in her peregrinations and watch the unfolding and examining of all those old treasures and heirlooms of bygone Laurances.

Of Aunt Winnifred I was less in awe, possibly because she dressed in a modern way and so looked to my small eyes more human and natural. As Winnifred Laurance she had been the beauty of the family and was a handsome woman still, with brilliant dark eyes and cameo-like features. She always looked very sad, spoke in a low sweet voice, and was my childish ideal of all that was high-bred and graceful.

I had many beloved haunts at the Grange, but I liked the garret best. It was a roomy old place, big enough to have comfortably housed a family in itself, and was filled with cast-off furniture and old trunks and boxes of discarded finery. I was never tired of playing there, dressing up in the old-fashioned gowns and hats and practising old-time dance steps before the high, cracked mirror that hung at one end. That old garret was a veritable fairyland to me.

There was one old chest which I could not explore and, like all forbidden things, it possessed a great attraction for me. It stood away back in a dusty, cobwebbed corner, a strong, high wooden box, painted blue. From some words which I had heard Grandmother let fall I was sure it had a history; it was the one thing she never explored in her periodical overhaulings. When I grew tired of playing I liked to creep up on it and sit there, picturing out my own fancies concerning it – of which my favourite one was that some day I should solve the riddle and open the chest to find it full of gold and jewels with which I might restore the fortune of the Laurances and all the traditionary splendours of the old Grange.

I was sitting there one day when Aunt Winnifred and Grandmother Laurance came up the narrow dark staircase, the latter jingling her keys and peering into the dusty corners as she came along the room. When they came to the old chest, Grandmother rapped the top smartly with her keys.

"I wonder what is in this old chest," she said. "I believe it really should be opened. The moths may have got into it through that crack in the lid."

"Why don't you open it, Mother?" said Mrs. DeLisle. "I am sure that key of Robert's would fit the lock."

"No," said Grandmother in the tone that nobody, not even Aunt Winnifred, ever dreamed of disputing. "I will not open that chest without Eliza's permission. She confided it to my care when she went away, and I promised that it should never be opened until she came for it."

"Poor Eliza," said Mrs. DeLisle thoughtfully. "I wonder what she is like now. Very much changed, like all the rest of us, I suppose. It is almost thirty years since she was here. How pretty she was!"

"I never approved of her," said Grandmother brusquely. "She was a sentimental, fanciful creature. She might have married well but she preferred to waste her life pining over the memory of a man who was not worthy to untie the shoelace of a Laurance."

Mrs. DeLisle sighed softly and made no reply. People said that she had had her own romance in her youth and that her mother had sternly repressed it. I had heard that her marriage with Mr. DeLisle was loveless on her part and proved very unhappy. But he had been dead many years, and Aunt Winnifred never spoke of him.

"I have made up my mind what to do," said Grandmother decidedly. "I will write to Eliza and ask her if I may open the chest to see if the moths have got into it. If she refuses, well and good. I have no doubt that she *will* refuse. She will cling to her old sentimental ideas as long as the breath is in her body."

I rather avoided the old chest after this. It took on a new significance in my eyes and seemed to me like the tomb of something – possibly some dead and buried romance of the past.

Later on a letter came to Grandmother; she passed it over the table to Mrs. DeLisle.

"That is from Eliza," she said. "I would know her writing anywhere – none of your modern sprawly, untidy hands, but a fine lady-like script, as regular as copperplate. Read the letter, Winnifred; I haven't my glasses and I dare say Eliza's rhapsodies would tire me very much. You need not read them aloud – I can imagine them all. Let me know what she says about the chest."

Aunt Winnifred opened and read the letter and laid it down with a brief sigh.

"This is all she says about the chest. 'If it were not for one thing that is in it, I would ask you to open the chest and burn all its contents. But I cannot bear that anyone but myself should see or touch that one thing. So please leave the chest as it is, dear Aunt. It is no matter if the moths do get in.' That is all," continued Mrs. DeLisle, "and I must confess that I am disappointed. I have always had an almost childish curiosity about that old chest, but I seem fated not to have it gratified. That 'one thing' must be her wedding dress. I have always thought that she locked it away there."

"Her answer is just what I expected of her," said Grandmother impatiently. "Evidently the years have not made her more sensible. Well, I wash my hands of her belongings, moths or no moths."

It was not until ten years afterwards that I heard anything more of the old chest. Grandmother Laurance had died, but Aunt Winnifred still lived at the Grange. She was very lonely, and the winter after Grandmother's death she sent me an invitation to make her a long visit.

When I revisited the garret and saw the old blue chest in the same dusty corner, my childish curiosity revived and I begged Aunt Winnifred to tell me its history.

"I am glad you have reminded me of it," said Mrs. DeLisle. "I have intended to open the chest ever since Mother's death but I kept putting it off. You know, Amy, poor Eliza Laurance died five years ago, but even then Mother would not have the chest opened. There is no reason why it should not be examined now. If you like, we will go and open it at once and afterwards I will tell you the story."

We went eagerly up the garret stairs. Aunt knelt down before the old chest and selected a key from the bunch at her belt.

"Would it not be too provoking, Amy, if this key should not fit after all? Well, I do not believe you would be any more disappointed than I."

She turned the key and lifted the heavy lid. I bent forward eagerly. A layer of tissue paper revealed itself, with a fine tracing of sifted dust in its crinkles.

"Lift it up, child," said my aunt gently. "There are no ghosts for you, at least, in this old chest."

I lifted the paper up and saw that the chest was divided into two compartments. Lying on the top of one was a small, square, inlaid box. This Mrs. DeLisle took up and carried to the window. Lifting up the cover she laid it in my lap.

"There, Amy, look through it and let us see what old treasures have lain hidden there these forty years."

The first thing I took out was a small square case covered with dark purple velvet. The tiny clasp was almost rusted away and yielded easily. I gave a little cry of admiration. Aunt Winnifred bent over my shoulder.

"That is Eliza's portrait at the age of twenty, and that is Willis Starr's. Was she not lovely, Amy?"

Lovely indeed was the face looking out at me from its border of tarnished gilt. It was the face of a young girl, in shape a perfect oval, with delicate features and large dark-blue eyes. Her hair, caught high on the crown and falling on her neck in the long curls of a bygone fashion, was a warm auburn, and the curves of her bare neck and shoulders were exquisite.

"The other picture is that of the man to whom she was betrothed. Tell me, Amy, do you think him handsome?"

I looked at the other portrait critically. It was that of a young man of about twenty-five; he was undeniably handsome, but there was something I did not like in his face and I said so.

Aunt Winnifred made no reply – she was taking out the remaining contents of the box. There was a white silk fan with delicately carved ivory sticks, a packet of old letters and a folded paper containing some dried and crumpled flowers. Aunt laid the box aside and unpacked the chest in silence. First came a ball dress of pale-yellow satin brocade, made with the trained skirt, "baby" waist and full puffed sleeves of a former generation. Beneath it was a case containing a necklace of small but perfect pearls and a pair of tiny satin slippers. The rest of the compartment was filled with household linen, fine and costly but yellowed with age – damask table linen and webs of the uncut fabric.

In the second compartment lay a dress. Aunt Winnifred lifted it out reverently. It was a gown of rich silk that had once been white, but now, like the linen, it was yellow with age. It was simply made and trimmed with cobwebby old lace. Wrapped around it was a long white bridal veil, redolent with some strange, old-time perfume that had kept its sweetness all through the years.

"Well, Amy, this is all," said Aunt Winnifred with a quiver in her voice. "And now for the story. Where shall I begin?"

"At the very beginning, Aunty. You see I know nothing at all except her name. Tell me who she was and why she put her wedding dress away here."

"Poor Eliza!" said Aunt dreamily. "It is a sorrowful story, Amy, and it seems so long ago now. I must be an old woman. Forty years ago – and I was only twenty then. Eliza Laurance was my cousin, the only daughter of Uncle Henry Laurance. My father – your grandfather, Amy, you don't remember him – had two brothers, each of whom had an only daughter. Both these girls were called Eliza after your great-grandmother. I never saw Uncle George's Eliza but once. He was a rich man and his daughter was much sought after, but she was no beauty, I promise you that, and proud and vain to the last degree. Her home was in a distant city and she never came to Wyther Grange.

"The other Eliza Laurance was a poor man's daughter. She and I were of the same age and did not look unlike each other, although I was not so pretty by half. You can see by the portrait how beautiful she was, and it does her scant justice, for half her charm lay in her arch expression and her vivacious ways. She had her little faults, of course, and was rather over much given to romance and sentiment. This did not seem much of a defect to me then, Amy, for I was young and romantic too. Mother never cared much for Eliza, I think, but everyone else liked her. One winter Eliza came to Wyther Grange for a long visit. The Grange was a very lively place then, Amy. Eliza kept the old house ringing with merriment. We went out a great deal and she was always the belle of any festivity we attended. Yet she wore her honours easily; all the flattery and homage she received did not turn her head.

"That winter we first met Willis Starr. He was a newcomer, and nobody knew much about him, but one or two of the best families took him up, and his own fascinations did the rest. He became what you would call the rage. He was considered very handsome, his manners were polished and easy, and people said he was rich.

"I don't think, Amy, that I ever trusted Willis Starr. But like all the rest, I was blinded by his charm. Mother was almost the only one who did not worship at his shrine, and very often she dropped hints about penniless adventurers that made Eliza very indignant.

"From the first he had paid Eliza marked attention and seemed utterly bewitched by her. Well, his was an easy winning. Eliza loved him with her whole impulsive, girlish heart and made no attempt to hide it.

"I shall never forget the night they were first engaged. It was Eliza's birthday, and we were invited to a ball that evening. This yellow gown is the very one she wore. I suppose that is why she put it away here – the gown she wore on the happiest night of her life. I had never seen her look more beautiful – her neck and arms were bare, and she wore this string of pearls and carried a bouquet of her favourite white roses.

"When we reached home after the dance, Eliza had her happy secret to tell us. She was engaged to Willis Starr, and they were to be married in early spring.

"Willis Starr certainly seemed to be an ideal lover, and Eliza was so perfectly happy that she seemed to grow more beautiful and radiant every day.

"Well, Amy, the wedding day was set. Eliza was to be married from the Grange, as her own mother was dead, and I was to be bridesmaid. We made her wedding dress together, she and I. Girls were not above making their own gowns then, and not a stitch was set in Eliza's save those put there by loving fingers and blessed by loving wishes. It was I who draped the veil over her sunny curls – see how yellow and creased it is now, but it was as white as snow that day.

"A week before the wedding, Willis Starr was spending the evening at the Grange. We were all chattering gaily about the coming event, and in speaking of the invited guests Eliza said something about the other Eliza Laurance, the great heiress, looking archly at Willis over her shoulder as she spoke. It was some merry badinage about the cousin whose namesake she was but whom she so little resembled.

"We all laughed, but I shall never forget the look that came over Willis Starr's face. It passed quickly, but the chill fear that it gave me remained. A few minutes later I left the room on some trifling errand, and as I returned through the dim hall I was met by Willis Starr. He laid his hand on my arm and bent his evil face – for it *was* evil then, Amy – close to mine.

" 'Tell me,' he said in a low but rude tone, 'is there another Eliza Laurance who is an heiress?'

" 'Certainly there is,' I said sharply. 'She is our cousin and the daughter of our Uncle George. Our Eliza is not an heiress. You surely did not suppose she was!'

"Willis stepped aside with a mocking smile.

" 'I did – what wonder? I had heard much about the great heiress, Eliza Laurance, and the great beauty, Eliza Laurance. I supposed they were one and the same. You have all been careful not to undeceive me.'

" 'You forget yourself, Mr. Starr, when you speak so to me,' I retorted coldly. 'You have deceived yourself. We have never dreamed of allowing anyone to think that Eliza was an heiress. She is sweet and lovely enough to be loved for her own sake.'

"I went back to the parlour full of dismay. Willis Starr remained gloomy and taciturn all the rest of the evening, but nobody seemed to notice it but myself.

"The next day we were all so busy that I almost forgot the incident of the previous evening. We girls were up in the sewing room putting the last touches to the wedding gown. Eliza tried it and her veil on and was standing so, in all her silken splendour, when a letter was brought in. I guessed by her blush who was the writer. I laughed and ran downstairs, leaving her to read it.

"When I returned she was still standing just where I had left her in the middle of the room, holding the letter in her hand. Her face was as white as her veil, and her wide-open eyes had a dazed, agonized look as of someone who had been stricken a mortal blow. All the soft happiness and sweetness had gone out of them. They were the eyes of an old woman, Amy.

" 'Eliza, what is the matter?' I said. 'Has anything happened to Willis?'

"She made no answer, but walked to the fireplace, dropped the letter in a bed of writhing blue flame and watched it burn to white ashes. Then she turned to me.

" 'Help me take off this gown, Winnie,' she said dully. 'I shall never wear it again. There will be no wedding. Willis is gone.'

" 'Gone!' I echoed stupidly.

" 'Yes. I am not the heiress, Winnie. It was the fortune, not the girl, he loved. He says he is too poor for us to dream of marrying when I have nothing. Oh, such a cruel, heartless letter! Why did he not kill me? It would have been so much more merciful! I loved him so – I trusted him so! Oh, Winnie, Winnie, what am I to do!'

"There was something terrible in the contrast between her passionate words and her calm face and lifeless voice. I wanted to call Mother, but she would not let me. She went away to her own room, trailing along the dark hall in her dress and veil, and locked herself in.

"Well, I told it all to the others in some fashion. You can imagine their anger and dismay. Your father, Amy – he was a hot-blooded, impetuous young fellow then – went at once to seek Willis Starr. But he was gone, no one knew where, and the whole country rang with the gossip and scandal of the affair. Eliza knew nothing of this, for she was ill and unconscious for many a day. In a novel or story she would have died, I suppose, and that would have been the end of it. But this was in real life, and Eliza did not die, although many times we thought she would.

"When she did recover, how frightfully changed she was! It almost broke my heart to see her. Her very nature seemed to have changed too – all her joyousness and light-heartedness were dead. From that time she was a faded, dispirited creature, no more like the Eliza we had known than the merest stranger. And then after a while came other news – Willis Starr was married to the other Eliza Laurance, the true heiress. He had made no second mistake. We tried to keep it from Eliza but she found it out at last. That was the day she came up here alone and packed this old chest. Nobody ever knew just what she put into it. But you and I see now, Amy – her ball dress, her wedding gown, her love letters and, more than all else, her youth and happiness – this old chest was the tomb of it all. Eliza Laurance was really buried here.

"She went home soon after. Before she went she exacted a promise from Mother that the old chest should be left at the Grange unopened until she came for it herself. But she never came back, and I do not think she ever intended to, and I never saw her again.

"That is the story of the old chest. It was all over so long ago – the heartbreak and the misery – but it all seems to come back to me now. Poor Eliza!"

My own eyes were full of tears as Aunt Winnifred went down the stairs, leaving me sitting dreamily there in the sunset light, with the old yellowed bridal veil across my lap and the portrait of Eliza Laurance in my hand. Around me were the relics of her pitiful story – the old, oft-repeated story of a faithless love and a woman's broken heart – the gown she had worn, the slippers in which she had danced light-heartedly at her betrothal ball, her fan, her pearls, her gloves – and it somehow seemed to me as if I were living in those old years myself, as if the love and happiness, the betrayal and pain were part of my own life. Presently Aunt Winnifred came back through the twilight shadows.

"Let us put all these things back in their grave, Amy," she said. "They are of no use to anyone now. The linen might be bleached and used, I dare say – but it would seem like a sacrilege. It was Mother's wedding present to Eliza. And the pearls – would you care to have them, Amy?"

"Oh, no, no," I said with a little shiver. "I would never wear them, Aunt Winnifred. I should feel like a ghost if I did. Put everything back just as we found it – only her portrait. I would like to keep that."

Reverently we put gowns and letters and trinkets back into the old blue chest. Aunt Winnifred closed the lid and turned the key softly. She bowed her head over it for a minute and then we went together in silence down the shadowy garret stairs of Wyther Grange.

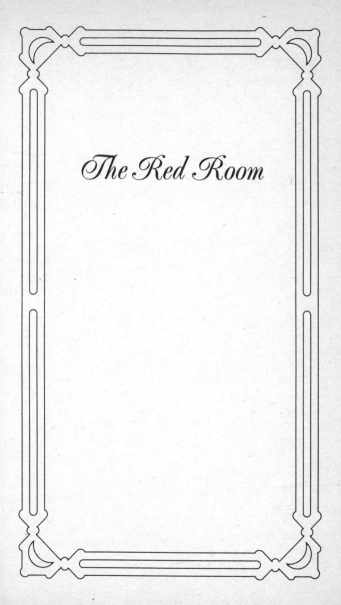

The Red Room

OU WOULD HAVE me tell you the story, Grand-child? 'Tis a sad one and best forgotten – few remember it now. There are always sad and dark stories in old families such as ours.

Yet I have promised and must keep my word. So sit down here at my feet and rest your bright head on my lap, that I may not see in your young eyes the shadows my story will bring across their bonny blue.

I was a mere child when it all happened, yet I remember it but too well, and I can recall how pleased I was when my father's stepmother, Mrs. Montressor – she not liking to be called grandmother, seeing she was but turned of fifty and a handsome woman still – wrote to my mother that she must send little Beatrice up to Montressor Place for the Christmas holidays. So I went joyfully, though my mother grieved to part with me; she had little to love save me, my father, Conrad Montressor, having been lost at sea when but three months wed.

My aunts were wont to tell me how much I resembled him, being, so they said, a Montressor to the backbone; and this I took to mean commendation, for the Montressors were a well-descended and well-thought-of family, and the women were noted for their beauty. This I could well believe, since of all my aunts there was not one but was counted a pretty woman. Therefore I took heart of grace when I thought of my dark face and spindling shape, hoping that when I should be grown up I might be counted not unworthy of my race.

The Place was an old-fashioned, mysterious house, such as I delighted in, and Mrs. Montressor was ever kind to me, albeit a little stern, for she was a proud woman and cared but little for children, having none of her own.

But there were books there to pore over without let or

hindrance – for nobody questioned of my whereabouts if I but kept out of the way – and strange, dim family portraits on the walls to gaze upon, until I knew each proud old face well, and had visioned a history for it in my own mind – for I was given to dreaming and was older and wiser than my years, having no childish companions to keep me still a child.

There were always some of my aunts at the Place to kiss and make much of me for my father's sake – for he had been their favourite brother. My aunts – there were eight of them – had all married well, so said people who knew, and lived not far away, coming home often to take tea with Mrs. Montressor, who had always gotten on well with her stepdaughters, or to help prepare for some festivity or other – for they were notable housekeepers, every one.

They were all at Montressor Place for Christmas, and I got more petting than I deserved, albeit they looked after me somewhat more strictly than did Mrs. Montressor, and saw to it that I did not read too many fairy tales or sit up later at nights than became my years.

But it was not for fairy tales and sugarplums nor yet for petting that I rejoiced to be at the Place at that time. Though I spoke not of it to anyone, I had a great longing to see my Uncle Hugh's wife, concerning whom I had heard much, both good and bad.

My Uncle Hugh, albeit the oldest of the family, had never married until now, and all the countryside rang with talk of his young wife. I did not hear as much as I wished, for the gossips took heed to my presence when I drew anear and turned to other matters. Yet, being some-what keener of comprehension than they knew, I heard and understood not a little of their talk.

And so I came to know that neither proud Mrs. Montressor nor my good aunts, nor even my gentle mother, looked with overmuch favour on what my Uncle Hugh had done.

And I did hear that Mrs. Montressor had chosen a wife for her stepson, of good family and some beauty, but that my Uncle Hugh would none of her – a thing Mrs. Montressor found hard to pardon, yet might so have done had not my uncle, on his last voyage to the Indies – for he went often in his own vessels – married and brought home a foreign bride, of whom no one knew aught save that her beauty was a thing to dazzle the day and that she was of some strange alien blood such as ran not in the blue veins of the Montressors.

Some had much to say of her pride and insolence, and wondered if Mrs. Montressor would tamely yield her mistress-ship to the stranger. But others, who were taken with her loveliness and grace, said that the tales told were born of envy and malice, and that Alicia Montressor was well worthy of her name and station.

So I halted between two opinions and thought to judge for myself, but when I went to the Place my Uncle Hugh and his bride were gone for a time, and I had even to swallow my disappointment and bide their return with all my small patience.

But my aunts and their stepmother talked much of Alicia, and they spoke slightingly of her, saying that she was but a light woman and that no good would come of my Uncle Hugh's having wed her, with other things of a like nature. Also they spoke of the company she gathered around her, thinking her to have strange and unbecoming companions for a Montressor. All this I heard and pondered much over, although my good aunts supposed that such a chit as I would take no heed to their whisperings.

When I was not with them, helping to whip eggs and stone raisins, and being watched to see that I ate not more than one out of five, I was surely to be found in the wing hall, poring over my book and grieving that I was no more allowed to go into the Red Room.

The wing hall was a narrow one and dim, connecting the main rooms of the Place with an older wing, built in a curious way. The hall was lighted by small, square-paned windows, and at its end a little flight of steps led up to the Red Room.

Whenever I had been at the Place before – and this was often – I had passed much of my time in this same Red Room. It was Mrs. Montressor's sitting-room then, where she wrote her letters and examined household accounts, and sometimes had an old gossip in to tea. The room was low-ceilinged and dim, hung with red damask, and with odd, square windows high up under the eaves and a dark wainscoting all around it. And there I loved to sit quietly on the red sofa and read my fairy tales, or talk dreamily to the swallows fluttering crazily against the tiny panes.

When I had gone this Christmas to the Place I soon bethought myself of the Red Room – for I had a great love for it. But I had got no further than the steps when Mrs. Montressor came sweeping down the hall in haste and, catching me by the arm, pulled me back as roughly as if it had been Bluebeard's chamber itself into which I was venturing.

Then, seeing my face, which I doubt not was startled enough, she seemed to repent of her haste and patted me gently on the head.

"There, there, little Beatrice! Did I frighten you, child? Forgive an old woman's thoughtlessness. But be not too ready to go where you are not bidden, and never venture foot in the Red Room now, for it belongs to your Uncle Hugh's wife, and let me tell you she is not over fond of intruders."

I felt sorry overmuch to hear this, nor could I see why my new aunt should care if I went in once in a while, as had been my habit, to talk to the swallows and misplace nothing. But Mrs. Montressor saw to it that I obeyed her, and I went no more to the Red Room, but busied myself with other matters.

For there were great doings at the Place and much coming and going. My aunts were never idle; there was to be much festivity Christmas week and a ball on Christmas Eve. And my aunts had promised me – though not till I had wearied them of my coaxing – that I should stay up that night and see as much of the gaiety as was good for me. So I did their errands and went early to bed every night without complaint – though I did this the more readily for that, when they thought me safely asleep, they would come in and talk around my bedroom fire, saying that of Alicia which I should not have heard.

At last came the day when my Uncle Hugh and his wife were expected home – though not until my scanty patience was well nigh wearied out – and we were all assembled to meet them in the great hall, where a ruddy firelight was gleaming.

My Aunt Frances had dressed me in my best white frock and my crimson sash, with much lamenting over my skinny neck and arms, and bade me behave prettily, as became my bringing up. So I slipped in a corner, my hands and feet cold with excitement, for I think every drop of blood in my body had gone to my head, and my heart beat so hardly that it even pained me.

Then the door opened and Alicia – for so I was used to hearing her called, nor did I ever think of her as my aunt in my own mind – came in, and a little in the rear my tall, dark uncle.

She came proudly forward to the fire and stood there superbly while she loosened her cloak, nor did she see me at all at first, but nodded, a little disdainfully, it seemed, to Mrs. Montressor and my aunts, who were grouped about the drawing-room door, very ladylike and quiet.

But I neither saw nor heard aught at the time save her

only, for her beauty, when she came forth from her crimson cloak and hood, was something so wonderful that I forgot my manners and stared at her as one fascinated – as indeed I was, for never had I seen such loveliness and hardly dreamed it.

Pretty women I had seen in plenty, for my aunts and my mother were counted fair, but my uncle's wife was as little like to them as a sunset glow to pale moonshine or a crimson rose to white day-lilies.

Nor can I paint her to you in words as I saw her then, with the long tongues of firelight licking her white neck and wavering over the rich masses of her red-gold hair.

She was tall – so tall that my aunts looked but insignificant beside her, and they were of no mean height, as became their race; yet no queen could have carried herself more royally, and all the passion and fire of her foreign nature burned in her splendid eyes, that might have been dark or light for aught that I could ever tell, but which seemed always like pools of warm flame, now tender, now fierce.

Her skin was like a delicate white rose leaf, and when she spoke I told my foolish self that never had I heard music before; nor do I ever again think to hear a voice so sweet, so liquid, as that which rippled over her ripe lips.

I had often in my own mind pictured this, my first meeting with Alicia, now in one way, now in another, but never had I dreamed of her speaking to me at all, so that it came to me as a great surprise when she turned and, holding out her lovely hands, said very graciously:

"And is this the little Beatrice? I have heard much of you – come, kiss me, child."

And I went, despite my Aunt Elizabeth's black frown, for the glamour of her loveliness was upon me, and I no longer wondered that my Uncle Hugh should have loved her.

Very proud of her was he too; yet I felt, rather than saw –

for I was sensitive and quick of perception, as old-young children ever are – that there was something other than pride and love in his face when he looked on her, and more in his manner than the fond lover – as it were, a sort of lurking mistrust.

Nor could I think, though to me the thought seemed as treason, that she loved her husband overmuch, for she seemed half condescending and half disdainful to him; yet one thought not of this in her presence, but only remembered it when she had gone.

When she went out it seemed to me that nothing was left, so I crept lonesomely away to the wing hall and sat down by a window to dream of her; and she filled my thoughts so fully that it was no surprise when I raised my eyes and saw her coming down the hall alone, her bright head shining against the dark old walls.

When she paused by me and asked me lightly of what I was dreaming, since I had such a sober face, I answered her truly that it was of her – whereat she laughed, as one not ill pleased, and said half mockingly:

"Waste not your thoughts so, little Beatrice. But come with me, child, if you will, for I have taken a strange fancy to your solemn eyes. Perchance the warmth of your young life may thaw out the ice that has frozen around my heart ever since I came among these cold Montressors."

And, though I understood not her meaning, I went, glad to see the Red Room once more. So she made me sit down and talk to her, which I did, for shyness was no failing of mine; and she asked me many questions, and some that I thought she should not have asked, but I could not answer them, so 'twere little harm.

After that I spent a part of every day with her in the Red Room. And my Uncle Hugh was there often, and he would kiss her and praise her loveliness, not heeding my presence – for I was but a child.

Yet it ever seemed to me that she endured rather than welcomed his caresses, and at times the ever-burning flame in her eyes glowed so luridly that a chill dread would creep over me, and I would remember what my Aunt Elizabeth had said, she being a bitter-tongued woman, though kind at heart – that this strange creature would bring on us all some evil fortune yet.

Then would I strive to banish such thoughts and chide myself for doubting one so kind to me.

When Christmas Eve drew nigh my silly head was full of the ball day and night. But a grievous disappointment befell me, for I awakened that day very ill with a most severe cold; and though I bore me bravely, my aunts discovered it soon, when, despite my piteous pleadings, I was put to bed, where I cried bitterly and would not be comforted. For I thought I should not see the fine folk and, more than all, Alicia.

But that disappointment, at least, was spared me, for at night she came into my room, knowing of my longing – she was ever indulgent to my little wishes. And when I saw her I forgot my aching limbs and burning brow, and even the ball I was not to see, for never was mortal creature so lovely as she, standing there by my bed.

Her gown was of white, and there was nothing I could liken the stuff to save moonshine falling athwart a frosted pane, and out from it swelled her gleaming breast and arms, so bare that it seemed to me a shame to look upon them. Yet it could not be denied they were of wondrous beauty, white as polished marble.

And all about her snowy throat and rounded arms, and in the masses of her splendid hair, were sparkling, gleaming stones, with hearts of pure light, which I know now to have been diamonds, but knew not then, for never had I seen aught of their like.

And I gazed at her, drinking in her beauty until my soul

was filled, as she stood like some goddess before her worshipper. I think she read my thought in my face and liked it – for she was a vain woman, and to such even the admiration of a child is sweet.

Then she leaned down to me until her splendid eyes looked straight into my dazzled ones.

"Tell me, little Beatrice – for they say the word of a child is to be believed – tell me, do you think me beautiful?"

I found my voice and told her truly that I thought her beautiful beyond my dreams of angels – as indeed she was. Whereat she smiled as one well pleased.

Then my Uncle Hugh came in, and though I thought that his face darkened as he looked on the naked splendour of her breast and arms, as if he liked not that the eyes of other men should gloat on it, yet he kissed her with all a lover's fond pride, while she looked at him half mockingly.

Then said he, "Sweet, will you grant me a favour?"

And she answered, "It may be that I will."

And he said, "Do not dance with that man tonight, Alicia. I mistrust him much."

His voice had more of a husband's command than a lover's entreaty. She looked at him with some scorn, but when she saw his face grow black – for the Montressors brooked scant disregard of their authority, as I had good reason to know – she seemed to change, and a smile came to her lips, though her eyes glowed balefully.

Then she laid her arms about his neck and – though it seemed to me that she had as soon strangled as embraced him – her voice was wondrous sweet and caressing as she murmured in his ear.

He laughed and his brow cleared, though he said still sternly, "Do not try me too far, Alicia."

Then they went out, she a little in advance and very stately.

After that my aunts also came in, very beautifully and

modestly dressed, but they seemed to me as nothing after Alicia. For I was caught in the snare of her beauty, and the longing to see her again so grew upon me that after a time I did an undutiful and disobedient thing.

I had been straitly charged to stay in bed, which I did not, but got up and put on a gown. For it was in my mind to go quietly down, if by chance I might again see Alicia, myself unseen.

But when I reached the great hall I heard steps approaching and, having a guilty conscience, I slipped aside into the blue parlour and hid me behind the curtains lest my aunts should see me.

Then Alicia came in, and with her a man whom I had never before seen. Yet I instantly bethought myself of a lean black snake, with a glittering and evil eye, which I had seen in Mrs. Montressor's garden two summers agone, and which was like to have bitten me. John, the gardener, had killed it, and I verily thought that if it had a soul, it must have gotten into this man.

Alicia sat down and he beside her, and when he had put his arms about her, he kissed her face and lips. Nor did she shrink from his embrace, but even smiled and leaned nearer to him with a little smooth motion, as they talked to each other in some strange, foreign tongue.

I was but a child and innocent, nor knew I aught of honour and dishonour. Yet it seemed to me that no man should kiss her save only my Uncle Hugh, and from that hour I mistrusted Alicia, though I understood not then what I afterwards did.

And as I watched them – not thinking of playing the spy – I saw her face grow suddenly cold, and she straightened herself up and pushed away her lover's arms.

Then I followed her guilty eyes to the door, where stood my Uncle Hugh, and all the pride and passion of the Montressors sat on his lowering brow. Yet he came forward quietly as Alicia and the snake drew apart and stood up.

At first he looked not at his guilty wife but at her lover, and smote him heavily in the face. Whereat he, being a coward at heart, as are all villains, turned white and slunk from the room with a muttered oath, nor was he stayed.

My uncle turned to Alicia, and very calmly and terribly he said, "From this hour you are no longer wife of mine!"

And there was that in his tone which told that his forgiveness and love should be hers nevermore.

Then he motioned her out and she went, like a proud queen, with her glorious head erect and no shame on her brow.

As for me, when they were gone I crept away, dazed and bewildered enough, and went back to my bed, having seen and heard more than I had a mind for, as disobedient people and eavesdroppers ever do.

But my Uncle Hugh kept his word, and Alicia was no more wife to him, save only in name. Yet of gossip or scandal there was none, for the pride of his race kept secret his dishonour, nor did he ever seem other than a courteous and respectful husband.

Nor did Mrs. Montressor and my aunts, though they wondered much among themselves, learn aught, for they dared question neither their brother nor Alicia, who carried herself as loftily as ever, and seemed to pine for neither lover nor husband. As for me, no one dreamed I knew aught of it, and I kept my own counsel as to what I had seen in the blue parlour on the night of the Christmas ball.

After the New Year I went home, but ere long Mrs. Montressor sent for me again, saying that the house was lonely without little Beatrice. So I went again and found all unchanged, though the Place was very quiet, and Alicia went out but little from the Red Room.

Of my Uncle Hugh I saw little, save when he went and came on the business of his estate, somewhat more gravely and silently than of yore, or brought to me books and sweetmeats from town.

But every day I was with Alicia in the Red Room, where she would talk to me, oftentimes wildly and strangely, but always kindly. And though I think Mrs. Montressor liked our intimacy none too well, she said no word, and I came and went as I listed with Alicia, though never quite liking her strange ways and the restless fire in her eyes.

Nor would I ever kiss her, after I had seen her lips pressed by the snake's, though she sometimes coaxed me, and grew pettish and vexed when I would not; but she guessed not my reason.

March came in that year like a lion, exceedingly hungry and fierce, and my Uncle Hugh had ridden away through the storm nor thought to be back for some days.

In the afternoon I was sitting in the wing hall, dreaming wondrous day-dreams, when Alicia called me to the Red Room. And as I went, I marvelled anew at her loveliness, for the blood was leaping in her face and her jewels were dim before the lustre of her eyes. Her hand, when she took mine, was burning hot, and her voice had a strange ring.

"Come, little Beatrice," she said, "come talk to me, for I know not what to do with my lone self today. Time hangs heavily in this gloomy house. I do verily think this Red Room has an evil influence over me. See if your childish prattle can drive away the ghosts that riot in these dark old corners – ghosts of a ruined and shamed life! Nay, shrink not – do I talk wildly? I mean not all I say – my brain seems on fire, little Beatrice. Come; it may be you know some grim old legend of this room – it must surely have one. Never was place fitter for a dark deed! Tush! never be so frightened, child – forget my vagaries. Tell me now and I will listen."

Whereat she cast herself lithely on the satin couch and turned her lovely face on me. So I gathered up my small wits and told her what I was not supposed to know – how that, generations agone, a Montressor had disgraced himself and his name, and that, when he came home to his mother, she had met him in that same Red Room and flung at him taunts and reproaches, forgetting whose breast had nourished him; and that he, frantic with shame and despair, turned his sword against his own heart and so died. But his mother went mad with her remorse, and was kept a prisoner in the Red Room until her death.

So lamely told I the tale, as I had heard my Aunt Elizabeth tell it, when she knew not I listened or understood. Alicia heard me through and said nothing, save that it was a tale worthy of the Montressors. Whereat I bridled, for I too was a Montressor, and proud of it.

But she took my hand soothingly in hers and said, "Little Beatrice, if tomorrow or the next day they should tell you, those cold, proud women, that Alicia was unworthy of your love, tell me, would you believe them?"

And I, remembering what I had seen in the blue parlour, was silent – for I could not lie. So she flung my hand away with a bitter laugh, and picked lightly from the table anear a small dagger with a jewelled handle.

It seemed to me a cruel-looking toy and I said so – whereat she smiled and drew her white fingers down the thin, shining blade in a fashion that made me cold.

"Such a little blow with this," she said, "such a little blow – and the heart beats no longer, the weary brain rests, the lips and eyes smile never again! 'Twere a short path out of all difficulties, my Beatrice."

And I, understanding her not, yet shivering, begged her to cast it aside, which she did carelessly and, putting a hand under my chin, she turned up my face to hers.

"Little, grave-eyed Beatrice, tell me truly, would it grieve you much if you were never again to sit here with Alicia in this same Red Room?"

And I made answer earnestly that it would, glad that I could say so much truly. Then her face grew tender and she sighed deeply.

Presently she opened a quaint, inlaid box and took from it a shining gold chain of rare workmanship and exquisite design, and this she hung around my neck, nor would suffer me to thank her but laid her hand gently on my lips.

"Now go," she said. "But ere you leave me, little Beatrice, grant me but the one favour – it may be that I shall never ask another of you. Your people, I know – those cold Montressors – care little for me, but with all my faults, I have ever been kind to you. So, when the morrow's come, and they tell you that Alicia is as one worse than dead, think not of me with scorn only but grant me a little pity – for I was not always what I am now, and might never have become so had a little child like you been always anear me, to keep me pure and innocent. And I would have you but the once lay your arms about my neck and kiss me."

And i did so, wondering much at her manner – for it had in it a strange tenderness and some sort of hopeless longing. Then she gently put me from the room, and I sat musing by the hall window until night fell darkly – and a fearsome night it was, of storm and blackness. And I thought how well it was that my Uncle Hugh had not to return in such a tempest. Yet, ere the thought had grown cold, the door opened and he strode down the hall, his cloak drenched and wind-twisted, in one hand a whip, as though he had but then sprung from his horse, in the other what seemed like a crumpled letter.

Nor was the night blacker than his face, and he took no heed of me as I ran after him, thinking selfishly of the sweetmeats he had promised to bring me – but I thought no more of them when I got to the door of the Red Room.

Alicia stood by the table, hooded and cloaked as for a journey, but her hood had slipped back, and her face rose from it marble-white, save where her wrathful eyes burned out, with dread and guilt and hatred in their depths, while she had one arm raised as if to thrust him back.

As for my uncle, he stood before her and I saw not his face, but his voice was low and terrible, speaking words I understood not then, though long afterwards I came to know their meaning.

And he cast foul scorn at her that she should have thought to fly with her lover, and swore that naught should again thwart his vengeance, with other threats, wild and dreadful enough.

Yet she said no word until he had done, and then she spoke, but what she said I know not, save that it was full of hatred and defiance and wild accusation, such as a mad woman might have uttered.

And she defied him even then to stop her flight, though he told her to cross that threshold would mean her death; for he was a wronged and desperate man and thought of nothing save his own dishonour.

Then she made as if to pass him, but he caught her by her white wrist; she turned on him with fury, and I saw her right hand reach stealthily out over the table behind her, where lay the dagger.

"Let me go!" she hissed.

And he said, "I will not."

Then she turned herself about and struck at him with the dagger – and never saw I such a face as was hers at the moment.

He fell heavily, yet held her even in death, so that she

had to wrench herself free, with a shriek that rings yet in my ears on a night when the wind wails over the rainy moors. She rushed past me unheeding, and fled down the hall like a hunted creature, and I heard the heavy door clang hollowly behind her.

As for me, I stood there looking at the dead man, for I could neither move nor speak and was like to have died of horror. And presently I knew nothing, nor did I come to my recollection for many a day, when I lay abed, sick of a fever and more like to die than live.

So that when at last I came out from the shadow of death, my Uncle Hugh had been long cold in his grave, and the hue and cry for his guilty wife was well nigh over, since naught had been seen or heard of her since she fled the country with her foreign lover.

When I came rightly to my remembrance, they questioned me as to what I had seen and heard in the Red Room. And I told them as best I could, though much aggrieved that to my questions they would answer nothing save to bid me to stay still and think not of the matter.

Then my mother, sorely vexed over my adventures – which in truth were but sorry ones for a child – took me home. Nor would she let me keep Alicia's chain, but made away with it, how I knew not and little cared, for the sight of it was loathsome to me.

It was many years ere I went again to Montressor Place, and I never saw the Red Room more, for Mrs. Montressor had the old wing torn down, deeming its sorrowful memories dark heritage enough for the next Montressor.

So, Grandchild, the sad tale is ended, and you will not see the Red Room when you go next month to Montressor Place. The swallows still build under the eaves, though – I know not if you will understand their speech as I did.

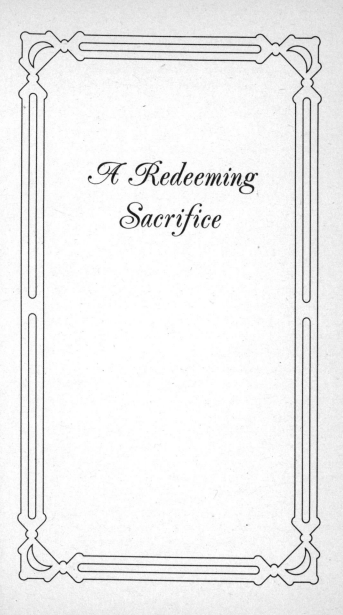

A Redeeming
Sacrifice

HE DANCE AT BYRON LYALL'S was in full swing. Toff Leclerc, the best fiddler in three counties, was enthroned on the kitchen table and from the glossy brown violin, which his grandfather brought from Grand Pré, was conjuring music which made even stiff old Aunt Phemy want to show her steps. Around the kitchen sat a row of young men and women, and the open sitting-room doorway was crowded with the faces of non-dancing guests who wanted to watch the sets.

An eight-hand reel had just been danced and the girls, giddy from the much swinging of the final figure, had been led back to their seats. Mattie Lyall came out with a dipper of water and sprinkled the floor, from which a fine dust was rising. Toff's violin purred under his hands as he waited for the next set to form. The dancers were slow about it. There was not the rush for the floor that there had been earlier in the evening, for the supper table was now spread in the dining-room and most of the guests were hungry.

"Fill up dere, boys," shouted the fiddler impatiently. "Bring out your gals for de nex' set."

After a moment Paul King led out Joan Shelley from the shadowy corner where they had been sitting. They had already danced several sets together; Joan had not danced with anybody else that evening. As they stood together under the light from the lamp on the shelf above them, many curious and disapproving eyes watched them. Connor Mitchell, who had been standing in the open outer doorway with the moonlight behind him, turned abruptly on his heel and went out.

Paul King leaned his head against the wall and watched the watchers with a smiling, defiant face as they waited for the set to form. He was a handsome fellow, with the easy, winning ways that women love. His hair curled in bronze masses about his head; his dark eyes were long and drowsy and laughing; there was a swarthy bloom on his round cheeks; and his lips were as red and beguiling as a girl's. A bad egg was Paul King, with a bad past and a bad future. He was shiftless and drunken; ugly tales were told of him. Not a man in Lyall's house that night but grudged him the privilege of standing up with Joan Shelley.

Joan was a slight, blossom-like girl in white, looking much like the pale, sweet-scented house rose she wore in her dark hair. Her face was colourless and young, very pure and softly curved. She had wonderfully sweet, dark blue eyes, generally dropped down, with notably long black lashes. There were many showier girls in the groups around her, but none half so lovely. She made all the rosy-cheeked beauties seem coarse and overblown.

She left in Paul's clasp the hand by which he had led her out on the floor. Now and then he shifted his gaze from the faces before him to hers. When he did, she always looked up and they exchanged glances as if they had been utterly alone. Three other couples gradually took the floor and the reel began. Joan drifted through the figures with the grace of a wind-blown leaf. Paul danced with rollicking abandon, seldom taking his eyes from Joan's face. When the last mad whirl was over, Joan's brother came up and told her in an angry tone to go into the next room and dance no more, since she would dance with only one man. Joan looked at Paul. That look meant that she would do as he, and none other, told her. Paul nodded easily – he did not want any fuss just then – and the girl went obediently into the room. As she turned from him, Paul coolly reached out his hand and took the rose from her hair; then, with a triumphant glance around the room, he went out.

The autumn night was very clear and chill, with a faint,

moaning wind blowing up from the northwest over the sea that lay shimmering before the door. Out beyond the cove the boats were nodding and curtsying on the swell, and over the shore fields the great red star of the lighthouse flared out against the silvery sky. Paul, with a whistle, sauntered down the sandy lane, thinking of Joan. How mightily he loved her – he, Paul King, who had made a mock of so many women and had never loved before! Ah, and she loved him. She had never said so in words, but eyes and tones had said it – she, Joan Shelley, the pick and pride of the Harbour girls, whom so many men had wooed, winning their trouble for their pains. He had won her; she was his and his only, for the asking. His heart was seething with pride and triumph and passion as he strode down to the shore and flung himself on the cold sand in the black shadow of Michael Brown's beached boat.

Byron Lyall, a grizzled, elderly man, half farmer, half fisherman, and Maxwell Holmes, the Prospect schoolteacher, came up to the boat presently. Paul lay softly and listened to what they were saying. He was not troubled by any sense of dishonour. Honour was something Paul King could not lose since it was something he had never possessed. They were talking of him and Joan.

"What a shame that a girl like Joan Shelley should throw herself away on a man like that," Holmes said.

Byron Lyall removed the pipe he was smoking and spat reflectively at his shadow.

"Darned shame," he agreed. "That girl's life will be ruined if she marries him, plum' ruined, and marry him she will. He's bewitched her – darned if I can understand it. A dozen better men have wanted her – Connor Mitchell for one. And he's a honest, steady fellow with a good home to offer her. If King had left her alone, she'd have taken Connor. She used to like him well enough. But that's all over. She's infatuated with King, the worthless scamp. She'll marry him and be sorry for it to her last day. He's bad clear through and always will be. Why, look you, Teacher, most men pull up a bit when they're courting a girl, no matter how wild they've been and will be again. Paul hasn't. It hasn't made any difference. He was dead drunk night afore last at the Harbour head, and he hasn't done a stroke of work for a month. And yet Joan Shelley'll take him."

"What are her people thinking of to let her go with him?" asked Holmes.

"She hasn't any but her brother. He's against Paul, of course, but it won't matter. The girl's fancy's caught and she'll go her own gait to ruin. Ruin, I tell ye. If she marries that handsome ne'er-do-well, she'll be a wretched woman all her days and none to pity her."

The two moved away then, and Paul lay motionless, face downward on the sand, his lips pressed against Joan's sweet, crushed rose. He felt no anger over Byron Lyall's unsparing condemnation. He knew it was true, every word of it. He *was* a worthless scamp and always would be. He knew that perfectly well. It was in his blood. None of his race had ever been respectable and he was worse than them all. He had no intention of trying to reform because he could not and because he did not even want to. He was not fit to touch Joan's hand. Yet he had meant to marry her!

But to spoil her life! Would it do that? Yes, it surely would. And if he were out of the way, taking his baleful charm out of her life, Connor Mitchell might and doubtless would win her yet and give her all he could not.

The man suddenly felt his eyes wet with tears. He had never shed a tear in his daredevil life before, but they came hot and stinging now. Something he had never known or thought of before entered into his passion and purified it. He loved Joan. Did he love her well enough to stand aside and let another take the sweetness and grace that was now his own? Did he love her well enough to save her from the poverty-stricken, shamed life she must lead with him? Did he love her better than himself?

"I ain't fit to think of her," he groaned. "I never did a decent thing in my life, as they say. But how can I give her up – God, how can I?"

He lay still a long time after that, until the moonlight crept around the boat and drove away the shadow. Then he got up and went slowly down to the water's edge with Joan's rose, all wet with his unaccustomed tears, in his hands. Slowly and reverently he plucked off the petals and scattered them on the ripples, where they drifted lightly off like fairy shallops on moonshine. When the last one had fluttered from his fingers, he went back to the house and hunted up Captain Alec Matheson, who was smoking his pipe in a corner of the verandah and watching the young folks dancing through the open door. The two men talked together for some time.

When the dance broke up and the guests straggled homeward, Paul sought Joan. Rob Shelley had his own girl to see home and relinquished the guardianship of his sister with a scowl. Paul strode out of the kitchen and down the steps at the side of Joan, smiling with his usual daredeviltry. He whistled noisily all the way up the lane.

"Great little dance," he said. "My last in Prospect for a spell, I guess."

"Why?" asked Joan wonderingly.

"Oh, I'm going to take a run down to South America in Matheson's schooner. Lord knows when I'll come back. This old place has got too deadly dull to suit me. I'm going to look for something livelier."

Joan's lips turned ashen under the fringes of her white fascinator. She trembled violently and put one of her small brown hands up to her throat. "You – you are not coming back?" she said faintly.

"Not likely. I'm pretty well tired of Prospect and I haven't got anything to hold me here. Things'll be livelier down south."

Joan said nothing more. They walked along the spruce-fringed roads where the moonbeams laughed down through the thick, softly swaying boughs. Paul whistled one rollicking tune after another. The girl bit her lips and clenched her hands. He cared nothing for her – he had been making a mock of her as of others. Hurt pride and wounded love fought each other in her soul. Pride conquered. She would not let him, or anyone, see that she cared. She would *not* care!

At her gate Paul held out his hand.

"Well, good-bye, Joan. I'm sailing tomorrow so I won't see you again – not for years likely. You will be some sober old married woman when I come back to Prospect, if I ever do."

"Good-bye," said Joan steadily. She gave him her cold hand and looked calmly into his face without quailing. She had loved him with all her heart, but now a fatal scorn of him was already mingling with her love. He was what they said he was, a scamp without principle or honour.

Paul whistled himself out of the Shelley lane and over the hill. Then he flung himself down under the spruces, crushed his face into the spicy frosted ferns, and had his black hour alone.

But when Captain Alec's schooner sailed out of the harbour the next day, Paul King was on board of her, the wildest and most hilarious of a wild and hilarious crew. Prospect people nodded their satisfaction.

"Good riddance," they said. "Paul King is black to the core. He never did a decent thing in his life."

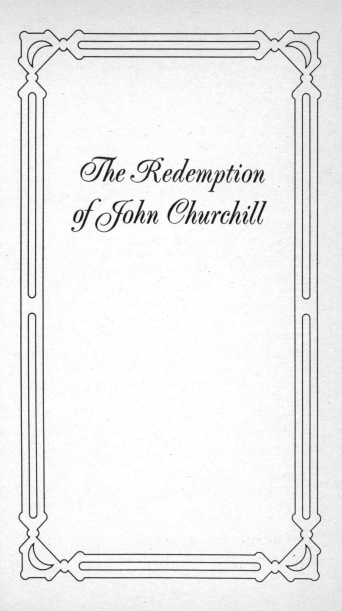

*The Redemption
of John Churchill*

OHN CHURCHILL walked slowly, not as a man walks who is tired, or content to saunter for the pleasure of it, but as one in no haste to reach his destination through dread of it. The day was well on to late afternoon in mid-spring, and the world was abloom. Before him and behind him wound a road that ran like a red ribbon through fields of lush clovery green. The orchards scattered along it were white and fragrant, giving of their incense to a merry south-west wind; fence-corner nooks were purple with patches of violets or golden-green with the curly heads of young ferns. The roadside was sprinkled over with the gold dust of dandelions and the pale stars of wild strawberry blossoms. It seemed a day through which a man should walk lightly and blithely, looking the world and his fellows frankly in the face, and opening his heart to let the springtime in.

But John Churchill walked laggingly, with bent head. When he met other wayfarers or was passed by them, he did not lift his face, but only glanced up under his eyebrows with a furtive look that was replaced by a sort of shamed relief when they had passed on without recognizing him. Some of them he knew for friends of the old time. Ten years had not changed them as he had been changed. They had spent those ten years in freedom and good repute, under God's blue sky, in His glad air and sunshine. He, John Churchill, had spent them behind the walls of a prison.

His close-clipped hair was grey; his figure, encased in an ill-fitting suit of coarse cloth, was stooped and shrunken; his face was deeply lined; yet he was not an old man in years. He was only forty; he was thirty when he had been convicted of embezzling the bank funds for purposes of speculation and had been sent to prison, leaving behind a wife and father who were broken-hearted and a sister whose pride had suffered more than her heart.

He had never seen them since, but he knew what had happened in his absence. His wife had died two months later, leaving behind her a baby boy; his father had died within the year. He had killed them; he, John Churchill, who loved them, had killed them as surely as though his hand had struck them down in cold blood. His sister had taken the baby, his little son whom he had never seen, but for whom he had prepared such a birthright of dishonour. She had never forgiven her brother and she never wrote to him. He knew that she would have brought the boy up either in ignorance of his father's crime or in utter detestation of it. When he came back to the world after his imprisonment, there was not a single friendly hand to clasp his and help him struggle up again. The best his friends had been able to do for him was to forget him.

He was filled with bitterness and despair and a gnawing hatred of the world of brightness around him. He had no place in it; he was an ugly blot on it. He was a friendless, wifeless, homeless man who could not so much as look his fellow men in the face, who must henceforth consort with outcasts. In his extremity he hated God and man, burning with futile resentment against both.

Only one feeling of tenderness yet remained in his heart; it centred around the thought of his little son.

When he left the prison he had made up his mind what to do. He had a little money which his father had left him, enough to take him west. He would go there, under a new name. There would be novelty and adventure to blot out the memories of the old years. He did not care what became of him, since there was no one else to care. He knew in his heart that his future career would probably lead him still further and further downward, but that did not matter. If there had been anybody to care, he might

have thought it worthwhile to struggle back to respectability and trample his shame under feet that should
henceforth walk only in the ways of honour and honesty.
But there was nobody to care. So he would go to his own
place.

But first he must see little Joey, who must be quite a big
boy now, nearly ten years old. He would go home and see
him just once, even although he dreaded meeting aversion in the child's eyes. Then, when he had bade him
good-bye, and, with him, good-bye to all that remained to
make for good in his desolated existence, he would go out
of his life forever.

"I'll go straight to the devil then," he said sullenly.
"That's where I belong, a jail-bird at whom everybody
except other jail-birds looks askance. To think what I was
once, and what I am now! It's enough to drive a man mad!
As for repenting, bah! Who'd believe that I really repented,
who'd give me a second chance on the faith of it? Not a
soul. Repentance won't blot out the past. It won't give me
back my wife whom I loved above everything on earth and
whose heart I broke. It won't restore me my unstained
name and my right to a place among honourable men.
There's no chance for a man who has fallen as low as I
have. If Emily were living, I could struggle for her sake. But
who'd be fool enough to attempt such a fight with no
motive and not one chance of success in a hundred. Not I.
I'm down and I'll stay down. There's no climbing up
again."

He celebrated his first day of freedom by getting drunk,
although he had never before been an intemperate man.
Then, when the effects of the debauch wore off, he took
the train for Alliston; he would go home and see little Joey
once.

Nobody at the station where he alighted recognized
him or paid any attention to him. He was as a dead man

who had come back to life to find himself effaced from recollection and his place knowing him no more. It was three miles from the station to where his sister lived, and he resolved to walk the distance. Now that the critical moment drew near, he shrank from it and wished to put it off as long as he could.

When he reached his sister's home he halted on the road and surveyed the place over its snug respectability of iron fence. His courage failed him at the thought of walking over that trim lawn and knocking at that closed front door. He would slip around by the back way; perhaps, who knew, he might come upon Joey without running the gauntlet of his sister's cold, offended eyes. If he might only find the boy and talk to him for a little while without betraying his identity, meet his son's clear gaze without the danger of finding scorn or fear in it – his heart beat high at the thought.

He walked furtively up the back way between high, screening hedges of spruce. When he came to the gate of the yard, he paused. He heard voices just beyond the thick hedge, children's voices, and he crept as near as he could to the sound and peered through the hedge, with a choking sensation in his throat and a smart in his eyes. Was that Joey, could that be his little son? Yes, it was; he would have known him anywhere by his likeness to Emily. Their boy had her curly brown hair, her sensitive mouth, above all, her clear-gazing, truthful grey eyes, eyes in which there was never a shadow of falsehood or faltering.

Joey Churchill was sitting on a stone bench in his aunt's kitchen yard, holding one of his black-stockinged knees between his small, brown hands. Jimmy Morris was standing opposite to him, his back braced against the trunk of a big, pink-blossomed apple tree, his hands in his pockets, and a scowl on his freckled face. Jimmy lived next door to Joey and as a rule they were very good friends, but this afternoon they had quarrelled over the right and proper way to construct an Indian ambush in the fir grove behind the pig-house. The argument was long and warm and finally culminated in personalities. Just as John Churchill dropped on one knee behind the hedge, the better to see Joey's face, Jimmy Morris said scornfully:

"I don't care what you say. Nobody believes you. Your father is in the penitentiary."

The taunt struck home as it always did. It was not the first time that Joey had been twitted with his father by his boyish companions. But never before by Jimmy! It always hurt him, and he had never before made any response to it. His face would flush crimson, his lips would quiver, and his big grey eyes darken miserably with the shadow that was on his life; he would turn away in silence. But that Jimmy, his best beloved chum, should say such a thing to him; oh, it hurt terribly.

There is nothing so merciless as a small boy. Jimmy saw his advantage and vindictively pursued it.

"Your father stole money, that's what he did! You know he did. I'm pretty glad *my* father isn't a thief. *Your* father is. And when he gets out of prison, he'll go on stealing again. My father says he will. Nobody'll have anything to do with him, my father says. His own sister won't have anything to do with him. So there, Joey Churchill!"

"There *will* somebody have something to do with him!" cried Joey hotly. He slid off the bench and faced Jimmy proudly and confidently. The unseen watcher on the other side of the hedge saw his face grow white and intense and set-lipped, as if it had been the face of a man. The grey eyes were alight with a steady, fearless glow.

"*I'll* have something to do with him. He is my father and I love him. I don't care what he did, I love him just as well as if he was the best man in the world. I love him better than if he was as good as your father, because he needs it

213

more. I've always loved him ever since I found out about him. I'd write to him and tell him so, if Aunt Beatrice would tell me where to send the letter. Aunt Beatrice won't ever talk about him or let me talk about him, but I *think* about him all the time. And he's going to be a good man yet, yes, he is, just as good as your father, Jimmy Morris. I'm going to *make* him good. I made up my mind years ago what I would do and I'm going to do it, so there, Jimmy."

"I don't see what you can do," muttered Jimmy, already ashamed of what he had said and wishing he had let Joey's father alone.

"I'll tell you what I can do!" Joey was confronting all the world now, with his head thrown back and his face flushed with his earnestness. "I can love him and stand by him, and I will. When he gets out of – of prison, he'll come to see me, I know he will. And I'm just going to hug him and kiss him and say, 'Never mind, Father. I know you're sorry for what you've done, and you're never going to do it any more. You're going to be a good man and I'm going to stand by you.' Yes, sir, that's just what I'm going to say to him. I'm all the children he has and there's nobody else to love him, because I know Aunt Beatrice doesn't. And I'm going with him wherever he goes."

"You can't," said Jimmy in a scared tone. "Your Aunt Beatrice won't let you."

"Yes, she will. She'll have to. I belong to my father. And I think he'll be coming pretty soon some way. I'm pretty sure the time must be most up. I wish he would come. I want to see him as much as can be, 'cause I know he'll need me. And I'll be proud of him yet, Jimmy Morris, yes, I'll be just as proud as you are of your father. When I get bigger, nobody will call my father names, I can tell you. I'll fight them if they do, yes, sir, I will. My father and I are going to stand by each other like bricks. Aunt Beatrice has lots of children of her own and I don't believe she'll be a bit sorry when I go away. She's ashamed of my father 'cause he did a bad thing. But I'm not, no, sir. I'm going to love him so much that it'll make up to him for everything else. And you can just go home, Jimmy Morris, so there!"

Jimmy Morris went home, and when he had gone, Joey flung himself face downward in the grass and fallen apple blossoms and lay very still.

On the other side of the spruce hedge knelt John Churchill with bowed head. The tears were running freely down his face, but there was a new, tender light in his eyes. The bitterness and despair had fallen out of his heart, leaving a great peace and a dawning hope in their place. Bless that loyal little soul! There was something to live for after all – there was a motive to make the struggle worthwhile. He must justify his son's faith in him; he must strive to make himself worthy of this sweet, pure, unselfish love that was offered to him, as a divine draught is offered to the parched lips of a man perishing from thirst. Aye, and, God helping him, he would. He would redeem the past. He would go west, but under his own name. His little son should go with him; he would work hard; he would pay back the money he had embezzled, as much of it as he could, if it took the rest of his life to do so. For his boy's sake he must cleanse his name from the dishonour he had brought on it. Oh, thank God, there was somebody to care, somebody to love him, somebody to believe him when he said humbly, "I repent." Under his breath he said, looking heavenward:

"God be merciful to me, a sinner."

Then he stood up erectly, went through the gate and over the grass to the motionless little figure with its face buried in its arms.

"Joey boy," he said huskily. "Joey boy."

Joey sprang to his feet with tears still glistening in his

eyes. He saw before him a bent, grey-headed man looking at him lovingly and wistfully. Joey knew who it was – the father he had never seen. With a glad cry of welcome he sprang into the outstretched arms of the man whom his love had already won back to God.

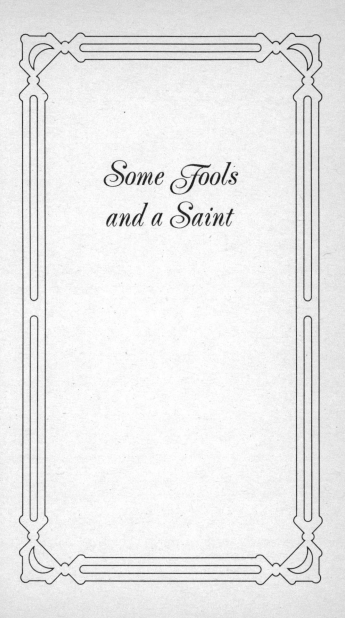

Some Fools
and a Saint

"YOU ARE GOING to board at Long Alec's!" exclaimed Mr. Sheldon in amazement.

The old minister of the Glen Donald congregation and the new minister were in the little church vestry. The old minister had looked kindly at the new minister . . . kindly and rather wistfully. This boy was so like what he himself had been fifty years before . . . young, enthusiastic, full of hope, energy and high purpose. Good-looking too. Mr. Sheldon smiled a bit in the back of his mind and wondered if Curtis Burns were engaged. Probably. Most young ministers were. If not, there would be some fluttering in the girlish hearts of Glen Donald. And small blame to them.

The induction service had been held in the afternoon and had been followed by a supper in the basement. Curtis Burns had met all his people and shaken hands with them. He was feeling a little confused and bewildered, and rather glad to find himself in the quiet, elm-shaded vestry with old Mr. Sheldon, his saintly predecessor, who had ministered to this congregation for over thirty years and whose resignation' in the preceding autumn had seemed cataclysmic to his adoring parish.

"You have a good church and a loyal people here, Mr. Burns," said Mr. Sheldon. "I hope your ministry among them will be happy and blessed."

Curtis Burns smiled. When he smiled his cheeks dimpled, which gave him a boyish, irresponsible look. Mr. Sheldon felt a momentary doubt. He could not recall any minister of his acquaintance who had dimples. Was it fitting? But Curtis Burns was saying, with just the right shade of diffidence and modesty:

"I am sure it will be my own fault, sir, if it is not. I feel my lack of experience. May I draw on yours occasionally for advice and help?"

"I shall be very glad to give you any assistance in my power," said Mr. Sheldon, his doubts disappearing promptly. "As for advice . . . bushels of it are at your disposal. I shall hand you out a piece at once. Go in the manse . . . don't board."

Curtis shook his brown head ruefully.

"I can't, Mr. Sheldon . . . not right away. I haven't a cent. It took my last penny to buy a suit for my ordination. I'll have to wait until I've saved enough out of my salary to put a few sticks of furniture in the manse."

"Oh, well . . . of course, if you can't, you can't. But do it as soon as you can. There is no place like his own home for a minister. The Glen Donald manse is a nice old house. It was a very happy home to me for thirty years . . . until the death of my dear wife five years ago. Since then I have been very lonely. However, you will have a good boarding place with Mrs. Richards. She will make you very comfortable."

"Unfortunately Mrs. Richards can't have me after all. She has to go to the hospital for a rather serious operation. I am going to board at Mr. Field's . . . Long Alec, I believe he is called. You seem to have odd nicknames in Glen Donald . . . I've heard a few already."

And then Mr. Sheldon had exclaimed: "Long Alec's!"

"Yes, I prevailed on him and his sister today to take me in for a few weeks on promise of good behaviour. I'm in luck. It's the only other place near the church. I had hard work to get them to consent."

"But . . . Long Alec's!" said Mr. Sheldon again.

It struck Curtis that Mr. Sheldon's surprise was rather surprising. Why shouldn't he board at Long Alec's?

Long Alec seemed a most respectable and rather attractive youngish man, with his fine-cut aquiline features, his high white forehead and soft dreamy grey eyes. And the sister . . . a sweet, little, brown thing, rather tired looking, with a flute-like voice. Her face was as brown as a nut, her hair and eyes were brown, her lips scarlet. Of all the girls that had clustered, flower-like, about the basement that day, casting shy glances of admiration at the handsome young minister, he remembered nothing. But he remembered Lucia Field.

"Why not Long Alec's?" he said. Recalling, too, that a few other people had seemed taken aback when he had mentioned his change of boarding-house. Mr. Sheldon looked embarrassed.

"Oh, it's all right, I suppose. Only . . . I shouldn't have thought them likely to take a boarder. Lucia has her hands full as it is. You know there's an invalid cousin there."

"Yes. I called to see her when I preached here in February. What a tragedy . . . that sweet, beautiful woman!"

"A beautiful woman indeed," said Mr. Sheldon emphatically. "And a wonderful woman. She is one of the greatest powers for good in this community. They call her the angel of Glen Donald. I tell you, Mr. Burns, the influence that Alice Harper wields from that bed of helplessness is amazing. I cannot tell you what she has been to me during these past ten years. Her wonderful life is an inspiration. The young girls of the congregation worship her. Do you know that for eight years she has taught a class of teenage girls? They go over to her room after the opening exercises of the Sunday school here. She enters into their lives . . . they take all their problems and perplexities to her. And it was entirely due to her that the church here was not hopelessly disrupted when Elder North went on a rampage because Lucia Field played a sacred violin solo for a collection piece one day. Alice sent for the Elder and talked him into sanity. She told me the whole interview later in confidence with her own inimitable little humorous touches. It was rich. She is full of fun. She suffers indescribably at times, but no one ever heard her utter a word of complaint."

"Has she always been so?"

"Oh, no. She fell from the barn loft ten years ago – hunting for eggs or something. She was unconscious for twenty-four hours, and has been paralyzed from the hips down ever since."

"Have they had good medical advice?"

"The best. Winthrop Field – Long Alec's father – had specialists from everywhere. They could do nothing for her. She is a daughter of Winthrop's sister. Her father and mother died when she was a baby – her father was a clever scamp who died a dipsomaniac like his father before him – and the Fields brought her up. Before her accident I really knew little of her . . . she was a slim, pretty, shy girl who liked to keep in the background and seldom went about with the other young people. I don't know that her existence on her uncle's charity was altogether easy. She feels her helplessness keenly – she can't even turn herself in bed, Mr. Burns – feels that she is a burden on Alec and Lucia. They are very good to her, but young and healthy people can't understand fully. Winthrop Field died seven years ago and his wife the next year. Then Lucia gave up her work in the city – she was a teacher in the high school – and came home to keep house for Alec and wait on Alice, who can't bear to have strangers handling her, poor soul. Lucia is a good girl, I think, and Alec's a fine fellow in many ways – a little stubborn perhaps. I've heard some talk of his being engaged to Edna Pollock, but it never comes to anything. Well, it's a fine old place – the Field farm is the best in Glen Donald – and Lucia is a good housekeeper. I hope you'll be comfortable . . . but . . ."

Mr. Sheldon stopped abruptly and stood up.

"Mr. Sheldon, what do you mean by that 'but'?" said

Curtis resolutely. "Some of the rest looked 'but' too, though they didn't say it. I want to understand. I don't like mysteries."

"Then you shouldn't go to Long Alec's," said Mr. Sheldon drily.

"Why not?"

"I suppose I'd better tell you. I suppose I ought to. Yet it always makes me feel like a fool. Mr. Burns, there is something very strange about the old Field place. Glen Donald people will tell you it is . . . haunted."

"Haunted!" Curtis almost laughed. His dimples ran riot. "Mr. Sheldon, you don't tell me that."

"I once said 'haunted' in just the same tone," said Mr. Sheldon a little sharply. Even if he were a saint he did not care to be laughed at by boys just out of college. "I never said it so after I spent a night there."

"But you don't, seriously, you don't believe it, Mr. Sheldon?"

"Of course I don't. That is, I don't believe the strange things that have happened there during the last five or six years are supernatural or caused by supernatural agency. But the things have happened, there is no doubt whatever about that."

"What things?"

Mr. Sheldon coughed.

"I . . . I . . . some of them sound a little ridiculous when put into words. But the cumulative effect is not ridiculous . . . at least, to those who have to live in the house and who cannot find the explanation of them – cannot, Mr. Burns. Rooms are turned upside down . . . a cradle is rocked in the garret where no cradle is . . . violins are played – there are no violins in the house except Lucia's, which is always kept her room . . . cold water is poured over people in bed . . . clothes pulled off them . . . shrieks ring through the garret . . . dead peoples' voices are heard talking in empty

rooms . . . bloody footprints are found on the floors . . .
white figures have been seen walking on the barn roof.
Oh, smile, Mr. Burns, I have smiled too. And I laughed
when I heard that all the eggs under their setting hens last
spring were discovered to be hard-boiled. But it was no
laughing matter when Long Alec's binder-house was
burned last fall with his new binder in it. It was off by itself – nobody had been near it for weeks."

"But, Mr. Sheldon, if anybody but you had told me those
things . . ."

"You wouldn't have believed them? And you don't . . .
quite . . . believe me. I don't blame you. I didn't believe the
yarns until I spent a night there."

"And did anything . . . what happened?"

"Well, I heard the cradle – it rocked all night in the
garret over my head. The dinner bell rang at midnight. I
heard a devilish sort of laugh . . . I can't say whether it was
in my room or out of it. There was a quality in it that filled
me with a sickening sort of horror . . . I admit it, Mr. Burns,
that laughter was not human. And just before dawn every
dish on one of the cupboard shelves was thrown to the
floor and smashed. Moreover," Mr. Sheldon's gentle old
mouth twitched, "the porridge at breakfast was literally
half salt."

"Somebody was playing tricks."

"Of course, I believe that as firmly as you do. But what
somebody? And how is it the somebody can't be caught?
You don't suppose Lucia and Long Alec haven't tried?"

"Do these performances go on every night?"

"No. Weeks will sometimes pass without incident. Then
there is an orgy. Moonlight nights are generally – not
always – quiet."

"Who lives in the house besides Miss Field and her
brother and Miss Harper?"

"Two people. Jock MacCree, a half-witted fellow who

has made his home with the Fields for thirty years – he must be close on fifty – and Julia Marsh, the servant girl. A lumpish, sulky sort of creature, one of the Glen Donald Road Marshes. Perhaps you've heard of them?"

"A half-wit, and a girl from a degenerate family! I don't think your ghosts should be very hard to locate, Mr. Sheldon."

"It's not so simple as that. Of course they were suspected at once. But the things go on when Jock is locked in his room. Julia would never have her door locked, I admit. But someone stood guard outside of it. Besides, these things happen nights she is away."

"Have you ever heard either of them laugh?"

"Yes. Jock giggles foolishly. Julia snorts. I cannot believe that either of them produced the sound I heard. Glen Donald people at first thought it was Jock. Now they believe it is ghosts, they really do, even those who won't admit they believe it."

"What reason do they have for supposing the house is haunted?"

"Well, there's a pitiful tale. Julia Marsh's sister Anna used to work there before Julia. Help is hard to get in Glen Donald, Mr. Burns. And Lucia must have help, she cannot do the work of that place and wait on Alice alone. Anna Marsh had had an illegitimate baby. It was about three years old and she used to have it there with her. It was a pretty little thing – they all liked the child. One day it was drowned in the barn cistern – Jock had left the top off. Anna seemed to take it coolly – didn't make a fuss, didn't even cry, I'm told. People said, 'Oh, she's glad to be rid of it. A bad lot, those Marshes.' But two weeks after the child was buried, Anna hanged herself in the garret."

Curtis gave a horrified exclamation.

"So you see there is a magnificent foundation for a ghost story. That's the reason Edna Pollock won't marry

Long Alec. The Pollocks are well off and Edna is a smart, capable girl, but a bit below the Fields socially and mentally. She wants Alec to sell and move. She insists that the place is under a curse. Well, as for that, a note was found one morning, written in blood, badly written and badly spelled – Anna Marsh was very illiterate – 'If ever children are born in this house they will be born accursed.' Alec won't sell. The place has been in his family since 1770 and he says he's not going to be driven out of it by spooks. A few weeks after Anna's death these performances began. The cradle was heard rocking in the garret – there was a cradle there then. They took it away, but the rocking went on just the same. Oh, everything has been done to solve the mystery. Neighbours have watched night after night. Sometimes nothing happened. Sometimes things happened but they couldn't find out why. Three years ago Julia took a sulky fit and left . . . said people were saying things about her. Also I believe she said a vase in the parlour made a face at her when she was dusting it. Lucia got Min Deacon from over Halston way. Min stayed three weeks and left because she was wakened by an icy hand on her face – though she had locked her door on the inside. Then they got Maggie Elgin – a young girl with splendid hair and no nerves. Maggie stood it for five weeks . . . icy hands and weird laughter and ghostly cradle couldn't bother her. But when she woke up one morning and found that her beautiful braid of black hair had been cut off in the night . . . well, that was too much for Maggie. Bobbed hair had not come in to Glen Donald then, and Maggie was proud of her hair. Anna Marsh, people will tell you, had very poor hair and was always bitterly jealous of girls with nice hair. Lucia prevailed on Julia to come back then, having disposed of the offending vase, and she's been there ever since. Personally, I feel sure Julia hasn't anything to do with it."

"Then . . . who has?"

"Oh, Mr. Burns, we can't answer that. And . . . who knows what the powers of evil can or cannot do? Some very strange things happened at Epworth Rectory, we are told. I don't think the mystery of them has ever been solved. And yet . . . I hardly think the devil – or even a malicious ghost – would empty out a dozen bottles of raspberry vinegar and fill them up with red ink, salt and water."

Mr. Sheldon laughed in spite of himself. Curtis didn't laugh . . . he frowned.

"It is intolerable that such things can go on for five years and the perpetrator escape. It must be a dreadful life for Miss Field."

"Lucia takes it coolly. Some people think a little too coolly. Of course, we have malicious people in Glen Donald as well as everywhere else, and some have hinted that she does the things herself. Of course, I cannot believe that."

"I should think not. What earthly motive could she have?"

"To prevent Long Alec's marriage with Edna Pollock. Lucia was never particularly fond of Edna. And the Field pride finds it hard to swallow a Pollock alliance. Besides, Lucia can play on the violin."

"I could never believe such a thing of Miss Field."

"No? I don't think I could either. Though I really don't know much about her. She hasn't taken any part in the church work . . . well, I suppose she couldn't. But it is hard to kill an insinuation. I have fought and ousted many a lie, Mr. Burns, but some insinuations have beaten me. Lucia is a reserved little thing – perhaps I am too old to get well acquainted with her. Well, I've told you all I know about our mystery. If you can put up with Long Alec's spooks for a few weeks, there is no reason why you shouldn't be very comfortable. I know Alice will be glad to have you there. She worries over the mystery – she thinks it keeps people away. Well, of course, it does, more or less . . . and she's fond of company, poor girl. Besides, she's very nervous about the goings-on. I hope I haven't made you nervous."

"No. You've interested me. I believe there's some quite simple solution."

"And you also believe that everything has been greatly exaggerated. Oh, not by me – I acquit you of that – but by my gossiping parishioners. Well, I dare say there has been a good deal of exaggeration. Stories can grow to huge proportions in five years, and we country folks are very fond of a spice of the dramatic. Twice two making four is dull . . . twice two making five is exciting. But my hard-headed ruling elder, old Malcolm Dinwoodie, heard Winthrop Field talking in the parlour there one night . . . years after he had been buried. Nobody who had once heard Winthrop Field's peculiar voice could mistake it . . . or the little nervous laugh he always ended up with."

"But I thought it was Anna Marsh's ghost that was supposed to walk?"

"Well, her voice has been heard too, Mr. Burns. I'm not going to talk any more about this. You'll think me a doddering idiot. Perhaps you won't be so sure when you've lived in that house for a while. And perhaps the spook will respect the cloth and behave while you are there. Perhaps you may even find out the truth."

Mr. Sheldon is a saint and a better man and minister than I'll ever be, mused Curtis as he walked across the road to his boarding place, but the old fellow believes Long Alec's house is haunted . . . in spite of the raspberry vinegar. Well, here's for a bout with the ghosts. And twice two is four.

He looked behind him at his church – a tranquil grey old building among sunken graves and mossy gravestones under the sharp silvery sky of the late spring evening. Beside it was the manse, a nice chubby old house of cream brick, looking lonely and appealing with its blindless windows. Directly opposite it across the road was "the Old Field place." The wide, rather low house, with its many porches, had an odd resemblance to a motherly old hen with little chickens peeping out from under her breast and wings. There was a peculiar strangeness of dormer windows in the roof. The window of a room in the main house was at right angles to one in the el and was so close to it that people could have shaken hands from window to window. There was something about this architectural trick that pleased Curtis. It gave the roof an individuality. Some great pine trees grew about it, stretching their boughs over it lovingly. The whole place had atmosphere, charm, suggestion. An old aunt of Curtis Burns' would have said, "There's family behind that."

Virginia creeper rioted over the porches. Gnarled apple trees, from which sounded faint, delicate notes of birds, bent over plots of old-fashioned flowers – thickets of white and fragrant sweet clover, beds of mint and southernwood, pansies, honeysuckles and blush roses. There was an old mossy path, bordered by clam shells, running up to the front door. Beyond were comfortable barns and a pasture field lying in the coolness of evening shadows, sprinkled over with the phantom-like globes of dandelions. A wholesome friendly old place. Nothing spookish about it. Mr. Sheldon was a saint but he was very old. Old people believed things too easily.

CURTIS BURNS had been boarding at the old Field place for five weeks and nothing had happened – except that he had fallen fathoms deep in love with Lucia Field. And he did not yet know that this had happened. Nobody knew it – except perhaps Alice Harper, who seemed to see things invisible to others with those clear beautiful blue eyes of hers. She and Curtis were close friends. Like everyone else he was racked alternately with inexpressible admiration for her spirit and courage, and fierce pity for her helplessness and sufferings. There was a pale, almost unearthly beauty about Alice Harper. In spite of her thin, lined face she had a strange look of youth, partly owing to her bobbed golden hair, kept cut to avoid tangles, partly to the splendour of her large eyes, which always seemed to have a laugh at the back of them, though she never laughed. She had a sweet smile with a hint of roguishness in it, especially when Curtis told her a joke. He was good at telling jokes and he carried every new one to her. She never complained, though there were occasional days when she moaned ceaselessly in almost unendurable agony and could see no one except Alec and Lucia. Some heart weakness made drugs dangerous and little could be done to relieve her, but in such attacks she could not endure to be alone.

On such days Curtis was left largely to the tender mercies of Julia Marsh, who served his meals properly but whom he could not bear. She was a rather handsome creature, though her clear red-and-white face was marred and rendered sinister by a birthmark – a deep red band across one cheek. Her eyes were small and amber-hued, her reddish-brown hair was splendid and untidy, and she moved with a graceful stealthiness of motion and limb like a cat in twilight. She was a great talker, save on days when she took tantrums and became possessed with a silent devil. Then not a word could be got out of her, and she glowered and lowered like a thunderstorm. Lucia did not seem to mind these moods – Lucia took everything that came with her sweet undisturbed serenity – but Curtis seemed to feel them all over the house. At such times Julia was a baffling, inhuman creature who might do anything.

Sometimes Curtis was sure that she was at the bottom of the spook business; at other times he was just as sure it was Jock MacCree. He had even less use for Jock than Julia and could not understand why Lucia and Long Alec seemed actually to have an affection for the uncanny fellow.

Jock was fifty and looked a hundred in some ways. He had staring filmy grey eyes, a skinny, sallow face, lank black hair, and a curiously protruding lower lip that made his profile singularly disagreeable. He was always arrayed in a motley collection of garments – of his own choice, it seemed, not of necessity – and spent most of his time carrying food to and looking after Long Alec's innumerable pigs. He made money for Long Alec out of the pigs, but of other work he could be trusted with nothing. When alone by himself he sang old Scotch songs in a surprisingly sweet true voice, but with something peculiar in its timbre. So Jock was musical, noted Curtis, remembering the violin. Jock's speaking voice was high-pitched and childish, and occasionally his expressionless face was shot through with gleams of Puck-like malice. When he smiled – which was rarely – he looked incredibly cunning. From the beginning he seemed to have an awe of the black-coated minister and kept out of his way as much as possible, though Curtis sought him out, determined to solve, if possible, the mystery of the place.

He had come to think lightly of the mystery. Everything had been normal and commonplace since his coming, except that one night when he sat up late in his dormer-windowed room to study, he had a curious, persistent feeling that he was being watched . . . by some inimical personality at that. He put it down to nerves. It was never repeated. Once, too, when he had risen in the night to lower his window against a high wind, he had looked across the road at the moonlit manse and for a moment thought he saw someone looking out of the study window. He examined the manse next day but found no traces of any intruder. The doors were locked, the windows securely closed. No one had a key except himself and Mr. Sheldon, who still kept most of his books and some other things in the manse, though he was boarding with Mrs. Carter at Glen Donald Station a mile away. Curtis concluded that some odd effect of moonlight and tree shadows had tricked him.

Evidently the perpetrator of the tricks knew when it was wise to lie low. A resident boarder, young and shrewd, was a different proposition from a transient guest, an old man or a sleepy, superstitious neighbour. So Curtis concluded in his youthful complacency. He was sorry nothing had happened. He wanted to have a chance at the spooks.

Neither Lucia nor Long Alec ever referred to their "ha'nts," nor did he. But he had talked the matter over thoroughly with Alice, who had mentioned it when he went in to see her on the evening of his arrival.

"So you are not afraid of our whow-whows? You know our garret is full of them," she said whimsically, as she gave him her very long, very slender, and very beautiful hand.

Curtis noticed that Lucia, who had just finished giving Alice's back and shoulders the half-hour's rub that was necessary every night, flushed suddenly and deeply.

"I'm afraid I don't take your whow-whows very seriously, Miss Harper," he said.

"Is there anything more you would like, Alice?" asked Lucia in a low voice.

"No, dear. I feel very comfortable. Run away and rest. I know you're tired. And I want to get really acquainted with my new minister."

Lucia went out, her face still flushed. Curtis felt a sudden upsetting thrill at his heart as he watched her. He wanted to comfort her, help her, wipe that tired patience from her sweet, brown little face, make her smile, make her laugh . . .

"Mr. Burns, you are so nice and young," Alice was saying. "I've never known any but an old minister. I like youth. And so you don't believe in our family ghosts?"

"I can't believe all the things I've heard."

"And yet they're all true. More things, too, than anyone has heard. Mr. Burns, may we have a frank talk about it? I've never been able to talk frankly to anyone about it. Lucia and Alec can't bear to talk of it . . . it made Mr. Sheldon nervous . . . and one can't talk to outsiders about such a matter, at least, I can't. When I heard you were coming here for a few weeks, I was glad, Mr. Burns. I can't help hoping that you will solve the mystery, especially for the sake of Lucia and Alec. It's ruining their lives. It's bad enough to have me on their hands, but ghosts and devilry plus me are really too much. And they writhe with humiliation over it – you know it's considered a kind of disgraceful thing to have ghosts in the family."

"What is your idea about the matter, Miss Harper?"

"Oh, I suppose Jock does it, though no one can understand how. Jock, you know, isn't really half such a fool as he looks. And Jock used to prowl about the house after night long ago – Uncle Winthrop often caught him. But he never did anything but prowl then."

"How does he come to be here at all?"

"His father, Dave MacCree, was a hired man here years ago. He saved Henry Kildare's life when the black stallion attacked him."

"Henry Kildare?"

"A young boy of eighteen who also worked here. He went to the Klondike when the gold rush began. He isn't in the picture at all, but Uncle Winthrop was so grateful to Jock's father for preventing such a thing happening that when Dave died the next year Uncle Winthrop promised him that Jock should always have a home here. Lucia and Alec promised it in their turn. We Fields are a clannish crew, Mr. Burns, and always back each other up and keep fast hold of our traditions. Jock has become one of our long-established customs."

"Is it possible Julia Marsh is guilty?"

"I can't believe it's Julia. The things go on when she's away. The only time I've really suspected Julia was when the church supper money vanished the night after Alec brought it home. He was treasurer of the committee. A hundred dollars disappeared out of his desk. Jock wouldn't have taken it. Nobody in Lancaster knows about that. Of course Alec made it good. I heard there was an eruption of new dresses in the Marsh gang all that year. Julia herself came out resplendent in a purple silk. That is the only time money has been taken. Mr. Burns, did anyone ever hint to you that Lucia does the things?"

"Mr. Sheldon told me people have hinted it."

"Mr. Sheldon? Why should he have told you that? It is a cruel, malicious falsehood," exclaimed Alice emphatically – almost too emphatically, Curtis thought. "Lucia never could do such things, never. She is entirely incapable of it. Nobody knows that child as I do, Mr. Burns. Her sweetness, her patience, her . . . her . . . Fieldness. Think of what it must have meant to her to give up her life and work in the city and bury herself in Glen Donald. When I think that it was because of me, it almost drives me crazy. Never for one moment, Mr. Burns, let yourself believe that Lucia does the things that are done here."

"I don't believe it. But if it isn't Jock or Julia, who is it?"

"That is the question. Once an idea occurred to me, but it was so wild, so incredible . . . I won't even put it into words."

"Has anything happened lately?"

"The telephone has rung our call at midnight and three o'clock every night for a week. Alec found another curse, written in blood – written backwards so that it could be read only in the mirror – slipped under his bedroom door. Our ghost is strong on curses, Mr. Burns. This one was a peculiarly nasty one. You'll find it in that little table drawer. I made Lucia give it to me. I wanted to show it to you. Yes, that's it. Hold it up to my hand mirror."

" 'Heven and hell shall blast your happyness. You shall be smitten in the persens of those you love. Your life shall be recked and your house left unto you desalate.' Mmmm. The ghost has a poor taste in stationery," concluded Curtis, looking at the cheap, blue-lined sheet on which the words were scrawled. "Can Jock write?"

"Yes, a little. You notice the spelling is bad. But even so, the whole composition seems to me to be beyond Jock. The coal oil that was poured into the cold chicken broth in the pantry night before last was more in his line. Also the delicate humour of a jug of molasses spilled all over the parlour carpet. It cost poor Lucia a hard day's work to get it all cleaned up."

"But surely the doer of a trick like that could easily be caught."

"If we knew when it was going to be done, oh, yes. But we can't watch every night. And generally when anyone is watching, nothing like that happens."

"That proves that it must be someone in the house. An outsider wouldn't know when there was a watch."

"I suppose so. And yet, Mr. Burns, the cradle was rocked and the violin played weirdly all night in the garret two weeks ago when Julia was away and Jock was out in the stable with Alec, working over a sick cow."

"Is it true that the voices of dead people have been heard?"

"Yes." Alice shivered. "It doesn't happen often, but it

has happened. I don't like to talk of that. I heard Uncle Winthrop outside my door one night saying, 'Alice, would you like anything? Have they done everything you want?' He used to do that when he was alive, very gently, so as not to disturb me if I were really asleep. You see," she added, with a return of her whimsicality, "our ghost is so extremely versatile. If it would stick to one line . . . but eeriness and roguery together is a hard combination to solve. This 'curse' has worried Alec, Lucia tells me. His nerves are not good lately – things 'get on' them. And there have been so many curses – mostly Bible verses. Our spooks know their Bible, Mr. Burns, which is another count against the Jock and Julia theories."

"But it is intolerable, this persecution . . ."

"Oh, we're all used to it more or less. At least Lucia and Alec are. I didn't mind so much until the binder-house was burned last fall. Since then I've been haunted by the fear that the house will go next, and me locked in here."

"Locked!"

"Why, yes. I make Lucia lock my door every night. I could never sleep – I'm a wretched sleeper at any time except in the early morning. But I couldn't sleep at all with that door unlocked and goodness knows what prowling round the house."

"But the goodness-knows-what isn't baffled by locked doors if the Min Deacon and Maggie Elgin tales are to be believed."

"Oh, I don't believe Min or Maggie had their doors locked when the things happened to them. They thought they had, of course, but they must have been mistaken. At any rate, I am sure mine is always locked. Well, we won't talk of it any more just now. But I want you to keep your eyes open and we'll see what we can do together. And you'll let me help you as much as I can in the church work, won't you? Mr. Sheldon did."

"I'll be very glad to have your help and counsel, Miss Harper."

"I want to do what I can while I'm here. Some of these days I'll just go out – pouf! – as a candle flickers and dies. My heart won't behave. Now never mind hunting in your mind, Mr. Burns, for the proper and tactful thing to say. I've looked death too long in the face to be afraid of it. Only sometimes in the long, wakeful hours I shrink a little from it, even though life holds nothing for me."

"Miss Harper, is it certain nothing can be done for you?"

"Absolutely. Uncle Winthrop had a dozen specialists here. The last was Dr. Clifford – you know him. When he could do me no good, I simply told him I would have no more doctors. I would not have them spending money on me when they might as well burn it. Oh, I'm not so badly off as hundreds of others. Everyone is so good to me – I'm not altogether useless – and it's only once a week or so that I suffer much. So we'll let it go at that and never talk of it any more, Mr. Burns. I'm more interested in the church work and you. I want you to get along well."

"So do I," laughed Curtis.

"Don't be too good-tempered," said Alice solemnly, but with mischief in her eyes. "Mr. Sheldon was never put out about anything and he was scandalously imposed on. Saints generally are. Poor old man, he hated to give up his work, but it was really time. He has never been the same since the death of his wife. He took it terribly hard. Indeed, for a year after her death people thought his mind was affected. He would do and say such odd things with apparently no recollection of them afterwards. And he took such a spite to Alec – thought he wasn't orthodox. But that passed. Will you draw up my blind and lower my light, please? Thank you. What a majestic sweep of wind there is in those old pines tonight! And no moonlight. I don't like moonlight. It always reminds me of things I want to forget. Good-night. Don't dream, and don't see or hear any 'ha'nts.' "

Curtis neither dreamed nor saw "ha'nts," though he lay awake for a long time thinking of many things. He was a little disappointed that he did not. But as the weeks passed he almost forgot that he was living in a supposedly haunted house. He was very busy getting acquainted with his parish and organizing his church work. In this he found Alice Harper's assistance invaluable. He could never have reorganized the choir without her. She smoothed irritations and talked away jealousies. It was she who managed Elder Kirk when he tried to put his foot down on the Boy Scout business; it was she who smoothed Curtis out of his consequent bitterness and annoyance.

"You mustn't mind Mr. Kirk. He was born a nincompoop, you know. And he has his good points. He is a good man and would be quite a nice one if he didn't really think it was his Christian duty to be a little miserable and cantankerous all the time."

"I wish I could be as tolerant as you, Miss Harper."

"I've learned tolerance in a hard school. I wasn't always tolerant. But Mr. Kirk is funny – you should have heard him."

Her mimicry of the Elder sent Curtis into howls of laughter. Alice smiled over her success. Curtis got into the habit of talking all his problems over with her. He made a sort of idol of her and worshipped her like a Madonna in a shrine. Yet she had her small foibles. She must know everything that went on in house and community. It hurt her to be shut out of anything. He told her all his goings and comings, finding her oddly jealous about his little secrets. She must even know what he had to eat when he went out to tea. She was avid about the details of his June weddings.

"All weddings are interesting," she averred, "even the weddings of people I don't know."

She liked to talk over his sermons with him while he was preparing them and was childishly pleased when now and then he preached from a text of her choosing.

He was very happy. He loved his work. His boarding-house was most agreeable. Long Alec was an intelligent, well-read fellow, and Curtis had interesting conversations with him. When Mrs. Richards died in the hospital, it was taken for granted that Curtis should go on living at the Field place as long as he wanted to. Glen Donald people were resigned to it, although they did not approve of his falling in love with Lucia. Everybody in the congregation knew that he was in love with Lucia long before he knew it himself. He only knew that Lucia's silences were quite as enchanting as Long Alec's eloquence or Alice's trick of sly, humorous sayings. He only knew that other girls' faces seemed futile and insipid compared with her brown beauty. He only knew that the sight of her stepping about the neat, dignified old rooms, coming down the dark, shining staircase, cutting flowers in the garden, making salads and cakes in the pantry, affected him like a perfect chord of music and seemed to waken echoes in his soul that repeated the enchantment as he went to and fro among his people. Once he trembled on the verge of discovering his own secret – when Lucia brought Alice in some early roses one day. Mr. Sheldon was there too, having just returned to Glen Donald from a visit to some distant friends. He had been away ever since the day following Curtis' ordination.

Lucia had evidently been crying. Lucia was not a girl who cried easily. Curtis was suddenly seized with a desire to draw her head down on his shoulder and comfort her. He was following her rather blindly from the room when a spasm of pain twisted Alice's face.

"Lucia, come back . . . quick, please. I'm going to have . . . one of . . . my spells."

Curtis did not see Lucia again for twenty-four hours. Most of the time she was in Alice's darkened room, vainly trying to relieve the sufferer. So he went a little longer in ignorance.

As he returned from the garden after seeing Mr. Sheldon off, he noticed that a beautiful young white birch, which had been growing exquisitely among the pines in a corner, had been cut down. It was Lucia's favourite tree – she had spoken of her love for it on the preceding evening. It was lying on the ground, its limp leaves quivering pitifully. He spoke of it rather indignantly to Long Alec.

"The tree was all right last night," said Long Alec.

Curtis stared.

"Didn't you cut it down – or order it cut?"

"No. It was like this when we got up this morning."

"Then . . . who cut it?"

"Our dear ghost, I suppose," said Long Alec bitterly, turning away. Alec would never discuss the ghost. Curtis saw Julia's queer little amber eyes watching him from the back verandah. He remembered hearing her ask Jock the previous day to sharpen the axe kept sacred to the splitting of kindling.

For the next three weeks Curtis had plenty to think about. One night he was awakened by the telephone ringing the Field call. He sat up in bed. Over his head in the garret a cradle was rocking distinctly. Curtis rose, flung on a dressing gown, snatched up his flashlight, went down the hall, opened the door into the little recess at its end and went up the garret stair. The cradle had stopped. The long room was bare and quiet under its rafters, hung with bunches of herbs, bags of feathers and a few discarded garments. There was little in the garret – two big wooden chests, a spinning wheel, some bags of wool. A rat could easily have hidden in it. Curtis went down and, as he reached the foot of the stair, the weird strains of a violin floated down after him. He was conscious of a nasty crinkling of his nerves but he flashed up again. Nothing . . . nobody was there. The garret was as still and innocent as before. Yet as he went down, the music recommenced.

The telephone rang again in the dining-room. Curtis went down and answered it. There was no response. It was of no use to call up central. The line was a rural party one with twenty subscribers on it.

Curtis deliberately listened at the door of Long Alec's bedroom off the dining-room. He could hear Long Alec's breathing. He tiptoed up the kitchen stair to Jock's door. Jock was snoring. He went back through the house and up the front stair. The telephone rang again. The house was very still. Opposite the stair was Alice's door. Her light as usual was burning and she was repeating the twenty-third psalm to herself in her soft, clear voice. A few steps further down the hall was Julia's room, opposite his own. Curtis listened at the door but heard nothing. Lucia's room was beyond the stair railing. He did not listen there. But he could not help the thought that everyone in the house was accounted for but Julia . . . and Lucia. He went back to his own room, shut the door, stood for a minute in scowling reflection and got into bed. As he did so, an eerie, derisive laugh sounded distinctly just outside his door. For the first time in his life Curtis knew sickening fear and the peculiar clammy perspiration it induces. He remembered what Mr. Sheldon had said – "there was something not human in it."

For a minute he went down before his horror. Then he set his teeth, sprang out of bed and flung open his door.

There was nothing in the great empty hall. Julia's tight-shut door opposite him seemed to wear an air of stealthy triumph.

Lucia looked worried at the breakfast table.

"Were . . . were you disturbed last night?" she asked hesitatingly.

"Rather," said Curtis. "I spent considerable time prowling about your house and eavesdropping shamelessly. Wasn't a bit the wiser."

Lucia produced the forlorn little spectre of a smile.

"If prowling and eavesdropping could have solved our mystery, it would have been solved long ago. Alec and I have given up taking any notice of . . . of . . . the manifestations. Generally we sleep through them now unless something very startling occurs. I had . . . hoped . . . there wouldn't be any more . . . at least while you were here. We have never had such a long interval of freedom."

"Will you give me carte blanche for investigation?" said Curtis.

Lucia hesitated perceptibly.

"Oh, yes," she said at last. "Only . . . please don't talk to me about it. I can't endure to hear it mentioned. It's weak and foolish of me, I suppose. But it has got to be such a sore subject . . . and so many people have 'investigated.' "

"I understand," said Curtis. "But I'm going to nab your ghost, Miss Field. This thing has got to be cleared up. It's intolerable in this country. It will completely ruin your life and your brother's if you stay here."

"And we must stay here," said Lucia, with a rueful smile. "We love this old place too much to leave it."

"Is it true," Curtis asked hesitatingly, "that Miss Pollock won't marry Alec because of this? Don't answer me if you think me impertinent."

Lucia's face changed a little. Her scarlet lips seemed to thin a little. People who had known old Winthrop Field would have said she was looking like her father.

"If it is, I don't think Alec is to be pitied on that score.

242

Edna Pollock is his inferior in every way. The Pollocks are nobodies."

Curtis thought her little foible of family pride quite enchanting. She was so very human, this brown sweet lovable thing.

DURING THE WEEKS that followed, Curtis Burns sometimes thought that he would go crazy. Sometimes he thought that they were all crazy together. He prowled, he investigated, he passed sleepless hours on guard, he spent whole nights in the garret, and he got nowhere. Things happened almost continually – ridiculous and horrible things all jumbled up together in a very orgy of impish devilment. Twelve dozen eggs packed for market were found broken all over the kitchen floor; Lucia's new georgette dress was found ruined with bloodstains in the closet of her bedroom; the violin played and the cradle rocked. The place seemed possessed by diabolical laughter. Several times everything in the parlour and dining-room was piled in the middle of the floor, involving a day's work of restoration for Lucia. Outer doors, locked at night, were found wide open in the morning; the spigot was pulled out of the churn in the dairy and a week's cream spilled on the floor; the spare-room bed was tumbled and dented as if slept in overnight; pigs and calves were let out to riot in the garden; ink was spattered all over the walls of the newly papered hall; plentiful curses were scattered about; voices sounded in that exasperating, commonplace garret. Finally Lucia's pet kitten, a beautiful little Persian Curtis had brought her from the city, was found hung on the back verandah, its poor limp little body dangling pitifully from the fretwork.

"I knew this would happen when you gave it to me," said Lucia. "I've never tried to have a pet since my dog was strangled four years ago. Everything I dare to love dies or is destroyed. My white calf, my dog, my birch tree, now my kitten."

For the most part Curtis carried on his investigations alone. Long Alec bluntly stated that he was fed up with spook stalking. He had had five years of it and had given it up. As long as the ghosts left his roof over his head, he would leave them alone. Once or twice Curtis got Mr. Sheldon to watch with him. Nothing at all happened those nights. Another night he had Henry Kildare. Henry was quite confident at first.

"I'll have that spook's hide nailed to the barn door by morning, preacher," he boasted.

But Henry capitulated in blind terror when he heard Winthrop Field's voice talking in the garret.

"I'll go ghosting no more, preacher. Don't tell me . . . I know old Winthrop's voice well enough – I worked here for three years. That's him, sure as sin. Preacher, you'd better get out of this house. Believe me, it ain't healthy."

Henry Kildare's reappearance in Glen Donald had created quite a sensation. He had made a fortune in the Klondike and announced that he could live on millionaire's row for the rest of his life. He stopped with a cousin but spent a good deal of his time at the old Field place. They liked him there. He was a big, bluff, hearty man, not over-refined, rather handsome, generous, boastful. Alice was never tired of hearing his tales of the Klondike and the days of the gold rush. To her, imprisoned within four walls for years, it was as if she could look out into a wonderful freedom of adventure and peril. But Henry, who had fronted the northern silences, cold and terrors undauntedly, could not front the Field spooks. He flatly refused to stay another night in the house.

"Preacher, this place is full of devils, not a doubt of it.

That Anna Marsh doesn't stay proper in her grave – she never would behave herself, and she drags old Winthrop out with her. Alec'd better give the place away if anyone will take it. I wish I could get Alice and Lucia out of it. They'll be found strangled like the kitten some night.''

Curtis was thoroughly exasperated. He had long ago given up theorizing about the matter. It seemed just as impossible that any one person in the house could have done all the things as that any person out of the house could have done them. Sometimes, so befuddled and bamboozled did he feel, he was almost tempted to believe that the place was haunted. If not, he was being made a fool of. Either conclusion was intolerable. It was tacitly understood in the household that the occurrences were not to be talked of outside. Curtis discussed the matter only with Mr. Sheldon, who spent a good deal of time with his books in the manse, sometimes reading there till late at night. But all his talks and guesses and researches left him just exactly where he was at first. He developed insomnia and couldn't sleep even when the house was quiet. He was under an obsession. Mr. Sheldon noticed it and advised him to find another boarding place. Curtis knew he could not do this. He could not leave Lucia. For by now he knew that he loved Lucia.

He had realized this one night when the banging of the big front door had aroused him from some late studies. He put his book aside and went downstairs. The door was shut but not locked as it had been when the household retired. As he tried the knob Lucia came out of the dining-room carrying a small candle. She was crying; he had never seen Lucia cry before, although once or twice he had suspected tears. Her hair hung over her shoulder in a thick braid. It made her look like a child – a tired, broken-hearted child. All at once he knew what she meant to him.

"What is the matter, Lucia?" he asked gently, unconscious that for the first time he had used her Christian name.

"Look," sobbed Lucia, holding the candle up in the dining-room doorway.

At first Curtis could not exactly understand what had happened. The room seemed to be a perfect maze of . . . of . . . what was it? Coloured yarns! They crossed and recrossed it. They were wound in and out of the furniture, around the chair rungs, about the table legs. The room looked like a huge spider's web.

"My afghan," said Lucia. "My new afghan! I finished it yesterday. It's completely ravelled out. I've been working at it since New Year's. Oh, I'm a fool to mind this, so many worse things have happened. But I have so little time to do anything like that. And the malice of it! What is it that hates me so?"

She broke away from Curtis' outstretched hand and ran upstairs, still sobbing. Curtis stood rather dazedly in the hall, looking after her until she disappeared. He knew now that he had loved her from their first meeting. He could have laughed at himself for his long blindness. Love her . . . of course he loved her . . . he had known it the moment he had seen tears in her brave, sweet eyes. Lucia in tears – tears that he had no right or power to wipe away. The thought was unbearable.

Alice called to him as he passed her door. He unlocked it and went in. A fresh, sweet wind of dawn was blowing through her window and a faint light was breaking behind the church.

"I've had a bad night," said Alice, "but it has been quiet, hasn't it, except for that door?"

"Quiet enough," said Curtis grimly. "Our ghost has amused itself with a nice quiet job – ravelling out Lucia's afghan. Miss Harper, I am at my wit's end."

"It must be Julia who has done this. She was very sulky all day yesterday. Lucia had scolded her about something. This is her revenge."

"I don't believe it is Julia. But I'm going to make one last effort. You said once, I remember, that an idea had occurred to you. What idea?"

Alice made a restless gesture with her beautiful hands.

"And I also said that it was too incredible to be put in words. I repeat that. If it has never occurred to you yourself, I will not utter it."

He could not move her and he went back to his own room with his head in a whirl.

"There are only two things I am sure of," he said as he watched the sun rise. "Twice two are four. And I'm going to marry Lucia."

Lucia, it developed, had a different opinion. When Curtis asked her to be his wife, she told him that it was impossible.

"Why? Don't you . . . can't you care for me?"

Lucia looked at him with a deepening of colour.

"I could – yes, I could. There is no use in denying that. One should not deny the truth. But as things are, I cannot marry. I cannot leave Alice and Alec."

"Alice could come with us. I would be very glad to have such a woman in our home. She is a constant inspiration to me."

"No. Such an arrangement would not be fair to you."

It was useless to plead or argue, though Curtis did both. Lucia was a Field. So Alice told him when he carried his woes to her.

"And to think . . . if it were not for me!" she said bitterly.

"It isn't only you. I've told her how glad I would be to have you with us. It's just as much Alec . . . and those infernal spooks!"

"S'sh . . . don't let Elder Kirk hear you," said Alice

whimsically. "I'm sorry, Mr. Burns . . . sorry for you and Lucia. I'm afraid she won't change her mind. We Fields do not when we've once made it up. Your only hope is to run the ghost to earth."

Nobody, it seemed, could do that. Curtis bitterly owned himself defeated. Two weeks of moonlit and peaceful nights followed. When the dark nights returned, the manifestations began anew. This time Curtis seemed to have become the object of the "ha'nts' " hatred. Repeatedly he found his sheets wet or well sanded when he got in between them at night; twice on going to don his ministerial suit on Sunday mornings he found all the buttons cut off; and the special anniversary service he had prepared with such care vanished from his desk Saturday night before he had time to memorize it. As a result he made rather a mess of things before a crowded church next day and was young and human enough to feel bitterly about it.

"You'd better go away, Mr. Burns," said Alice. "That is unselfish advice if any ever was given, for I shall miss you more than I can say. But you must. You haven't Lucia's phlegm or Alec's stubbornness, or even my faith in a locked door. They won't leave you alone now they've begun. Look how they've persecuted Lucia for years."

"I can't go away and leave her in this predicament," said Curtis stubbornly.

"What good can you do? You've tried . . . failed. I really think you'd have a better chance with Lucia if you went away. She'd find out what you really meant to her then – if you mean anything."

"Sometimes I think I don't," said Curtis passionately.

"Oh, yes, you do. But, Mr. Burns, don't expect Lucia to love you as you love her. The Fields don't. They're rather cool-blooded, you know. Look at Alec. He's fond of Edna, he'd like to marry her, but he doesn't lose sleep or appetite over it. Neither would Lucia. She'd make a dear little wife for you, faithful and devoted, but she won't break her heart over it if she can't marry you. You don't like to hear that. You want to be loved more romantically and passionately. But it's true."

There were times when Curtis thought that Alice was about right in her summing up of Lucia. To his ardent nature Lucia did seem too composed and resigned. But the thought of giving her up was torture.

She's like little red rose just out of reach. I must reach her, he thought.

He could not bear the thought of going away. He would see her so seldom then, for he knew she would elude his visits. Gossip was already busy with their names, and Mr. Sheldon had hinted disapprobation. Curtis ignored his hints and was a trifle brusque with the old man. He knew Mr. Sheldon had never approved of his boarding at Long Alec's.

His perplexity suddenly received a new twist. One night, returning home late from a meeting in a distant section, he stood for a long time at his dormer window before going to bed. He had found a treasured volume on his desk – a book his dead mother had given him on a boyish birthday – with half its leaves cut to pieces and ink spilled over the rest. He was angry with the impatient anger of a man who is buffeted by the blows of an unseen antagonist. The situation was growing more intolerable every day. Perhaps he had better go, although he hated to admit defeat. Lucia didn't care for him; she avoided him; he hadn't been able to exchange a word with her for days except at the table. From something Long Alec had said, Curtis knew that Lucia wished him to find another domicile.

"It would be a bit easier for her, I guess," said Long Alec. "She worries over things so."

Well, if she wanted to get rid of him! Curtis was petulant just then. He was a failure in everything; his sermons were beginning to be flat; he was losing interest in his work; he wished he had never come to Lancaster.

He leaned out of his window to inhale the scented summer air. The night was rather ghostly. The trees about the lawn put on the weird shapes trees can assume in dim, uncertain light such as clouded moonlight. Cool, elusive night smells came up from the garden. He felt soothed, cheered. After all, there must be some way out. He was young; the world was good just because Lucia was in it. He wouldn't give up yet a while.

The moon suddenly broke out between the parting clouds. Curtis found himself looking through the opposite dormer window into the spare-room, the blind of which happened to be up. The room was quite clear to him in the sudden radiance, and in the mirror on the wall Curtis saw a face looking at him – sharply outlined against the darkness of the doorway which framed it. He saw it only for a moment before the clouds again swallowed up the moon, but he recognized it. The face was Lucia's. He thought nothing of it . . . then. Doubtless she had heard some noise and had gone to the spare-room to investigate. But when at breakfast the next morning he asked her what had disturbed her she looked at him blankly.

"When you went to the spare-room door last night," he explained.

"I wasn't near the spare-room last night," she said. "I went to bed very early – I was tired – and slept soundly all night."

She rose as she spoke and went out. She did not return, nor did she make any further reference to the matter. Why had she . . . lied? An ugly word, but Curtis could not soften it. He had seen her. True, it was but for a moment in the moonlit mirror, but he could not be mistaken. It was Lucia's face . . . and she had lied to him!

Curtis decided to leave Long Alec's. He would board at the station, which would be inconvenient, but go he must. He was sick at heart. He no longer wanted to find out who or what the Field ghost was. He was afraid to find out.

Lucia turned a little pale when he told her, but said nothing. Long Alec, in his usual easy-going fashion, agreed that it would be best. Alice approved with tear-filled eyes.

"Of course you must go. The situation here is impossible for you. But oh, what shall I do?"

"I'll come to see you often, dear."

"It won't be the same. You don't know what you've meant to me, Curtis. You don't mind my calling you Curtis, do you? You seem like a young cousin or nephew or something like that. You're a dear boy. I ought to be glad you're going. This accursed house is no place for you. When do you go?"

"In four days, after I come back from Presbytery."

Curtis missed his regular train after the meeting of Presbytery – missed it hunting in the bookstores for a book Alice wanted to see – and came back on the owl train that dumped him off at Glen Donald at one o'clock. It did not stop as a rule, but he knew the conductor, who was an obliging man. Henry Kildare got off too. He had expected to have to go on to Rexbridge, not having the advantage of a pull with the conductor.

"It's only three miles, I can hoof it easy," he said as they left the platform.

"Might as well come to Long Alec's for the rest of the night," suggested Curtis.

"Not me," said Henry emphatically. "I wouldn't stay

another night in that house for half my pile. I hear you're getting out, preacher. Wise boy!"

Curtis did not answer. He was not desirous of any company on his walk, much less Henry Kildare's. He strode along in moody silence, unheeding Henry's stream of conversation. It was a night of high winds and heavy clouds, with outbursts of brilliant moonlight between them. Curtis felt wretched, hopeless, discouraged. He had failed to solve the mystery he had tackled so cocksurely; he had failed to win his love or rescue her; he had . . .

"Yes, I'm going to get out of this and hike back to the coast," Henry was saying. "Ain't no sense in my hanging round Glen Donald any longer. I can't get the girl I want."

So Henry had love troubles of his own.

"Sorry," said Curtis automatically.

"Sorry! It's a case to be sorry. Preacher, I don't mind talking to you about it. You seem like a human being and you're a mighty good friend to Alice."

"Alice!" Curtis was amazed. "Do you mean . . . is it Miss Harper?"

"Sure thing. Never was anyone else. Preacher, I've always worshipped the ground that girl walked on. Years ago when I was working for old Winthrop, I was crazy mad about her. She never knew it. Didn't think I could ever get her, of course. She was one of the aristocratic Fields and I was a hired boy. But I never forgot her, never could get interested in anybody else. When I struck luck in the Yukon, I says to myself, 'Now I'm going straight back to Glen Donald and if Alice Harper isn't married yet, I'll see if she'll have me.' You see, I'd never heard from the place for years, never heard of Alice's accident. Preacher, it was an awful jolt when I came home and found her like she is. And the worst of it is, I'm just as fond of her as ever – too fond of her to take up with anyone else. Since I can't get Alice, I don't want anyone. And me wanting to marry, with lots of cash to give my woman the dandiest house at the coast! Hard luck, ain't it?"

Curtis agreed that it was. Privately he thought it did not matter much, as far as Henry Kildare was concerned, whether Alice could or could not marry. Surely she could never care for this brusque, boastful man. But there was real feeling in Kildare's voice, and Curtis felt very sympathetic just then with anyone who lived in vain.

"What's that in the Field orchard?" demanded Henry in a startled tone.

Curtis saw it at the same moment. The moon had burst out and the orchard was day-clear in its radiance. A slender light-clad figure stood among the trees.

"Good Lord, it's the spook," said Henry.

As he spoke, the figure began to run. Curtis voicelessly bounded over the fence in pursuit. After a second's hesitation Henry followed him.

"No preacher is going where I dassn't follow him," he muttered.

He caught up with Curtis just as the other rounded the corner of the house and the object of their pursuit darted through the front door. Curtis had a sickening flash of conviction that the solution of the mystery which had seemed within his grasp had again evaded him. Then a wild gust of wind swept through the hall of the house; the heavy door clanged shut with a bang; and caught in it hard and fast was the skirt of the fleeing figure's garment.

Curtis bounded up the steps, clutched the dress, flung open the door, confronted the woman inside.

"You! You!" he cried in a terrible voice. "You!"

ALICE HARPER looked at him, her white face distorted with rage and hatred.

"You dog," she hissed venomously.

"It's been you . . . you?" gasped Curtis. "You . . . devil!"

"Easy on, preacher." Henry Kildare closed the door softly. "Remember, you're speaking to a lady. Don't let's have too much of a fuss. It might disturb the folks. Let's go in the parlour here and talk it over quiet like."

Curtis did as he was told. In the daze of the moment he would probably have done anything he was told. Henry followed and closed the door. Alice confronted them defiantly. Amid all Curtis' bewilderment one idea came out clearly in his confusion of thought. How much she looked like Lucia! In daylight the difference in colouring kept the resemblance hidden; in the moonlit room it was clearly seen.

Curtis was shaken with the soul-sickness of a horrible disillusionment. He tried to say something, but Henry Kildare interrupted.

"Preacher, you'd better let me handle this. You've had a bit of a shock. Sit down there."

Curtis sat down. Kildare seemed suddenly changed into a quiet, powerful fellow whom it would be well to obey.

"Now, Alice, you sit down too." He wheeled an easy chair out from the wall and put her gently in it. She sat gazing at both of them, a beautiful woman in the moonlight, the pale blue silk wrapper she wore falling about her slim form in graceful folds. Curtis wished he might wake up. This was the worst nightmare he had ever had.

Henry leaned forward from the sofa.

"Now, Alice, tell us all about it. You have to, you know. Then we'll see what can be done. The game's up, you know."

"Yes, I know," Alice laughed hysterically. "But I've had five glorious years. Oh, I've ruled them – from my sickbed I've ruled them. I pulled the strings and they danced – my puppets. Black Lucia and condescending Alec, and that love-sick boy there."

"Yes, it must have been fun," agreed Henry. "But why, Alice?"

"I was sick of being patronized and snubbed and condescended to," said Alice bitterly. "That's what my youth was. I was just the poor relation. Why, when they had company I had to wait and eat afterwards. I was not good enough to talk to their company. No, I was only good enough to lay their table and cook their food. I hated every one of them, Lucia most of all. She was their petted darling. Her father wouldn't let the winds of heaven visit her too roughly. I slept in a dark, stuffy back room. She had the sunny look-out. She was four years younger than I was but she thought she was my superior in everything. They sent her away to school. No one ever thought of educating me, though I was far cleverer than she was."

"Clever, yes," agreed Henry with curious emphasis. Curtis felt that he should not let Alice Harper say such things of Lucia, but a temporary paralysis seemed to have descended upon him. It was a dream . . . a nightmare . . . one couldn't . . . Alice went on.

"Uncle Winthrop was always saying sarcastic things to me. I remember them, every one. Do you remember them, Henry?"

"Yes. The old chap had a habit that way. Didn't mean much by it. I did think he wasn't so nice to you as he might have been. But your aunt was good to you."

"She slapped me one day before company. I hated her after that. I never spoke a word to her for ten weeks. And she never noticed it. One day, when I was nineteen, she said, 'I was married at your age.' Whose fault was it I was not married? I hated going about with the young people. I knew they looked down on me."

"Nonsense," said Henry. "You just imagined that."

"Laura Gregor taunted me once with living on charity," retorted Alice, her voice shaking. "If I had been dressed like Lucia, Roy Major would have noticed me. But I was shabby . . . dowdy. I . . . I loved him . . . I would have done anything to win him."

"I remember how jealous I was of him," said Henry reflectively.

Alice swept on as if she had not heard him.

"When Marian Lister told me she and Roy were going to be married and asked me to be her bridesmaid, I could have killed her. But I consented. She should not suspect and triumph over me. I thought my heart would break the day of the wedding. I prayed that God would give me the power to avenge my suffering on somebody."

"You poor kid," said Henry.

"That was my life for twenty years. Then I fell from the loft. I was paralyzed at first. For months I couldn't move. Then I found that I could. But I wouldn't. An idea came to me. I had found a way to punish them – rule them. Oh, I laughed when I thought of it."

Alice laughed again. Curtis remembered he had never heard her laugh before. There was an unpleasant something in it which reminded him of the haunted nights.

"My idea worked well. I was afraid I could not deceive the doctors. But it was easy, so easy. I could never have believed it would be so easy to fool supposedly intelligent people. How I laughed to myself as they consulted over me with solemn faces! I never complained. I must be patient, saintly, heroic. Uncle Winthrop had several specialists. He had to spend some money at last on his despised niece. They were all easy to hoodwink, except Dr. Clifford. I felt that he was vaguely suspicious. So I would have no more doctors. The household waited on me hand and foot. Oh, how I gloried in feeling such power over them, I, whom they had disdained. I had never been of any importance to them. I was the most important person in the house now. Lucia came home to wait on me.

She thought it her 'duty.' Lucia always took herself very seriously."

Alice shot a malicious glance at Curtis.

"People said my patience was angelic. Mr. Sheldon said I was a saint. They began to call me the angel of Glen Donald. Once I did not speak a word for four days. The household was terribly alarmed. And I made Lucia rub my back and shoulders every night for half an hour. It was excellent exercise for her and amused me. Some days I pretended to suffer horribly. Had the room darkened, moaned occasionally for hours. I had those attacks whenever I thought Lucia needed a little discipline. Then I discovered that Alec wanted to marry Edna Pollock. This didn't suit me. Lucia would be free to go then and Edna would not wait on me properly. Besides, a Pollock was not good enough for a Field. Then the idea of playing spook came to me."

"Now we're coming to the interesting part," said Henry. "How did you manage those stunts, locked in your room?"

"There's a closet in my room, and its back wall is not plastered. It's merely a partition of boards between the closet and the alcove where the garret stairs are. When I was a child I discovered that two of those boards could be easily and noiselessly slipped back. I kept it a secret, liking to know something nobody else of all the wise Fields knew. It was very easy to slip out and in through that space. Nobody ever suspected me with my locked door."

"But how could you get out of the garret? There's only one way up and down."

"Haven't I told you people were easy to fool? There's a big chest up there supposed to be packed full of quilts, my quilts. Old Grandmother Field left them to me, so nobody ever disturbed them. The chest isn't really full. There's quite a space between the quilts and the back. I used to slip in there. Nobody could ever get up the garret stairs without my hearing them. Two of the steps creaked. I never stepped on those. When I heard anyone coming I shut the lid and pulled one of those thick folded quilts over my head. Dozens of people lifted the lid of that chest, saw it apparently full of woollen quilts, and put the lid down again. Mr. Burns there did it twice. I was in it laughing at him. Oh, they were all such fools. But I was clever – you can't deny that I was a good actress. When I was a girl I wanted to go on the stage and Uncle Winthrop put his foot down on it contemptuously. 'Do you suppose you could act, girl?' he jeered. I wonder what he would think now. It was amusing to terrify people with his laugh. I could mimic it and his voice to the life, his and Anna Marsh's."

"You were always a good mimic," agreed Henry. "But how did you rock the cradle after it was taken out?"

"I never touched the cradle. I made a rocking noise by wriggling a loose board on the floor. I could easily manipulate it without getting out of the chest. Of course I took chances. Dozens of times I was almost caught, but never quite. I didn't often play tricks on moonlight nights. Once for fun I climbed a ladder and walked along the flat ridge-roof of the barn. But that was too dangerous. I was seen by some passer-by. Sometimes when people watched I did nothing. At other times it amused me to outwit them. Generally I slid down the bannister. It was quieter and quicker. I never made any noise below stairs until I was through for the night. I never did anything without planning out a way of escape beforehand. There were plenty of hiding places if I could not get back to the closet in time. It was your old fiddle I played on, Henry. I hid it behind the closet boards when you went away. When people began to suspect Lucia, I raved so vehemently that they thought I protested too much."

"What about those bloody footprints and the curses?" asked Henry.

"Oh, the Fields kept so many hens they never counted them. The curses cost me some pains of composition. I found some very effective ones in the Bible. 'There shall not be an old man in thine house.' That made Alec think he was going to die young."

"Was it you cut Maggie Elgin's hair?"

"Of course. For once she forgot to lock her door. I wanted Julia back. One night I thought I was caught at last. I thought you saw the reflection of my face in the spare-room window."

She gestured towards Curtis, but he did not look up. A spark of malice came into her face.

"My greatest amusement was to worry Lucia. One morning I pretended to feel feverish and Lucia put a thermometer under my tongue. When she went out I stuck it into a cup of tea on my tray and slipped it back when I heard her coming. My temperature was a hundred and six. Lucia rushed in great alarm to phone for the doctor. When he came he declared my temperature was normal. Lucia believed she had made a foolish mistake and her face burned. Oh, the Field pride got a bit of a humbling then. When I cut down the birch tree she loved, every blow was a delight to me."

Still Curtis made no sign. Alice continued to address him.

"I was glad when you came here to board. I liked a young minister. I was so tired of old Mr. Sheldon. As long as his wife lived, there was some amusement in making him worship at my shrine, for old as they were she was jealous of his devotion to me. When nobody cared how much he reverenced my saintliness, I didn't want his reverence. And I was not afraid of you. I knew you would be just as easily fooled as the rest. But I decided that I would keep quiet for a while so that you would not become disgusted and leave us. It was very amusing to talk seriously to you about our ghosts. And then you fell in love with my lady cousin and I decided that you must go. I knew Lucia was secretly crazy about you, though, like all the Fields, she can hide her feelings very successfully. And yet, do you know, when you told me you were going, my tears of regret were very real ones. You have no idea how much I really liked you."

Alice laughed again. Her eyes were sparkling in the moonlight.

"How did you manage the telephone business?" asked Henry. "I was in the hall when it was ringing. There was no one near it."

"Oh, I had nothing to do with that. Some boys along the line must have been playing a trick for the fun of it. They often do, but it's never noticed in a house that isn't supposed to be haunted. It helped things on nicely. And I didn't take Alec's money. Some of the Marsh gang did that without a doubt. Not Julia perhaps, but some of them. Neither did I set fire to the binder-house. Likely it was some prowling tramp – anyway, I know nothing of it."

"Come now, I'm glad to hear that," said Henry in a tone of relief. "Somehow, that kinder stuck in my crop. Now I see my way. And you really can walk as well as anyone?"

"Of course I can. I've had enough exercise at nights to keep well in practice walking. Well, what are you going to do, gentlemen, my judges? Tell silly Alec and little black Lucia, I suppose, and have me turned out on the road. I wouldn't live here now even if they'd let me. I'd starve first."

"Why, no, you ain't going to starve," said Henry soothingly. "The preacher here can tell Alec and Lucia – I'm not hankering for that job. It's you I'm concerned with. I'm going to marry you and take you away. That's what I came home to do. I s'posed I couldn't when I found you were bed-rid. But since you ain't, what's to hinder?"

"Do you . . . want me . . . now?" said Alice slowly.

"By the nine gods I do," said Henry emphatically. "I don't care what you've done, you're the girl I've wanted all my life. I'm going to have you. I'll take you out to the coast – you need never see any of the folks round here again."

"Will you take me away from here tonight . . . now?" demanded Alice.

"Sure," said Henry. "We'll go right to the station. It'll be time for the early train when we get there. We'll go into Rexbridge and be married. That's all right, preacher, ain't it?"

"I . . . suppose so," said poor Curtis.

Henry bent forward and tapped Alice gently on the arm.

"It's settled. Come along. I'll house and dress you like a queen, but listen, my girl, listen. There's to be no more tricks . . . no more tricks with Henry Kildare. Understand?"

"I . . . understand," said Alice.

"Go upstairs and get ready. Got anything to wear besides that wrapper?"

"I have my old navy blue suit and hat," said Alice meekly.

"Well, preacher, what have you got to say?" demanded Henry when she had gone.

"Nothing," said Curtis.

Henry nodded. "Best line to take, I guess. This is one of the things there don't seem to be any language to fit, and that's a fact."

The door closed upon Henry Kildare and Alice Harper. Curtis had not spoken a word even when Alice halted for a moment as she passed him in the hall.

"Hate me . . . hate me," she said passionately. "I don't mind your hate but I won't have your tolerance."

Mr. Sheldon came up the next night, having heard the incredible rumour that flew like flame through Glen Donald. He listened to Curtis' story and shook his head.

"Well, I suppose after a time I'll get this through my noodle and accept it. Just at present I can't believe it, that's all. We've dreamed it."

"I think we all feel like that," said Curtis. "Alec and Lucia have gone about in a helpless daze all day."

"What hurts me worst," said Mr. Sheldon tremulously, "is her . . . her hypocrisy. She pretended to be so interested in our work."

"That may not have been hypocrisy, Mr. Sheldon. It may have been a real side of her nature."

"That is incredible."

"Nothing is incredible with abnormality. Remember, you cannot judge her as you would a normal person. She has never been normal – her story proves that. She was hampered by heredity. Her father and grandfather were dipsomaniacs. You can't reform your ancestors. The shock of repressed feeling at the wedding of the man she loved evidently played havoc with her soul."

"Poor Henry Kildare."

Curtis grinned boyishly.

"Not so poor. He's got the woman he always wanted and, take my word for it, Mr. Sheldon, he'll manage her. Besides, marriage and a home and wealth – all she craved – may have a very salutary effect on her mind. But she'll never come back to show off her diamonds in Glen Donald."

When Curtis came back from the gate in the twilight, he met Lucia in the porch. She would have slipped away but he caught her exultantly.

"Sweetheart, you'll listen to me now . . . you will . . . you will."

Jock was coming across the lawn. Lucia twisted herself from Curtis' grasp and ran. But before she ran, Curtis heard the most charming sound in the world – the little yielding laugh of a woman caught by her lover.

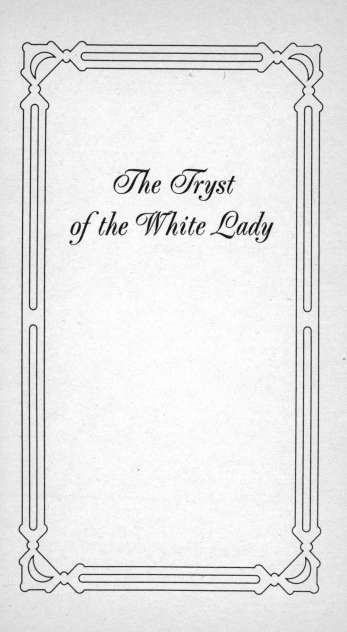

*The Tryst
of the White Lady*

"I WISHT YE'D GIT MARRIED, Roger," said Catherine Ames. "I'm gitting too old to work – seventy last April – and who's going to look after ye when I'm gone. Git married, b'y – git married."

Roger Temple winced. His aunt's harsh, disagreeable voice always jarred horribly on his sensitive nerves. He was fond of her after a fashion, but always that voice made him wonder if there could be anything harder to endure.

Then he gave a bitter little laugh.

"Who'd have me, Aunt Catherine?" he asked.

Catherine Ames looked at him critically across the supper table. She loved him in her way, with all her heart, but she was not in the least blind to his defects. She did not mince matters with herself or with other people. Roger was a sallow, plain-featured fellow, small and insignificant looking. And, as if this were not bad enough, he walked with a slight limp and had one thin shoulder a little higher than the other – "Jarback" Temple he had been called in school, and the name still clung to him. To be sure, he had very fine grey eyes, but their dreamy brilliance gave his dull face an uncanny look which girls did not like, and so made matters rather worse than better. Of course looks didn't matter so much in the case of a man; Steve Millar was homely enough, and all marked up with smallpox to boot, yet he had got for wife the prettiest and smartest girl in South Bay. But Steve was rich. Roger was poor and always would be. He worked his stony little farm, from which his father and grandfather had wrested a fair living, after a fashion, but Nature had not cut him out for a successful farmer. He hadn't the strength for it and his heart wasn't in it. He'd rather be hanging over a book. Catherine secretly thought Roger's matrimonial chances very poor, but it would not do to discourage the b'y. What he needed was spurring on.

"Ye'll git someone if ye don't fly too high," she announced loudly and cheerfully. "Thar's always a gal or two here and thar that's glad to marry for a home. 'Tain't no use for *you* to be settin' your thoughts on anyone young and pretty. Ye wouldn't git her and ye'd be worse off if ye did. Your grandfather married for looks, and a nice useless wife he got – sick half her time. Git a good strong girl that ain't afraid of work, that'll hold things together when ye're reading po'try – that's as much as you kin expect. And the sooner the better. I'm done – last winter's rheumatiz has about finished *me*. An' we can't afford hired help."

Roger felt as if his raw, quivering soul were being seared. He looked at his aunt curiously – at her broad, flat face with the mole on the end of her dumpy nose, the bristling hairs on her chin, the wrinkled yellow neck, the pale, protruding eyes, the coarse, good-humoured mouth. She was so extremely ugly – and he had seen her across the table all his life. For twenty-five years he had looked at her so. Must he continue to go on looking at ugliness in the shape of a wife all the rest of his life – he, who worshipped beauty in everything?

"Did my mother look like you, Aunt Catherine?" he asked abruptly.

His aunt stared – and snorted. Her snort was meant to express kindly amusement, but it sounded like derision and contempt.

"Yer ma wasn't so humly as me," she said cheerfully, "but she wan't no beauty either. None of the Temples was ever better lookin' than was necessary. We was *workers*. Yer pa wa'n't bad looking. You're humlier than either of 'em. Some ways ye take after yer grandma – though *she* was counted pretty at one time. She was yaller and spindlin' like you, and you've got her eyes. What yer so int'rested in yer ma's looks all at once fer?"

"I was wondering," said Roger coolly, "if Father ever looked at her across the table and wished she were prettier."

Catherine giggled. Her giggle was ugly and disagreeable like everything else about her – everything except a certain odd, loving, loyal old heart buried deep in her bosom, for the sake of which Roger endured the giggle and all the rest.

"Dessay he did – dessay he did. Men al'ays has a hankerin' for good looks. But ye've got to cut yer coat 'cording to yer cloth. As for yer poor ma, she didn't live long enough to git as ugly as me. When I come here to keep house for yer pa, folks said as it wouldn't be long 'fore he married me. *I* wouldn't a-minded. But yer pa never hinted it. S'pose he'd had enough of ugly women likely."

Catherine snorted amiably again. Roger got up – he couldn't endure any more just then. He must escape.

"Now you think over what I've said," his aunt called after him. "Ye've gotter git a wife soon, however ye manage it. 'Twon't be so hard if ye're reasonable. Don't stay out as late as ye did last night. Ye coughed all night. Where was ye – down at the shore?"

"No," said Roger, who always answered her questions even when he hated to. "I was down at Aunt Isabel's grave."

"Till eleven o'clock! Ye ain't wise! I dunno what hankering ye have after that unchancy place. *I* ain't been near it for twenty year. I wonder ye ain't scairt. What'd ye think ye'd do if ye saw her ghost?"

Catherine looked curiously at Roger. She was very superstitious and she believed firmly in ghosts, and saw no absurdity in her question.

"I wish I *could* see it," said Roger, his great eyes flashing. He believed in ghosts too, at least in Isabel Temple's ghost. His uncle had seen it; his grandfather had seen it;

he believed he would see it – the beautiful, bewitching, mocking, luring ghost of lovely Isabel Temple.

"Don't wish such stuff," said Catherine. "Nobody ain't never the same after they've seen her."

"Was Uncle different?" Roger had come back into the kitchen and was looking curiously at his aunt.

"Diff'rent? He was another man. He didn't even *look* the same. Sich eyes! Al'ays looking past ye at something behind ye. They'd give anyone creeps. He never had any notion of flesh-and-blood women after that – said a man wouldn't, after seeing Isabel. His life was plumb ruined. Lucky he died young. I hated to be in the same room with him – he wa'n't canny, that was all there was to it. *You* keep away from that grave – *you* don't want to look odder than ye are by nature. And when ye git married, ye'll have to give up roamin' about half the night in graveyards. A wife wouldn't put up with it, as I've done."

"I'll never get as good a wife as you, Aunt Catherine," said Roger with a little whimsical smile that gave him the look of an amused gnome.

"Dessay you won't. But someone ye have to have. Why'n't ye try 'Liza Adams. She *might* have ye – she's gittin' on."

"'Liza . . . Adams!"

"That's what I said. Ye needn't repeat it – 'Liza . . . Adams – 's if I'd mentioned a hippopotamus. I git out of patience with ye. I b'lieve in my heart ye think ye ought to git a wife that'd look like a picter."

"I do, Aunt Catherine. That's just the kind of wife I want – grace and beauty and charm. Nothing less than that will ever content me."

ROGER LAUGHED BITTERLY again and went out. It was sunset. There was no work to do that night except to milk the cows, and his little home boy could do that. He felt a glad freedom. He put his hand in his pocket to see if his beloved Wordsworth was there and then he took his way across the fields, under a sky of purple and amber, walking quickly despite his limp. He wanted to get to some solitary place where he could forget Aunt Catherine and her abominable suggestions and escape into the world of dreams where he habitually lived and where he found the loveliness he had not found nor could hope to find in his real world.

Roger's mother had died when he was three and his father when he was eight. His little, old, bedridden grandmother had lived until he was twelve. He had loved her passionately. She had not been pretty in his remembrance – a tiny, shrunken, wrinkled thing – but she had beautiful grey eyes that never grew old and a soft, gentle voice – the only woman's voice he had ever heard with pleasure. He was very critical as regards women's voices and very sensitive to them. Nothing hurt him quite so much as an unlovely voice – not even unloveliness of face. Her death had left him desolate. She was the only human being who had ever understood him. He could never, he thought, have got through his tortured school days without her. After she died he would not go to school. He was not in any sense educated. His father and grandfather had been illiterate men and he had inherited their underdeveloped brain cells. But he loved poetry and read all he could get of it. It overlaid his primitive nature with a curious iridescence of fancy and furnished him with ideals and hungers his environment could never satisfy. He loved beauty in everything. Moonrises hurt him with their loveliness and he could sit for hours gazing at a white narcissus – much to his aunt's exasperation. He was solitary by nature. He felt horribly alone in a crowded building but never in the woods or in the wild places along the shore. It was because of this that his aunt could not get him to go to church – which was a horror to her orthodox soul. He told her he would like to go to church if it were empty but he could not bear it when it was full – full of smug, ugly people. Most people, he thought, were ugly – though not so ugly as he was – and ugliness made him sick with repulsion. Now and then he saw a pretty girl at whom he liked to look but he never saw one that wholly pleased him. To him, the homely, crippled, poverty-stricken Roger Temple whom they all would have scorned, there was always a certain subtle something wanting, and the lack of it kept him heartwhole. He knew that this probably saved him from much suffering, but for all that he regretted it. He wanted to love, even vainly; he wanted to experience this passion of which the poets sang so much. Without it he felt he lacked the key to a world of wonder. He even tried to fall in love; he went to church for several Sundays and sat where he could see beautiful Elsa Carey. She was lovely – it gave him pleasure to look at her; the gold of her hair was so bright and living; the pink of her cheek so pure, the curve of her neck so flawless, the lashes of her eyes so dark and silken. But he looked at her as at a picture. When he tried to think and dream of her, it bored him. Besides, he knew she had a rather nasal voice. He used to laugh sarcastically to himself over Elsa's feelings if she had known how desperately he was trying to fall in love with her and failing – Elsa the queen of hearts, who believed she had only to look to reign. He gave up trying at last, but he still longed to love. He knew he would never marry; he could not marry plainness, and beauty would have none of him; but he did not want to miss everything and he had moments when he was very bitter and rebellious because he felt he must miss it forever.

He went straight to Isabel Temple's grave in the remote shore field of his farm. Isabel Temple had lived and died eighty years ago. She had been very lovely, very wilful, very fond of playing with the hearts of men. She had married William Temple, the brother of his great-grandfather, and as she stood in her white dress beside her bridegroom, at the conclusion of the wedding ceremony, a jilted lover, crazed by despair, had entered the house and shot her dead. She had been buried in the shore field, where a square space had been dyked off in the centre for a burial lot because the church was then so far away. With the passage of years the lot had grown up so thickly with fir and birch and wild cherry that it looked like a compact grove. A winding path led through it to its heart where Isabel Temple's grave was, thickly overgrown with long, silken, pale green grass. Roger hurried along the path and sat down on the big grey boulder by the grave, looking about him with a long breath of delight. How lovely – and witching – and unearthly it was here. Little ferns were growing in the hollows and cracks of the big boulder where clay had lodged. Over Isabel Temple's crooked, lichened gravestone hung a young wild cherry in its delicate bloom. Above it, in a little space of sky left by the slender tree tops, was a young moon. It was too dark here after all to read Wordsworth, but that did not matter. The place, with its moist air, its tang of fir balsam, was like a perfumed room where a man might dream dreams and see visions. There was a soft murmur of wind in the boughs over him, and the faraway moan of the sea on the bar crept in. Roger surrendered himself utterly to the charm of the place. When he entered that grove, he had left behind the realm of daylight and things known and come into the realm of shadow and mystery and enchantment. Anything might happen – anything might be true.

Eighty long years had come and gone, but Isabel Temple, thus cruelly torn from life at the moment when it had promised her most, did not even yet rest calmly in her grave; such at least was the story, and Roger believed it. It was in his blood to believe it. The Temples were a superstitious family, and there was nothing in Roger's upbringing to correct the tendency. His was not a sceptical or scientific mind. He was ignorant and poetical and credulous. He had always accepted unquestioningly the tale that Isabel Temple had been seen on earth long after the red clay was heaped over her murdered body. Her bridegroom had seen her, when he went to visit her on the eve of his second and unhappy marriage; his grandfather had seen her. His grandmother, who had told him Isabel's story, had told him this too, and believed it. She had added, with a bitterness foreign to his idea of her, that her husband had never been the same to her afterwards; his uncle had seen her – and had lived and died a haunted man. It was only to men the lovely, restless ghost appeared, and her appearance boded no good to him who saw. Roger knew this, but he had a curious longing to see her. He had never avoided her grave as others of his tribe did. He loved the spot, and he believed that some time he would see Isabel Temple there. She came, so the story went, to one in each generation of the family.

He gazed down at her sunken grave; a little wind, that came stealing along the floor of the grove, raised and swayed the long, hair-like grass on it, giving the curious suggestion of something prisoned under it trying to draw a long breath and float upward.

Then, when he lifted his eyes again, he saw her!

She was standing behind the gravestone, under the cherry tree, whose long white branches touched her head; standing there, with her head drooping a little, but looking steadily at him. It was just between dusk and dark now, but he saw her very plainly. She was dressed in white, with some filmy scarf over her head, and her hair hung in a dark heavy braid over her shoulder. Her face was small and ivory-white, and her eyes were very large and dark. Roger looked straight into them and they did something to him – drew something out of him that was never to be his again – his heart? his soul? He did not know. He only knew that lovely Isabel Temple had now come to him and that he was hers forever.

For a few moments that seemed years he looked at her – looked till the lure of her eyes drew him to his feet as a man rises in sleep-walking. As he slowly stood up, the low-hanging bough of a fir tree pushed his cap down over his face and blinded him. When he snatched it off, she was gone.

ROGER TEMPLE did not go home that night till the spring dawn was in the sky. Catherine was sleepless with anxiety about him. When she heard him come up the stairs, she opened her door and peeped out. Roger went along the hall without seeing her. His brilliant eyes stared straight before him, and there was something in his face that made Catherine steal back to her bed with a little shiver of fear. He looked like his uncle. She did not ask him, when they met at breakfast, where or how he had spent the night. He had been dreading the question and was relieved beyond measure when it was not asked. But, apart from that, he was hardly conscious of her presence. He ate and drank mechanically and voicelessly. When he had gone out, Catherine wagged her uncomely grey head ominously.

"He's bewitched," she muttered. "I know the signs. He's seen her – drat her! It's time she gave up that kind of work. Well, I dunno what to do – thar ain't anything I can do, I reckon. He'll never marry now – I'm as sure of that as of any mortal thing. He's in love with a ghost."

It had not yet occurred to Roger that he was in love. He thought of nothing but Isabel Temple – her lovely, lovely face, sweeter than any picture he had ever seen or any ideal he had dreamed, her long dark hair, her slim form and, more than all, her compelling eyes. He saw them wherever he looked – they drew him – he would have followed them to the end of the world, heedless of all else.

He longed for night, that he might again steal to the grave in the haunted grove. She might come again – who knew? He felt no fear, nothing but a terrible hunger to see her again. But she did not come that night – nor the next – nor the next. Two weeks went by and he had not seen her. Perhaps he would never see her again – the thought filled him with anguish not to be borne. He knew now that he loved her – Isabel Temple, dead for eighty years. This was love – this searing, torturing, intolerably sweet thing – this possession of body and soul and spirit. The poets had sung but weakly of it. He could tell them better if he could find words. Could other men have loved at all – could any man love those blowzy, common girls of earth? It seemed impossible – absurd. There was only one thing that could be loved – that white spirit. No wonder his uncle had died. He, Roger Temple, would soon die too. That would be well. Only the dead could woo Isabel. Meanwhile he revelled in his torment and his happiness – so madly commingled that he never knew whether he was in heaven or hell. It was beautiful – and dreadful – and wonderful – and exquisite – oh, so exquisite. Mortal love could never be so exquisite. He had never lived before – now he lived in every fibre of his being.

He was glad Aunt Catherine did not worry him with questions. He had feared she would. But she never asked any questions now and she was afraid of Roger, as she had been afraid of his uncle. She dared not ask questions. It was a thing that must not be tampered with. Who knew what she might hear if she asked him questions? She was very unhappy. Something dreadful had happened to her poor boy – he had been bewitched by that hussy – he would die as his uncle had died.

"Mebbe it's best," she muttered. "He's the last of the Temples, so mebbe she'll rest in her grave when she's killed 'em all. I dunno what she's sich a spite at *them* for – there's be more sense if she'd haunt the Mortons, seein' as a Morton killed her. Well, I'm mighty old and tired and worn out. It don't seem that it's been much use, the way I've slaved and fussed to bring that b'y up and keep things together for him – and now the ghost's got him. I might as well have let him die when he was a sickly baby."

If this had been said to Roger he would have retorted that it was worthwhile to have lived long enough to feel what he was feeling now. He would not have missed it for a score of other men's lives. He had drunk of some immortal wine and was as a god. Even if she never came again, he had seen her once, and she had taught him life's great secret in that one unforgettable exchange of eyes. She was his – his in spite of his ugliness and his crooked shoulder. No man could ever take her from him.

But she did come again. One evening, when the darkening grove was full of magic in the light of the rising yellow moon shining across the level field, Roger sat on the big boulder by the grave. The evening was very still; there was no sound save the echoes of noisy laughter that seemed to come up from the bay shore – drunken fishermen, likely as not. Roger resented the intrusion of such a sound in such a place – it was a sacrilege. When he came here to dream of her, only the loveliest of muted sounds should be heard – the faintest whisper of trees, the half-heard, half-felt moan of surf, the airiest sigh of wind. He never read Wordsworth now or any other book. He only sat there and thought of her, his great eyes alight, his pale face flushed with the wonder of his love.

She slipped through the dark boughs like a moonbeam and stood by the stone. Again he saw her quite plainly – saw and drank her in with his eyes. He did not feel surprise – something in him had known she would come again. He would not move a muscle lest he lose her as he had lost her before. They looked at each other – for how long? He did not know; and then – a horrible thing happened. Into that place of wonder and revelation and mystery reeled a hiccoughing, laughing creature, a drunken sailor from a harbour ship, with a leering face and desecrating breath.

"Oh, you're here, my dear – I thought I'd catch you yet," he said.

He caught hold of her. She screamed. Roger sprang forward and struck him in the face. In his fury of sudden rage the strength of ten seemed to animate his slender body and pass into his blow. The sailor reeled back and put up his hands. He was a coward – and even a brave man might have been daunted by that terrible white face and those blazing eyes. He backed down the path.

"Shorry – shorry," he muttered. "Didn't know she was your girl – shorry I butted in. Shentlemans never butt in – shorry – shir – shorry."

He kept repeating his ridiculous "shorry" until he was out of the grove. Then he turned and ran stumblingly across the field. Roger did not follow; he went back to Isabel Temple's grave. The girl was lying across it; he thought she was unconscious. He stooped and picked her up – she was light and small, but she was warm flesh and blood; she clung uncertainly to him for a moment and he felt her breath on his face. He did not speak – he was too sick at heart. She did not speak either. He did not think this strange until afterwards. He was incapable of thinking just then; he was dazed, wretched, lost. Presently he became aware that she was timidly pulling his arm. It seemed that she wanted him to go with her – she was evidently frightened of that brute – he must take her to safety. And then –

She moved on down the little path and he followed. Out in the moonlit field he saw her clearly. With her drooping head, her flowing dark hair, her great brown eyes, she looked like the nymph of a wood-brook, a haunter of shadows, a creature sprung from the wild. But she was mortal maid, and he – what a fool he had been! Presently he would laugh at himself, when this dazed agony should clear away from his brain. He followed her down the long field to the bay shore. Now and then she paused and looked back to see if he were coming, but she never spoke. When she reached the shore road she turned and went along it until they came to an old grey house fronting the calm grey harbour. At its gate she paused. Roger knew now who she was. Catherine had told him about her a month ago.

She was Lilith Barr, a girl of eighteen, who had come to live with her uncle and aunt. Her father had died some months before. She was absolutely deaf as the result of some accident in childhood, and she was, as his own eyes told him, exquisitely lovely in her white, haunting style. But she was not Isabel Temple; he had tricked himself – he had lived in a fool's paradise – oh, he must get away and laugh at himself. He left her at her gate, disregarding the little hand she put timidly out – but he did not laugh at himself. He went back to Isabel Temple's grave and flung himself down on it and cried like a boy. He wept his stormy, anguished soul out on it; and when he rose and went away, he believed it was forever. He thought he could never, never go there again.

CATHERINE LOOKED AT HIM curiously the next morning. He looked wretched – haggard and hollow-eyed. She knew he had not come in till the summer dawn. But he had lost the rapt, uncanny look she hated; suddenly she no longer felt afraid of him. With this, she began to ask questions again.

"What kept ye out so late again last night, b'y?" she said reproachfully.

Roger looked at her in her morning ugliness. He had not really seen her for weeks. Now she smote on his tortured senses, so long drugged with beauty, like a physical blow. He suddenly burst into a laughter that frightened her.

"Preserve's, b'y, have ye gone mad? Or," she added, "have ye seen Isabel Temple's ghost?"

"No," said Roger loudly and explosively. "Don't talk any more about that damned ghost. Nobody ever saw it. The whole story is balderdash."

He got up and went violently out, leaving Catherine aghast. Was it possible Roger had sworn? What on earth had come over the b'y? But come what had or come what would, he no longer looked *fey* – there was that much to be thankful for. Even an occasional oath was better than that. Catherine went stiffly about her dish-washing, resolving to have 'Liza Adams to supper some night.

For a week Roger lived in agony – an agony of shame and humiliation and self-contempt. Then, when the edge of his bitter disappointment wore away, he made another dreadful discovery. He still loved her and longed for her just as keenly as before. He wanted madly to see her – her flower-like face, her great, asking eyes, the sleek, braided flow of her hair. Ghost or woman – spirit or flesh – it mattered not. He could not live without her. At last his hunger for her drew him to the old grey house on the bay shore. He knew he was a fool – she would never look at him; he was only feeding the flame that must consume him. But go he must and did, seeking for his lost paradise.

He did not see her when he went in, but Mrs. Barr received him kindly and talked about her in a pleasant garrulous fashion which jarred on Roger, yet he listened greedily. Lilith, her aunt told him, had been made deaf by the accidental explosion of a gun when she was eight years old. She could not hear a sound but she could talk.

"A little, that is – not much, but enough to get along with. But she don't like talking somehow – dunno why. She's shy – and we think maybe she don't like to talk much because she can't hear her own voice. She don't ever speak except just when she has to. But she's been trained to lip-reading something wonderful – she can understand anything that's said when she can see the person that's talking. Still, it's a terrible drawback for the poor child – she's never had any real girl-life and she's dreadful sensitive and retiring. We can't get her to go out anywhere, only for lonely walks along shore by herself. We're much obliged for what you did the other night. It ain't safe for her to wander about alone as she does, but it ain't often anybody from the harbour gets up this far. She was dreadful upset about it – hasn't got over her scare yet."

When Lilith came in, her ivory-white face went scarlet all over at the sight of Roger. She sat down in a shadowy corner. Mrs. Barr got up and went out. Roger was mute; he could find nothing to say. He could have talked glibly enough to Isabel Temple's ghost in some unearthly tryst by her grave, but he could not find a word to say to this slip of flesh and blood. He felt very foolish and absurd, and very conscious of his twisted shoulder. What a fool he had been to come!

Then Lilith looked up at him – and smiled. A little shy, friendly smile. Roger suddenly saw her not as the tantalizing, unreal, mystic thing of the twilit grove, but as a little human creature, exquisitely pretty in her young-moon beauty, longing for companionship. He got up, forgetting his ugliness, and went across the room to her.

"Will you come for a walk," he said eagerly. He held out

his hand like a child; as a child she stood up and took it; like two children they went out and down the sunset shore. Roger was again incredibly happy. It was not the same happiness as had been his in that vanished fortnight; it was a homelier happiness with its feet on the earth. The amazing thing was that he felt she was happy too – happy because she was walking with *him*, "Jarback" Temple, whom no girl had even thought about. A certain secret well-spring of fancy that had seemed dry welled up in him sparklingly again.

Through the summer weeks the odd courtship went on. Roger talked to her as he had never talked to anyone. He did not find it in the least hard to talk to her, though her necessity of watching his face so closely while he talked bothered him occasionally. He felt that her intent gaze was reading his soul as well as his lips. She never talked much herself; what she did say she spoke so low that it was hardly above a whisper, but she had a voice as lovely as her face – sweet, cadenced, haunting. Roger was quite mad about her, and he was horribly afraid that he could never get up enough courage to ask her to marry him. And he was afraid that if he did, she would never consent. In spite of her shy, eager welcomes he could not believe she could care for him – for *him*. She liked him, she was sorry for him, but it was unthinkable that she, white, exquisite Lilith, could marry him and sit at his table and his hearth. He was a fool to dream of it.

To the existence of romance and glamour in which he lived, no gossip of the countryside penetrated. Yet much gossip there was, and at last it came blundering in on Roger to destroy his fairy world a second time. He came downstairs one night in the twilight, ready to go to Lilith. His aunt and an old crony were talking in the kitchen; the crony was old, and Catherine, supposing Roger was out of the house, was talking loudly in that horrible voice of hers with still more horrible zest and satisfaction.

"Yes, I'm guessing it'll be a match as ye say. Oh, the b'y's doing well. He ain't for every market, as I'm bound to admit. Ef she wan't deaf she wouldn't look at him, no doubt. But she has scads of money – they won't need to do a tap of work unless they like – and she's a good house-keeper too, her aunt tells me. She's pretty enough to suit him – he's as particular as never was – and he wan't crooked and she wan't deaf when they was born, so it's likely their children will be all right. I'm that proud when I think of the match."

Roger fled out of the house, white of face and sick of heart. He went, not to the bay shore, but to Isabel Temple's grave. He had never been there since the night when he had rescued Lilith, but now he rushed to it in his new agony. His aunt's horrible practicalities had filled him with disgust – they dragged his love in the dust of sordid things. And Lilith was rich; he had never known that – never suspected it. He could never ask her to marry him now; he must never see her again. For the second time he had lost her, and this second losing could not be borne.

He sat down on the big boulder by the grave and dropped his poor grey face in his hands, moaning in anguish. Nothing was left him, not even dreams. He hoped he could soon die.

He did not know how long he sat there – he did not know when she came. But when he lifted his miserable eyes, he saw her, sitting just a little way from him on the big stone and looking at him with something in her face that made his heart beat madly. He forgot Aunt Catherine's sacrilege – he forgot that he was a presumptuous fool. He bent forward and kissed her lips for the first time. The wonder of it loosed his bound tongue.

"Lilith," he gasped, "I love you."

She put her hand into his and nestled closer to him.

"I thought you would have told me that long ago," she said.

White Magic

NE SEPTEMBER AFTERNOON in the year of grace 1840 Avery and Janet Sparhallow were picking apples in their Uncle Daniel Sparhallow's big orchard. It was an afternoon of mellow sunshine; about them, beyond the orchard, were old harvest fields, mellowly bright and serene, and beyond the fields the sapphire curve of the St. Lawrence Gulf was visible through the groves of spruce and birch. There was a soft whisper of wind in the trees, and the pale purple asters that feathered the orchard grass swayed gently towards each other. Janet Sparhallow, who loved the outdoor world and its beauty, was, for the time being at least, very happy, as her little brown face, with its fine, satiny skin, plainly showed. Avery Sparhallow did not seem so happy. She worked rather abstractedly and frowned oftener than she smiled.

Avery Sparhallow was conceded to be a beauty, and had no rival in Burnley Beach. She was very pretty, with the obvious, indisputable prettiness of rich black hair, vivid, certain colour, and laughing, brilliant eyes. Nobody ever called Janet a beauty, or even thought her pretty. She was only seventeen – five years younger than Avery – and was rather lanky and weedy, with a rope of straight dark-brown hair, long, narrow, shining brown eyes and very black lashes, and a crooked, clever little mouth. She had visitations of beauty when excited, because then she flushed deeply, and colour made all the difference in the world to her; but she had never happened to look in the glass when excited, so that she had never seen herself beautiful; and hardly anybody else had ever seen her so, because she was always too shy and awkward and tongue-tied in company to feel excited over anything. Yet very little could bring that transforming flush to her face: a wind off the gulf, a sudden glimpse of blue upland, a

287

flame-red poppy, a baby's laugh, a certain footstep. As for Avery Sparhallow, she never got excited over anything – not even her wedding dress, which had come from Charlottetown that day, and was incomparably beyond anything that had ever been seen in Burnley Beach before. For it was made of an apple-green silk, sprayed over with tiny rosebuds, which had been specially sent for to England, where Aunt Matilda Sparhallow had a brother in the silk trade. Avery Sparhallow's wedding dress was making far more of a sensation in Burnley Beach than her wedding itself was making. For Randall Burnley had been dangling after her for three years, and everybody knew that there was nobody for a Sparhallow to marry except a Burnley and nobody for a Burnley to marry except a Sparhallow.

"Only one silk dress – and I want a dozen," Avery had said scornfully.

"What would you do with a dozen silk dresses on a farm?" Janet asked wonderingly.

"Oh – what indeed?" agreed Avery, with an impatient laugh.

"Randall will think just as much of you in drugget as in silk," said Janet, meaning to comfort.

Again Avery laughed.

"That is true. Randall never notices what a woman has on. I like a man who does notice – and tells me about it. I like a man who likes me better in silk than in drugget. I will wear this rosebud silk when I'm married, and it will be supposed to last me the rest of my life and be worn on all state occasions, and in time become an heirloom like Aunt Matilda's hideous blue satin. I want a new silk dress every month."

Janet paid little attention to this kind of raving. Avery had always been more or less discontented. She would be contented enough after she was married. Nobody could be discontented who was Randall Burnley's wife. Janet was sure of that.

Janet liked picking apples; Avery did not like it; but Aunt Matilda had decreed that the red apples should be picked that afternoon, and Aunt Matilda's word was law at the Sparhallow farm, even for wilful Avery. So they worked and talked as they worked – of Avery's wedding, which was to be as soon as Bruce Gordon should arrive from Scotland.

"I wonder what Bruce will be like," said Avery. "It is eight years since he went home to Scotland. He was sixteen then – he will be twenty-four now. He went away a boy – he will come back a man."

"I don't remember much about him," said Janet. "I was only nine when he went away. He used to tease me – I do remember that." There was a little resentment in her voice. Janet had never liked being teased. Avery laughed.

"You were so touchy, Janet. Touchy people always get teased. Bruce was very handsome – and as nice as he was handsome. Those two years he was here were the nicest, gayest time I ever had. I wish he had stayed in Canada. But of course he wouldn't do that. His father was a rich man and Bruce was ambitious. Oh, Janet, I wish I could live in the old land. That would be life."

Janet had heard all this before and could not understand it. She had no hankering for either Scotland or England. She loved the new land and its wild, virgin beauty. She yearned to the future, never to the past.

"I'm tired of Burnley Beach," Avery went on passionately, shaking apples wildly off a laden bough by way of emphasis. "I know all the people – what they are – what they can be. It's like reading a book for the twentieth time. I know where I was born and who I'll marry – and where I'll be buried. That's knowing too much. All my days will be alike when I marry Randall. There will never be anything

unexpected or surprising about them. I tell you, Janet,"
Avery seized another bough and shook it with a vengeance, "I hate the very thought of it."

"The thought of – what?" said Janet in bewilderment.

"Of marrying Randall Burnley – or marrying anybody
down here – and settling down on a farm for life."

Then Avery sat down on the rung of her ladder and
laughed at Janet's face.

"You look stunned, Janet. Did you really think I wanted
to marry Randall?"

Janet was stunned, and she did think that. How could
any girl not want to marry Randall Burnley if she had the
chance?

"Don't you love him?" she asked stupidly.

Avery bit into a nut-sweet apple.

"No," she said frankly. "Oh, I don't hate him, of course. I
like him well enough. I like him very well. But we'll quarrel
all our lives."

"Then what are you marrying him for?" asked Janet.

"Why, I'm getting on – twenty-two – all the girls of my
age are married already. I won't be an old maid, and
there's nobody but Randall. Nobody good enough for a
Sparhallow, that is. You wouldn't want me to marry Ned
Adams or John Buchanan, would you?"

"No," said Janet, who had her full share of the Sparhallow pride.

"Well, then, of course I must marry Randall. That's
settled and there's no use making faces over the notion.
I'm not making faces, but I'm tired of hearing you talk as if
you thought I adored him and must be in the seventh
heaven because I was going to marry him, you romantic
child."

"Does Randall know you feel like this?" asked Janet in a
low tone.

"No. Randall is like all men – vain and self-satisfied – and believes I'm crazy about him. It's just as well to let him think so, until we're safely married anyhow. Randall has some romantic notions too, and I'm not sure that he'd marry me if he knew, in spite of his three years' devotion. And I have no intention of being jilted three weeks before my wedding day."

Avery laughed again, and tossed away the core of her apple.

Janet, who had been very pale, went crimson and lovely. She could not endure hearing Randall criticized. "Vain and self-satisfied" – when there was never a man less so! She was horrified to feel that she almost hated Avery – Avery who did not love Randall.

"What a pity Randall didn't take a fancy to you instead of me, Janet," said Avery teasingly. "Wouldn't you like to marry him, Janet? Wouldn't you now?"

"No," cried Janet angrily. "I just like Randall, I've liked him ever since that day when I was a little thing and he came here and saved me from being shut up all day in that dreadful dark closet because I broke Aunt Matilda's blue cup – when I hadn't meant to break it. He wouldn't let her shut me up! He is like that – he understands! I want you to marry him because he wants you, and it isn't fair that you – that you –"

"Nothing is fair in this world, child. Is it fair that I, who am so pretty – you know I am pretty, Janet – and who love life and excitement, should have to be buried on a P.E. Island farm all my days? Or else be an old maid because a Sparhallow mustn't marry beneath her? Come, Janet, don't look so woebegone. I wouldn't have told you if I'd thought you'd take it so much to heart. I'll be a good wife to Randall, never fear, and I'll keep him up to the notch of prosperity much better than if I thought him a little lower than the angels. It doesn't do to think a man perfection, Janet, because he thinks so too, and when he finds some-one who agrees with him he is inclined to rest on his oars."

"At any rate, you don't care for anyone else," said Janet hopefully.

"Not I. I like Randall as well as I like anybody."

"Randall won't be satisfied with that," muttered Janet. But Avery did not hear her, having picked up her basket of apples and gone. Janet sat down on the lower rung of the ladder and gave herself up to an unpleasant reverie. Oh, how the world had changed in half an hour! She had never been so worried in her life. She was so fond of Randall – she had always been fond of him – why, he was just like a brother to her! She couldn't possibly love a brother more. And Avery was going to hurt him; it would hurt him horribly when he found out she did not love him. Janet could not bear the thought of Randall being hurt; it made her fairly savage. He must not be hurt – Avery must love him. Janet could not understand why she did not.

Surely everyone must love Randall. It had never oc-curred to Janet to ask herself, as Avery had asked, if she would like to marry Randall. Randall could never fancy her – a little plain, brown thing, only half grown. Nobody could think of her beside beautiful, rose-faced Avery. Janet accepted this fact unquestioningly. She had never been jealous. She only felt that she wanted Randall to have everything he wanted – to be perfectly happy. Why, it would be dreadful if he did not marry Avery – if he went and married some other girl. She would never see him then, never have any more delightful talks with him about all the things they both loved so much – winds and deli-cate dawns, mysterious woods in moonlight and starry midnights, silver-white sails going out of the harbour in the magic of morning, and the grey of gulf storms. There would be nothing in life; it would just be one great, unbearable emptiness; for she, herself, would never marry. There was nobody for her to marry – and she didn't care. If she could have Randall for a real brother, she would not mind a bit being an old maid. And there was that beautiful new frame house Randall had built for his bride, which she, Janet, had helped him build, because Avery would not condescend to details of pantry and linen closet and cupboards. Janet and Randall had had such fun over the cupboards. No stranger must ever come to be mistress of that house. Randall must marry Avery, and she must love him. Could anything be done to make her love him?

"I believe I'll go and see Granny Thomas," said Janet desperately.

She thought this was a silly idea, but it still haunted her and would not be shaken off. Granny Thomas was a very old woman who lived at Burnley Cove and was reputed to be something of a witch. That is, people who were not Sparhallows or Burnleys gave her that name. Sparhallows or Burnleys, of course, were above believing in such nonsense. Janet was above believing it; but still – the sailors along shore were careful to "keep on the good side" of Granny Thomas, lest she brew an unfavourable wind for them, and there was much talk of love potions. Janet knew that people said Peggy Buchanan would never have got Jack McLeod if Granny had not given her a love potion. Jack had never looked at Peggy, though she was after him for years; and then, all at once, he was quite mad about her – and married her – and wore her life out with jealousy. And Peggy, the homeliest of all the Buchanan girls! There must be something in it. Janet made a sudden desperate resolve. She would go to Granny and ask her for a love potion to make Avery love Randall. If Granny couldn't do any good, she couldn't do any harm. Janet was a little afraid of her, and had never been near her house, but what wouldn't she do for Randall?

JANET NEVER LOST much time in carrying out any resolution she made. The next afternoon she slipped away to visit Granny Thomas. She put on her longest dress and did her hair up for the first time. Granny must not think her a child. She rowed herself down the long pond to the row of golden-brown sand dunes that parted it from the gulf. It was a wonderful autumn day. There were wild growths and colours and scents in sweet procession all around the pond. Every curve in it revealed some little whim of loveliness. On the left bank, in a grove of birch, was Randall's new house, waiting to be sanctified by love and joy and birth. Janet loved to be alone thus with the delightful day. She was sorry when she had walked over the stretch of windy weedy sea fields and reached Granny's little tumbledown house at the Cove – sorry and a little frightened as well. But only a little; there was good stuff in Janet; she lifted the latch boldly and walked in when Granny bade. Granny was curled up on a stool by her fireplace, and if ever anybody did look like a witch, she did. She waved her pipe at another stool, and Janet sat down, gazing a little curiously at Granny, whom she had never seen at such close quarters before.

Will I look like that when I am very old? she thought, beholding Granny's wizened, marvellously wrinkled face. I wonder if anybody will be sorry when you die.

"Staring wasn't thought good manners in my time," said Granny. Then, as Janet blushed crimson under the rebuke, she added, "Keep red like that instead o' white, and you won't need no love ointment."

Janet felt a little cold thrill. How did Granny know what she had come for? Was she a real witch after all? For a moment she wished she hadn't come. Perhaps it was not right to tamper with the powers of darkness. Peggy Buchanan was notoriously unhappy. If Janet had known how to get herself away, she would have gone without asking for anything.

Then a sound came from the lean-to behind the house.

"S-s-h. I hear the devil grunting like a pig," muttered Granny, looking very impish.

But Janet smiled a little contemptuously. She knew it was a pig and no devil. Granny Thomas was only an old fraud. Her awe passed away and left her cool Sparhallow.

"Can you," she said with her own directness, "make a – a person care for another person – care – very much?"

Granny removed her pipe and chuckled.

"What you want is toad ointment," she said.

Toad ointment! Janet shuddered. That did not sound very nice. Granny noticed the shudder.

"Nothing like it," she said, nodding her crone-like old grey head. "There's other things, but noan so sure. Put a li'l bit – oh, such a li'l bit – on his eyelids, and he's yourn for life. You need something powerful – you're noan so pretty – only when you're blushing."

Janet was blushing again. So Granny thought she wanted the charm for herself! Well, what did it matter? Randall was the only one to be considered.

"Is it very – expensive?" she faltered. She had not much money. Money was no plentiful thing on a P.E.I. farm in 1840.

"Oh, noa – oh, noa," Granny leered. "I don't sell it. I gives it. I like to see young folks happy. You don't need much, as I've said – just a li'l smootch and you'll have your man, and send old Granny a bite o' the wedding cake and fig o' baccy for luck, and a bid to the fir-r-st christening! Doan't forget that, dearie."

Janet was cold again with anger. She hated old Granny Thomas. She would never come near her again.

"I'd rather pay you its worth," she said coldly.

"You couldn't, dearie. What money could be eno' for such a treasure? But that's the Sparhallow pride. Well, go, see if the Sparhallow pride and the Sparhallow money will buy you your lad's love."

Granny looked so angry that Janet hastened to appease her.

"Oh, please forgive me – I meant no offence. Only – it must have cost you much trouble to make it."

Granny chuckled again. She was vastly pleased to see a Sparhallow suing to her – a Sparhallow!

"Toads am cheap," she said. "It's all in the knowing how and the time o' the moon. Here, take this li'l pill box – there's eno' in it – and put a li'l bit on his eyelids when you've getten the chance – and when he looks at you, he'll love you. Mind you, though, that he looks at no other first – it's the first one he sees that he'll love. That's the way it works."

"Thank you." Janet took the little box. She wished she dared to go at once. But perhaps this would anger Granny. Granny looked at her with a twinkle in her little, incredibly old eyes.

"Be off," she said. "You're in a hurry to go – you're as proud as any of the proud Sparhallows. But I bear you no grudge. I likes proud people – when they have to come to me to get help."

Janet found herself outside with a relieved heart in her bosom and her little box in her hand. For a moment she was tempted to throw it away. But no – Randall would be so unhappy if he found out Avery didn't love him! She would try the ointment at least – she would try to forget about the toads and not let herself think how it was made – something might come of it.

JANET HURRIED HOME along the shore, where a silvery wave broke in a little lovely silvery curve on the sand. She was so happy that her cheeks burned, and Randall Burnley, who was sitting on the edge of her flat when she reached the pond, looked at her with admiration. Janet dropped her box into her pocket stealthily when she saw him. What with her guilty secret, she hardly knew whether she was glad or not when he said he was going to row her up the pond.

"I saw you go down an hour ago and I've been waiting ever since," he said. "Where have you been?"

"Oh – I just – wanted a walk – this lovely day," said Janet miserably. She felt that she was telling an untruth and this hurt her horribly – especially when it was to Randall. This was what came of truck with witches – you were led into falsehood and deception straightway. Again Janet was tempted to drop Granny's pill box into the depths of Burnley Pond – and again she decided not to because she saw Randall Burnley's deep-set, blue-grey eyes, that could look tender or sorrowful or passionate or whimsical as he willed, and thought how they would look when he found Avery did not love him.

So Janet drowned the voice of conscience and was brazenly happy – happy because Randall Burnley rowed her up the pond – happy because he walked halfway home with her over the autumnal fields – happy because he talked of the day and the sea and the golden weather, as only Randall could talk. But she thought she was happy because she had in her pocket what might make Avery love him.

Randall went as far as the stile in the birch wood between the Burnley and the Sparhallow land – and he kept her there talking for another half-hour – and though he talked only of a book he had read and a new puppy he was training, Janet listened with her soul in her ears. She talked too – quite freely; she was never in the least shy or tongue-tied or awkward in Randall's company. There she was always at her best, with a delightful feeling of being understood. She wondered if he noticed she had her hair done up. Her eyes shone and her brown face was full of rosy, kissable hues. When he finally turned away homeward, life went flat. Janet decided she was very tired after her long walk and her trying interview. But it did not matter, since she had her love potion. That was so much nicer a name than toad ointment.

That night Janet rubbed mutton tallow on her hands. She had never done that before – she had thought it vain and foolish – though Avery did it every night. But that afternoon on the pond Randall had said something about the beautiful shape of her pretty slender hands. He had never paid her a compliment before. Her hands were brown and a little hard – not soft and white like Avery's. So Janet resorted to the mutton tallow. If one had a scrap of beauty, if only in one's hands, one might as well take care of it.

Having got her ointment, the next thing was to make use of it. This was not so easy – because, in the first place, it must not be done when there was any danger of Avery's seeing some other than Randall first – and it must be done without Avery's knowing it. The two problems combined were almost too much for Janet. She bided her chance like a watchful cat – but it did not come. Two weeks went by and it had not come. Janet was getting very desperate. The wedding day was only a week away. The bride's cake was made and the turkeys fattened. The invitations were sent out. Janet's own bridesmaid dress was ready. And still the little pill box in the till of Janet's blue chest was unopened. She had never even opened it, lest virtue escape.

Then her chance came at last, unexpectedly. One evening at dusk, when Janet was crossing the little dark upstairs hall, Aunt Matilda called up to her.

"Janet, send Avery down. There is a young man wanting to see her."

Aunt Matilda was laughing a little – as she always did when Randall came. It was a habit with her, hanging over from the early days of Randall's courtship. Janet went on into their room to tell Avery. And lo, Avery was lying asleep on her bed, tired out from her busy day. Janet, after one glance, flew to her chest. She took out her pill box and opened it, a little fearfully. The toad ointment was there, dark and unpleasant enough to view. Janet tiptoed breathlessly to the bed and gingerly scraped the tip of her finger in the ointment.

She said so little would be enough – oh, I hope I'm not doing wrong.

Trembling with excitement, she brushed lightly the white lids of Avery's eyes. Avery stirred and opened them. Janet guiltily thrust her pill box behind her.

"Randall is downstairs asking for you, Avery."

Avery sat up, looking annoyed. She had not expected Randall that evening and would greatly have preferred a continuance of her nap. She went down crossly enough, but looking very lovely, flushed from sleep. Janet stood in their room, clasping her cold hands nervously over her breast. Would the charm work? Oh, she must know – she must know. She could not wait. After a few moments that seemed like years she crept down the stairs and out into the dusk of the June-warm September night. Like a shadow she slipped up to the open parlour window and looked cautiously in between the white muslin curtains. The next minute she had fallen on her knees in the mint bed. She wished she could die then and there.

The young man in the parlour was not Randall Burnley. He was dark and smart and handsome; he was sitting on the sofa by Avery's side, holding her hands in his, smiling into her rosy, delighted, excited face. And he was Bruce Gordon – no doubt of that. Bruce Gordon, the expected cousin from Scotland!

"Oh, what have I done? What have I done?" moaned poor Janet, wringing her hands. She had seen Avery's face quite plainly – had seen the look in her eyes. Avery had never looked at Randall Burnley like that. Granny Thomas' abominable ointment had worked all right – and Avery had fallen in love with the wrong man.

Janet, cold with horror and remorse, dragged herself up to the window again and listened. She must know – she must be sure. She could hear only a word here and there, but that word was enough.

"I thought you promised to wait for me, Avery," Bruce said reproachfully.

"You were so long in coming back – I thought you had forgotten me," cried Avery.

"I think I did forget a little, Avery. I was such a boy. But now – well, thank Heaven, I haven't come too late."

There was a silence, and shameless Janet, peering above the window sill, saw what she saw. It was enough. She crept away upstairs to her room. She was lying there across the bed when Avery swept in – a splendid, transfigured Avery, flushed triumphant. Janet sat up, pallid, tear-stained, and looked at her.

"Janet," said Avery, "I am going to marry Bruce Gordon next Wednesday night instead of Randall Burnley."

Janet sprang forward and caught Avery's hand.

"You must not," she cried wildly. "It's all my fault – oh, if I could only die – I got the love ointment from Granny Thomas to rub on your eyes to make you love the first man you would see. I meant it to be Randall – I thought it was Randall – oh, Avery!"

Avery had been listening, between amazement and anger. Now anger mastered amazement.

"Janet Sparhallow," she cried, "are you crazy? Or do you mean that you went to Granny Thomas – you, a Spar-

hallow! – and asked her for a love philtre to make me love
Randall Burnley?"

"I didn't tell her it was for you – she thought I wanted it
for myself," moaned Janet. "Oh, we must undo it – I'll go to
her again – no doubt she knows of some way to undo the
spell –"

Avery, whose rages never lasted long, threw back her
dark head and laughed ringingly.

"Janet Sparhallow, you talk as if you lived in the dark
ages! The idea of supposing that horrid old woman could
give you love philtres! Why, girl, I've always loved Bruce –
always. But I thought he'd forgotten me. And tonight
when he came I found he hadn't. There's the whole thing
in a nutshell. I'm going to marry him and go home with
him to Scotland."

"And what about Randall?" said Janet, corpse-white.

"Oh, Randall – pooh! Do you suppose I'm worrying
about Randall? But you must go to him tomorrow and tell
him for me, Janet."

"I will not – I will not."

"Then I'll tell him myself – and I'll tell him about you
going to Granny," said Avery cruelly. "Janet, don't stand
there looking like that. I've no patience with you. I shall be
perfectly happy with Bruce – I would have been miserable
with Randall. I know I shan't sleep a wink tonight – I'm so
excited. Why, Janet, I'll be Mrs. Gordon of Gordon Brae –
and I'll have everything heart can desire and the man of
my heart to boot. What has lanky Randall Burnley with his
little six-roomed house to set against that?"

If Avery did not sleep, neither did Janet. She lay awake
till dawn, suffering such misery as she had never endured
in her life before. She knew she must go to Randall Burnley tomorrow and break his heart. If she did not, Avery
would tell him – tell him what Janet had done. And he

must not know that – he must not. Janet could not bear that thought.

IT WAS A PALLID, dull-eyed Janet who went through the birch wood to the Burnley farm next afternoon, leaving behind her an excited household where the sudden change of bridegrooms, as announced by Avery, had rather upset everybody. Janet found Randall working in the garden of his new house – setting out rosebushes for Avery – Avery, who was to jilt him at the very altar, so to speak. He came over to open the gate for Janet, smiling his dear smile. It was a dear smile – Janet caught her breath over the dearness of it – and she was going to blot it off his face.

She spoke out, with plainness and directness. When you had to deal a mortal blow, why try to lighten it?

"Avery sent me to tell you that she is going to marry Bruce Gordon instead of you. He came last night – and she says that she has always liked him best."

A very curious change came over Randall's face – but not the change Janet had expected to see. Instead of turning pale Randall flushed; and instead of a sharp cry of pain and incredulity, Randall said in no uncertain tones, "Thank God!"

Janet wondered if she were dreaming. Granny Thomas' love potion seemed to have turned the world upside down. For Randall's arms were about her and Randall was pressing his lean bronzed cheek to hers and Randall was saying:

"Now I can tell you, Janet, how much I love you."

"Me? Me!" choked Janet.

"You. Why, you're in the very core of my heart, girl. Don't tell me you can't love me – you can – you must – why, Janet," for his eyes had caught and locked with hers for a minute, "you do!"

There were five minutes about which nobody can tell anything, for even Randall and Janet never knew clearly just what happened in those five minutes. Then Janet, feeling somehow as if she had died and then come back to life, found her tongue.

"Three years ago you came courting Avery," she said reproachfully.

"Three years ago you were a child. I did not think about you. I wanted a wife – and Avery was pretty. I thought I was in love with her. Then you grew up all at once – and we were such good friends – I never could talk to Avery – she wasn't interested in anything I said – and you have eyes that catch a man – I've always thought of your eyes. But I was honour-bound to Avery – I didn't dream you cared. You must marry me next Wednesday, Janet – we'll have a double wedding. You won't mind – being married – so soon?"

"Oh, no – I won't – mind," said Janet dazedly. "Only – oh, Randall – I must tell you – I didn't mean to tell you – I'd have rather died – but now – I must tell you about it now – because I can't bear anything hidden between us. I went to old Granny Thomas – and got a love ointment from her – to make Avery love you, because I knew she didn't – and I wanted you to be happy – Randall, don't – I can't talk when you do that! Do you think Granny's ointment could have made her care for Bruce?"

Randall laughed – the little, low laugh of the triumphant lover.

"If it did, I'm glad of it. But I need no such ointment on my eyes to make me love you – you carry your philtre in that elfin little face of yours, Janet."

Editorial Note

These stories were originally published in the following magazines and newspapers, and are listed here in the order of their appearance in this collection. Where the original illustrations accompanying the stories are available, they have been included. Obvious typographical errors have been corrected, spelling and punctuation normalized.

1. The Closed Door, *Family Herald*, June 1934.
2. Davenport's Story, *Waverley Magazine*, April 1902.
3. The Deacon's Painkiller, no information available.
4. Detected by the Camera, *Philadelphia Times*, June 1897.
5. From out the Silence, *Family Herald*, January 1934.
6. The Girl at the Gate, *National Magazine*, August 1906.
7. The House Party at Smoky Island, *Weird Tales Magazine*, August 1935.
8. The Man on the Train, *Canadian Courier*, July 1914.
9. The Martyrdom of Estella, *Waverley Magazine*, December 1902.
10. Min, *American Home*, December 1903.
11. Miriam's Lover, *Waverley Magazine*, June 1901.
12. Miss Calista's Peppermint Bottle, *Westminster Magazine*, November 1910. Also as Of Miss Calista's Peppermint, *Springfield Republican*, November 1900.

Acknowledgements

The late Dr. Stuart Macdonald gave me permission to begin the research that culminated in my collection of Montgomery's stories; Professors Mary Rubio and Elizabeth Waterston encouraged and advised me; C. Anderson Silber gave his always constant support. Librarians were unfailingly helpful.

L. M. Montgomery

For the most complete listing, see Russell, Russell, and Wilmshurst, *Lucy Maud Montgomery: A Preliminary Bibliography*, University of Waterloo Library Bibliography Series, No. 13 (Waterloo: University of Waterloo Library, 1986).

THE "ANNE" BOOKS (in order of Anne's life)

Anne of Green Gables, 1908
Anne of Avonlea, 1909
Anne of the Island, 1915
Anne of Windy Poplars, 1936
Anne's House of Dreams, 1917
Anne of Ingleside, 1939
Rainbow Valley, 1919
Rilla of Ingleside, 1920

THE "EMILY" BOOKS

Emily of New Moon, 1923
Emily Climbs, 1925
Emily's Quest, 1927

OTHER NOVELS (in chronological order)

Kilmeny of the Orchard, 1910

The Story Girl, 1911
The Golden Road, 1913
The Blue Castle, 1926
Magic for Marigold, 1929
A Tangled Web, 1931
Pat of Silver Bush, 1933
Mistress Pat, 1935
Jane of Lantern Hill, 1937

COLLECTIONS OF SHORT STORIES

Chronicles of Avonlea, 1912
Further Chronicles of Avonlea, 1920
The Road to Yesterday, 1974
The Doctor's Sweetheart, and Other Stories, 1979
Akin to Anne: Tales of Other Orphans, 1988
Along the Shore: Tales by the Sea, 1989

POETRY

The Watchman, and Other Poems, 1916
Poetry of Lucy Maud Montgomery, 1987

SPY WARS
Espionage and Canada from Gouzenko to Glasnost
by J. L. Granatstein and David Stafford

The Cold War may be over but the "great game" of spy vs. spy will continue, say the authors of this "path-breaking popular history."
"A fun read. Descriptions of the back-stabbing, blackmailing politics of spying are admirably well done." – *Quill and Quire*
0-7710-3511-X \$7.50 8 pages b&w photos

CHANGELINGS
by Tom Marshall

Fans of *The Three Faces of Eve* and *The Shining* will enjoy this eerie, critically acclaimed novel about an estranged brother and sister, each of whom suffers from multiple personality disorder.
"Fascinating fiction, controlled, assured … " – *Windsor Star*
"A chilling yarn … difficult to put down." – *The Gazette* (Montreal)
0-7710-5661-3 \$6.99

KICKING TOMORROW
by Daniel Richler

The remarkable debut novel from Canada's hottest new literary star. Four months on the national bestseller list.
"An exhilarating romp … It crackles with wit and insight." – *The Globe and Mail*
"A gutsy *Catcher in the Rye* for the nineties." – Susan Musgrave, CBC's *The Journal*
"Excellent … entertaining and ambitious." – *Calgary Herald*
0-7710-7470-0 \$6.99

Hot titles from
M&S Paperbacks

AFTER MANY DAYS
Tales of Time Passed
by L. M. Montgomery; edited by Rea Wilmshurst
Eighteen newly discovered classics penned by the author of the
immortal *Anne of Green Gables*, collected by the editor of *Akin to
Anne* and *Along the Shore*.
0-7710-6171-4 $6.99

CONSPIRACY OF SILENCE
by Lisa Priest
The powerful, award-winning best-seller about racism, murder, and
apathy in a Manitoba community. Basis of the acclaimed CBC-TV
movie. From the author of *Women Who Killed: Stories of Canadian
Female Murderers.*
0-7710-7152-3 $5.99 Photos

ELIZABETH
by Alexander Walker
The definitive biography of Hollywood's much-married biggest star,
Elizabeth Taylor, by the acclaimed author of *Vivien*.
"Informative, thoughtful, and understanding." – *The Listener*
0-7710-8781-0 $7.99 32 pages b&w photos

THE JACAMAR NEST
by David Parry and Patrick Withrow
Someone is out to bring corporate America to its knees and ex-CIA-
agent-turned-insurance-investigator Harry Bracken is determined
to find out who. Provided, of course, he isn't shot or blown up first.
"A fast-moving terrorist story leavened with sophistication and
wit." – *The New York Times*
"The action never stops and the authors have a nice way with
dialogue." – *The Globe and Mail*
0-7710-6931-6 $6.99